PLANTED

D.P. DART

PLANTED

Dedicated to my wife and kids.

Thank you to my wife, Sue; Erica Nunez; Carolyn Simi; and to those who provided guidance, encouragement, and proofreading assistance.

CONTENTS

THE SIGNAL

I t was a gray morning in early October 2010 when I returned from my second interview with the NYPD and the Manhattan District Attorney's office. The meeting had lasted more than two hours as 20 people—most with official-looking badges, uniforms, and legal pads—sat restlessly in a cold, windowless room. The tone wasn't hostile exactly, but it wasn't welcoming either. They weren't just looking for answers. They were fitting pieces together.

I answered their questions, but I left feeling drained. Cold in a way that had nothing to do with temperature.

I remember the hallway's silence. The smell of varnish and dust. The hum of the overhead lights. When I stepped outside into Manhattan's early afternoon, everything looked the same —but I didn't feel the same. Something inside me had shifted.

I walked for blocks without thinking, past Centre Street, through Chinatown, all the way to Battery Park. I sat on a bench, watching ferries cut through the harbor, trying to understand what I'd just been part of.

They hadn't accused me of anything. Not directly. But their questions had a shape, and that shape didn't point to the story we'd all agreed on. It hinted at gaps: gaps in access logs, VPN records that didn't match behavior, and anomalies that had been scrubbed too neatly.

They didn't offer a theory, but the absences told a story.

And something inside me turned cold again.

I wasn't sure what it meant yet, only that something was off. Too clean. Too precise. As if someone had wiped down a crime scene, but the air still smelled of bleach.

By the time I made it back to the office, I didn't go to my desk. I went to the archive room. The hum of drives. The soft flicker of fluorescent light. It was quiet there. Familiar. Safe. Or at least it used to be.

I started pulling logs. Snapshots. Firewall records. I didn't know what I was looking for, only that I'd know it when I saw it.

Then I found it.

A file that shouldn't have been there: *session_hook.dll*.

Obscure, buried in a legacy folder, invisible unless you were looking from the right angle.

I called Doug Saito, one of my best tech experts. He ran it in a sandbox.

We didn't get confirmation. But the shape of the thing— what it did, how it behaved—told me enough. It was subtle. Precise. Almost elegant. Not amateur work. Not random.

Something had been manipulated.

Warren hadn't told me everything. Not yet. That would come later, in a quiet office with a sealed envelope. But I knew, just from the way they'd asked the questions, from the stillness in that room, that someone was rewriting the past.

This wasn't about compliance failures, audit gaps, or sloppy security.

It was about control.

And fear.

And silence.

Someone had been removed, carefully and deliberately.

Maybe it was Alasdair. Maybe someone else. Maybe more than one person.

I didn't know yet.

But I knew what erasure looked like.

And as I sat at my desk that evening, the logs glowing on my monitor, I realized something I hadn't let myself admit before: this wasn't an accident.

Someone had made it look as if it had never happened.

And maybe I'd been part of it.

I didn't know what I was going to do. But I knew I wouldn't forget.

How the hell had I ended up here?

I thought I was taking a career-defining job, not walking into a war I didn't know was being fought. Not becoming part of a system that could burn someone alive and leave no smoke.

And yet, here I was. Numb. Complicit.

And just awake enough to feel it.

CHAPTER 1
THE SETUP

That morning, I came up from the subway near Wall Street. Jacket sharp and stride steady, I felt unstoppable. My return to New York. It was my first day with the Cambria Financial Group, North American branch. A new start, and I was buzzing.

But that confidence was a transient illusion, draining rapidly as I neared the office.

Something was bothering me. I had an intense sense of foreboding and a weight in my chest. *What have you walked into?* I asked myself.

A lack of self-belief was not something I was used to. I had escaped the council estates of inner London. We had lived on the top floor of a high-rise building, where the elevator rarely worked yet always smelled like piss.

My dad drove a bin lorry for the local council, and my mum stayed home to look after me and my six younger siblings. As the eldest, I was expected to set an example, contribute equally, and avoid causing problems. Life was loud, rough, and honest, and everyone knew everyone. Money was tight. Everyone had to earn respect. And if you wanted something, you grafted for it. Nothing came easy.

I left school at 16 with few qualifications and even fewer prospects. But I could hustle. I talked my way into several jobs, eventually finding my way into banking. I got married young. Sue and I had been together since secondary school. We didn't have much, but we had a plan. Or thought we did.

We had both our kids young, too: first our daughter Stephanie, then our son Chris. But we struggled financially. I landed a job at British Colonial Bank, where I was responsible for trading room technologies. How did I get it? Good question. But I worked hard and thrived.

In 1994, they offered me a transfer to New York, and I took it. The plan was to stay for two years. But when we were due to go back home, British Colonial asked if I would like to stay on. My family had settled, so it was a straightforward decision. My stock at the bank was high based on the success of the projects I had led. We agreed to stay, with the understanding that the bank would sponsor us for green cards.

Thirty interesting years later, and we are still here.

We bought a home in New Jersey. Sue built a life of her own —friends, volunteering, PTA meetings. She never said much about the missed dinners or long nights, but I knew it was a challenge for her. Professionally, I adapted well to life in the United States. Where my Cockney accent had always been a handicap in the UK, in New York, my "English" accent was a bonus. Combined with my relentless work ethic and strong delivery record, I did very well.

I had built a reputation as a deliverer. And then I got cocky.

When Global Financial Networks offered me a big job title and a bigger salary, I jumped. The job was in North Carolina. I commuted weekly. Sue stayed in Chatham. It was miserable. Worse, the job itself didn't exist, not really. The strategy was vapor. The politics were dense. I knew within weeks I'd made a mistake.

Then, out of the blue, I had a meeting that changed everything.

A friend had passed my name to Alasdair Stewart, the US general manager for a Welsh bank I had never heard of. He was sharp, calm, and carried authority without raising his voice. A quiet intensity that made you want to impress him, or fear disappointing him. We met for breakfast.

"What would you do?" he asked, "if the group's systems couldn't support your business?"

"Build what we need," I said. "Deliver results first. Ask forgiveness later."

He gave a single nod. That was all.

I knew little about Cambria then. Just that it was Welsh, conservative, and, somehow, had opened a full-service commercial bank in the heart of the Financial District. That alone intrigued me. Why would a regional lender from Swansea open a flagship branch in Manhattan?

I started digging.

Not on the clock, not officially. Just one of those late-night research rabbit holes, half out of interest, half out of instinct. What I found was ... strange.

Cambria had always played it safe. Founded in the cautious postwar years, its mandate had been stability. Serve the miners, the small shops, the working families of southwest Wales. It was partly council-owned, for God's sake. It had never posted a loss in its history, but it never made headlines, either. No scandals. No surprises. Just the banking equivalent of warm toast.

But in the mid-90s, something changed. Maybe it was shareholder pressure. Maybe it was ego. Whatever the reason, Cambria began reaching: London. Singapore. Sydney. The moves were bold, too bold for the bank's DNA, if you asked me. But the real shock came in the early 2000s, when they opened in New York. Not a token sales desk either. A fully autonomous, self-contained commercial operation. The kind of move that made no sense unless someone, somewhere, had a point to prove.

I didn't know it yet, but that decision, that branch, would end up defining the rest of my life.

Within weeks, I completed five interviews in New York; I was asked to fly to Head Office for a second set of meetings, this time with the board. I flew into Cardiff and took the train west. The station at Swansea smelled faintly of seaweed and diesel, the wind carrying seagull cries across cracked stone platforms. Outside, the town was a patchwork of soot-streaked brick, old industrial shells, and hopeful glass-front cafés. The Cambria building stood oddly modern against its surroundings, its mirrored panels reflecting the dull skies, as if it didn't want to see where it had been built.

Inside, everyone spoke English, but the melodic lilt of Welsh rippled beneath it, especially in the corridors, where you couldn't always tell if a joke was being shared or a warning delivered. It felt distant from London. It felt like a lifetime from New York.

After three days there, I was back at the New York office— three rented floors in the newly completed Freedom Tower— for my final interview with Carolyn Smith, the human resources director. I remember her poised presence: 5'8" in a sharply tailored suit, designer glasses reflecting the room's piercing fluorescent lights. She asked measured questions about my values and how I fit into Cambria's culture. It was clear she wasn't just vetting my résumé; she was judging my fit into the firm's heartbeat.

When the offer came, it had the weight of oxygen.

Chief Technology Officer of the US branch. I started in early 2007.

I distinctly recall the moment I realized I had made the right decision. It struck me as I was sitting on the subway, heading downtown, that morning. It felt right, calm, and certain, as if I had made a move that matched my skills. It wasn't just relief; it was a gut-level confidence I hadn't felt in years.

I wore my sharpest suit that morning, a made-to-measure, three-button Italian number with narrow lapels and tailored sleeves. Mod-inspired, but not a costume. Back in London, they knew me for it, sharp lines, polished Chelsea boots, and mohair-blend fabrics that caught the light just right. It wasn't vanity. It was identity—a way of walking into any room and owning it.

Even now, at the downtown office, I intended to be the best-dressed man in the building. And most days, I was. It was my way of saying, "I know who I am. You don't get to decide that."

What I didn't know that morning was that Cambria's New York office wasn't just a branch. It was a fortress. And I was walking into a war I didn't even know had started.

CHAPTER 2
THE ARRIVAL

"Wallace," I said. "David Wallace. I'm here to start as the new chief technology officer at Cambria Financial Group."

The guard, midfifties, heavyset, didn't look up. He just tapped something into the terminal with two fingers and frowned. That was all. Then, he slid a plastic badge across the desk without breaking his rhythm.

"29th floor," he said. "They're expecting you."

I wasn't so sure.

The badge felt oddly weighty in my hand. Not because of its size, but because of what it represented: authority, entry, belonging. It was a symbol of inclusion, or at least the illusion of it. I turned it over once, twice, as if expecting it to say something more. The edges were smooth, the plastic warm from the guard's hand.

I slipped the badge into my jacket pocket and headed to the elevator bank, taking a breath as I stepped into the brushed steel box. The doors slid shut with a hiss. I checked my reflection— crisp lines, sharp silhouette, ready for whatever waited upstairs. I wasn't nervous. But I had something to prove again.

Years of major project delivery, technical firefighting, and boardroom battles had brought me here. Still, in this new game, none of that would matter unless I made it count fast.

The elevator rose quickly, quietly. I was alone.

The 29th floor opened into silence. A man in shirtsleeves walked past holding two coffees, one for someone I'd never meet. He didn't make eye contact. No one did. It was as if I hadn't arrived; I'd intruded.

As I stepped out, the hush felt absolute, more like a vacuum than an office. For a moment, I just stood there.

The floor-to-ceiling windows looked out across Manhattan's sprawl, rivers framing the skyline, yellow taxis dotting the avenues like restless ants. But inside, there was no motion, no energy—only glass, air, and the stale buzz of anxiety humming through every light fixture. The view was pure velocity. The office, pure paralysis.

As I waited for someone to notice, my mind wandered. They hired me to fix things, but what exactly needed fixing was still opaque. This felt different. For some reason, it felt as if I were stepping into enemy territory, a sleek fortress with glass walls, hidden hierarchies, and watchers you never saw but always felt. Not the bustling energy I expected, not even the sterile hum of corporate efficiency. Just ... silence.

The reception desk was vacant. Phones rang distantly. The air smelled of new carpet and recycled ambition. Frosted glass offices lined the hallway like display cases, perfectly spaced, identically furnished, and utterly soulless.

I stood there for nearly a full minute, trying not to look lost. Each second stretched. I shifted my weight. Adjusted my tie. Looked for a clock. Nothing. The absence of a welcome felt deliberate, like a warning.

Eventually, a woman approached. She was tall, slim, and blond, wearing a navy dress with a precise hemline. Everything about her seemed measured: hair perfectly pinned, lanyard hanging like a badge of survival, and eyes that flicked between suspicion and fatigue.

"Mr. Wallace?" she said.

"That's me."

"I'm Karen. You're here to ... see Todd?"

I frowned. "I was told today was my first day. I'm here to start—chief technology officer."

Her expression didn't quite shift, but her eyes hesitated. That half-second pause said more than words ever could.

"Right," she said. "Of course. This way, please."

She turned and began walking briskly down the corridor. Her heels clicked like metronomes against the polished floor of the walkway, a soundtrack to my rising doubt. I followed, passing identical offices and identical people who didn't glance up. Every surface reflected light, but there was no warmth. It was as if the designers had created the entire floor to avoid disturbing the air.

We stopped in front of a large corner office. The kind with glass on two sides and a view over Lower Manhattan. The sort of office where people made decisions that moved markets. Karen opened the door, and someone was already sitting at the desk.

He didn't look up immediately. Just kept typing. His fingers moved with the mechanical confidence of someone who knew exactly where each key lived. Salt-and-pepper hair, glasses perched on the end of his nose, collar open one button too far. Middle-aged, like me, but with the air of someone who'd spent 20 years aging into a chair. When he finally glanced up, there was no welcome in his eyes—just calculation.

"Can I help you?" he asked, voice dry, crossing his arms.

I stepped forward and offered a hand. "David Wallace. Starting today—chief technology officer."

He didn't shake my hand. He didn't even uncross his arms. Just leaned back slightly, inspecting me.

"I run the technology here." His tone wasn't angry. It was possessive. I had been labeled, along with everything else in the room. He struck me as the kind of man who just wanted to finish out his career unbothered—retirement without risk.

Karen looked as if she might faint. "I'll ... get coffee," she mumbled, and vanished like smoke.

I closed the door behind her and walked farther into the room, glancing briefly at the skyline outside, then back at the man I now knew must be Todd Carter.

"I imagine they didn't communicate this very well," I said.

"No," he replied. "They didn't."

A long silence followed. Not hostile. Not yet. But charged, like the moment before a wire snaps.

As I would soon learn, Todd had been with Cambria's downtown office since it opened in 2000. A man who thrived in still waters, he was slow to anger, slower to act, but deeply territorial. He was not cruel. Habit, not strategy, kept him from politics. He simply didn't grasp how much the New York operation had evolved. How different its needs were from the head office's model. And that ignorance, more than malice, made him dangerous.

I knew after my first few days that the tech team felt it. You could see it in their restraint during meetings, their sidelong glances, their growing tendency to check with me after he'd spoken.

I learned that he had spent the last six months lobbying against my hire, convinced that Swansea was plotting his quiet removal. Maybe they were. As I later heard someone describe him, he was "part of the furniture" there. Not brilliant, not bad. Just there. Dependable. Safe. The kind of guy that the head office liked because he didn't make waves.

Until now.

I didn't claw my way up just to walk on eggshells around a man like Todd.

Over the next few weeks, we cohabited the role. It wasn't easy. Part of me hoped Todd would recognize the inevitability of the transition and step aside gracefully. But each day that passed made it clearer: I would have to be the one to force the change, and that didn't sit well with me. I took no pleasure in displacing someone. He wasn't malicious, just misplaced. Still, I had a responsibility to the team and the business, but that internal conflict wore on me more than I admitted at the time.

He showed up every morning as if nothing had changed. Still held team meetings. Still signed off on tickets. I let him—for a while. But behind the scenes, I started working around him. The first confrontation came on a Tuesday morning. He had overwritten one of my scheduled architecture review meetings with a staff huddle. I confronted him gently, hoping to de-escalate.

"Todd," I said, "we need to sync calendar coordination. I've had a meeting with the team leads booked all week."

He didn't look up. "They need direction. Theirs or yours, that's debatable."

I let the silence stretch. "Direction only works when the compass isn't spinning."

He looked up then. "We've been doing this for a long time without you."

"Clearly," I said. "That's why I'm here."

He didn't respond. But from that day on, the temperature dropped several degrees between us.

I met with Dmitry Ivanov, the head of infrastructure. Russian by birth, early thirties, quietly brilliant. He'd been at the bank since day one and knew every server, every wire, and every crack in the building's digital spine. He said little at first.

Just watched. Measured. But after our second meeting, he nodded and said, "You're not Todd. That's good."

Erica Cross, our razor-sharp head of back-office operations, invited me to a meeting during my first day. Medium build, early thirties, sharp-eyed. Her intelligence wasn't the kind you announced; it was the kind that disarmed quietly. She grew up in Y Wladfa, Argentina, spoke three languages fluently, and wielded silence like a blade. But what made her unforgettable was her ambition. Not the performative kind, but the kind that waited, watched, and learned the field before making its move.

At first, my role felt like navigating a minefield disguised as an office. Todd's cold indifference was palpable, but Dmitry's subtle nod of approval gave me a foothold. Slowly, I began stitching together an understanding of the culture here: fractured loyalties, whispered alliances, and a hierarchy as brittle as it was rigid.

One afternoon, while poring over server schematics with Dmitry, I asked, "What's Todd's story, anyway?" Dmitry raised an eyebrow, but didn't answer right away. Instead, he traced a finger along a network diagram, pausing only to tap lightly on the central hub. "He's just like that," Dmitry said finally. "Critical, but prone to overheat."

That evening, I found myself in the break room, grabbing an emergency dose of caffeine, when Erica appeared, a storm wrapped in an impeccable blazer. "Surviving Todd Day Four, I see," she said, grabbing her own mug. Before I could respond, she added, "Word is, he's been circling the wagons. If you're not careful, you'll find yourself on an island."

"I think I already am," I replied, taking a sip. Erica gave me a sly smile, one that hinted at battles already fought and won.

We started having coffee together each morning in the pantry, an unspoken ritual that turned into an alliance. Sometimes we gossiped about Swansea, sometimes we debated who'd survive the next round of budget cuts, and other times she'd grill me on macroeconomic policy between sips of dark roast as if we were on a quiz show.

"You know," she said on my third morning, "this place was better when everyone smoked indoors. At least then you knew who was plotting against you, because they all stood in the same cloud."

I laughed. I couldn't help it. Erica was a force, strategic, unreadable, and always ten moves ahead. She once pulled me aside after a tense budget meeting and said, "You're not here to fit in, David. You're here to make it work. Just don't mistake applause for protection." There was a chill in her delivery that made me realize she'd seen people fall, maybe even nudged a few of them along the way. A war-tested professional who didn't blink under pressure and never wasted a breath pretending to be impressed.

But it always ended with an honest exchange.

"You've got two weeks, max," she told me one day, handing me a mug. "If Todd doesn't walk himself out by then, you'll have to push."

"I'm not here to humiliate anyone."

"You're in banking," she said, deadpan. "Humiliation is a feature, not a bug."

She stirred her coffee with exaggerated care, then leaned in, dropping her voice. "I once saw Todd freeze up because someone asked him how many CPUs were in our main server. He blinked as if he'd just heard something spoken in French."

I grinned. "What did he say?"

"Nothing. He pretended he had a phone call and left the room."

We both laughed. One could almost believe I had found an ally in a city of strangers.

She sipped, smirking. "He once filed an incident ticket because a spreadsheet didn't load. Didn't even try to reboot."

"Really?"

"He's terrified of losing control. He clearly does not know what it's like to have already lost it."

By the start of week three, I had full admin access. Systems were being restructured. Meetings were being routed to me, not Todd. People noticed. He noticed. And then, just like that, he was gone.

I came in on a rainy Monday and found his desk empty. His chair pushed in, his nameplate gone, and his access badge clipped to a Post-it with the word "Thanks."

No farewell. No email. No ceremony.

Just absence.

I met with Alasdair the following week—after Todd had already cleared out his desk—though, of course, it wasn't our first meeting. It was, however, unusual that my first meeting with my new boss only took place a few weeks after I started.

Six weeks prior, he'd interviewed me over breakfast, which felt more like a cross-examination. He'd arrived ten minutes late, wearing an immaculate suit and a faint sneer. He didn't ask about my résumé; he had clearly already read it. What he wanted to know was how I handled the pressure, how I handled politics, and especially, whether I would be able to handle the Welsh?

One question struck at the heart of my resolve. I gave him the truth, unvarnished and sincere. All I received in return was a quiet nod, the lone acknowledgment that my words had found their mark.

When he saw me again, his handshake wasn't an introduction; it was confirmation. His eyes flicked over me like a scanner. Every part of him screamed: I see everything.

"David Wallace," he said, with a slight Scottish accent. "The new chief technology officer."

"That's me."

"So, Todd Carter."

"He left quietly," I said. "No goodbyes."

Alasdair nodded, unsurprised. "It was time."

"Understood."

He gestured to a chair and sat across from me in a glass-walled office with the blinds half-drawn.

"Tell me something," he said. "Do you need Swansea's permission to do your job?"

"No."

"Good," he said, standing again. "Then don't ask."

There was something in the way he said it, like a warning buried inside permission. I didn't know it then, but that conversation would echo through every major decision I made in that building.

He didn't smile. Didn't nod. Just turned away and opened his laptop. That was the end of the meeting.

People feared Alasdair as much as they respected him. His title was United States country general manager, and everyone knew he ran the branch. His unofficial motto? "Make money or make room."

He protected the people who delivered. He expected blood from the stone and loyalty in return.

He liked me—at least for now.

Todd's departure felt like a collective exhale. The tension in the office softened. Karen even smiled at me the next time she passed my door, something I hadn't seen from her before. But I couldn't shake the image of him from last Friday. He was sitting at his desk, back straight, staring out the window. I passed by and nodded. He didn't return it.

"They never called," he said, still looking at the glass. "No explanation. No thanks. Just a new name on the org chart."

I didn't know what to say.

"Twenty years," he added, his voice thin. "Gone as if it were nothing."

I opened my mouth. Closed it again.

He turned to look at me finally. "Watch your back, Wallace."

And then he was gone.

This was not the start I was hoping for. But in this place, hope didn't get you very far. Results did. And enemies didn't wait for you to find your footing. I knew I had to move quickly, tighten the infrastructure, build trust with Dmitry, deepen the alliance with Erica, and prepare for whatever Swansea threw my way. The actual work was just beginning.

CHAPTER 3
THE FAULT LINES

There's a moment after the chaos of a new job settles, when the fog lifts just enough to reveal the real landscape. Not the one from the onboarding decks and welcome speeches, but the one people don't talk about—the fault lines. That moment arrived quickly at the Cambria.

Before I joined in March 2007, Alasdair and his management team had already done something remarkable: they had built a New York operation that *worked*, consistently profitable even when nearly the entire bank was sputtering. Financially speaking, the branch was punching above its weight. Politically, that made it risky.

At the board level, New York was considered the bank's jewel in the crown. Our consistent profitability earned admiration, and many saw Alasdair in particular as a future group CEO, perhaps even the front-runner. But below that rarefied air, on the operational level, things were different. Senior executives in Swansea mistrusted New York's independence and especially resented Alasdair's outspoken style. It wasn't open hostility, not yet, but it was friction, quiet and persistent.

A consensus—scrutinized by a board blending private shareholders with state overseers, anchored the executive order in Swansea. Alasdair knew how to bend those constraints without breaking them. Owen, his chief of staff, moved quietly in the shadows, each step calculated. Together they embodied a dual mantle: entrepreneurial spark and Welsh exactitude. But every victory magnified their sway, and in a culture steeped in caution, such power inevitably left casualties behind.

Above all, Alasdair had the unwavering support of the Group CEO, Edward Thomas, who ran the whole global group from Head Office in Swansea. This had made Alasdair untouchable and only added to the friction he experienced when engaging with the senior executives at Head Office.

I should have felt inspired, lucky, even, to land in such a high-performing outpost. But beneath the surface, I couldn't shake the feeling that this success story was a house built too close to a fault line. Something was going to shift.

By the end of my first month, I understood I had walked into a battle zone. Not a firefight, at least not yet, but something colder. A quiet, smoldering conflict between two incompatible forces: Swansea and New York. One obsessed with control; the other built on performance. One allergic to autonomy; the other thriving on it. It wasn't just a culture clash. It was a battle over who would define the future.

I quickly realized that the central IT team, based in Swansea, viewed the New York IT team not as a partner, but as a rogue branch to be reined in—a wild outpost that operated outside their control and threatened their illusion of uniformity. The head office IT team reported directly to the group operations officer—not to the business units—reinforcing the sense of top-down enforcement. Their memos to me asked nothing. They instructed.

My job, it turned out, was to sit dead center, trying to help the New York business stay profitable while dealing with a head office IT team that seemed more focused on control than collaboration. At times, it felt as if their goal wasn't to help us succeed, but to ensure we didn't stand out.

To them, our autonomy wasn't just inconvenient; it was insubordination. If Alasdair rose any further, he'd become a symbol that performance mattered more than politics. And for executives who'd built careers playing by committee, that was a dangerous idea.

Officially, I was the chief technology officer for the New York branch. In practice? They had just conscripted me into an underground resistance, one lacking uniforms and badges but with a proper battle to fight. They didn't draw the lines in blood, but in budgets, technical systems, and whispered alliances. And my job? Navigate it all without losing the branch or myself in the crossfire. I had to learn quickly, or I wouldn't last the quarter.

It started the morning after my first actual clash with Todd, my predecessor. My inbox pinged with a stream of "welcome" emails, every single one from the head office IT team. Not HR, not leadership, not even a line from the group CEO. Just Swansea's tech department, opening fire: deeper integration plans, system migration dates, plans to reduce our local software, and mandates for central finance and risk systems.

Swansea's memos kept coming: technocratic, irrelevant, and increasingly absurd. We stopped treating them as guidance and started treating them as noise.

Each email arrived with the urgency of a ticking clock.

I scanned the attachments. The corporate language in most of them was so confusing that it gave me a headache. The ones I could decipher were even worse. The systems appeared to be designed for mid-sized European retail banking branches, rather than the aggressive, client-driven world we operated in New York. Trying to implement them here would be like installing tractor tires on a Formula One car: all traction, no speed.

I forwarded one to the head of back-office operations. "Do we use this?" I asked.

The response was immediate: "God, no. We tried once. Nearly brought the business to a halt," Erica explained.

Erica managed the back office and possessed a subtle sense of humor, as well as extensive knowledge of the bank's operations. She had an accent that didn't quite belong to any one country, somewhere between Buenos Aires and Cardiff. Her proficiency in the Welsh language, combined with her exceptional intellect, rendered her an unlikely candidate for internal political maneuvering.

At first glance, she seemed above it all. She had previously been a senior accountant for one of the largest accounting firms in the nation, KPMG, and knew every accounting and operational loophole in the book. I came to rely on her like a compass; she kept me grounded. Erica wasn't just clever; she was fearless in a way that made other executives cautious around her. She suffered no fools, and she didn't flinch.

She showed up at my office that afternoon with two coffees and a sideways smile.

"You've seen Swansea's memos?"

"I have."

"You planning on following them?"

"I'd prefer not to bankrupt the branch in my first month."

She let out a laugh. "Good answer. You'll do fine."

That laugh felt like a lifeline. Until that moment, I didn't realize how alone I'd felt. One sip of terrible coffee and suddenly I wasn't a stranger anymore. We quickly became co-conspirators—a quiet alliance in a place where such things mattered more than organizational charts or official titles.

Erica was a long-term employee and had been with the bank from the start. She knew who was pulling which strings, and which ones were worn thin. Over the next months, she would become one of my closest allies, always ready with the numbers, and always three steps ahead of the gossip. Looking back, maybe she was always three steps ahead of me, too. That day, though, she gave me something more valuable: permission.

"Don't be afraid to piss them off," she said. "If Alasdair backs you, you're untouchable." It was the first time anyone had said his name out loud.

I didn't sleep well that night. Not from fear, exactly, but from the weight of it all, the sense that the actual job had just begun. The mask had come off. I wasn't the new guy anymore. I was the man standing between two worlds, and both were already calculating my odds.

CHAPTER 4
THE PACT

Alasdair Stewart, US general manager—really the master of this outpost—was the sun around which everything in the New York office orbited. Tall, muscular, tanned year-round. He wasn't loud, but his presence filled every room. When he asked questions, they came clipped, loaded, precise. When he said nothing, you paid closer attention.

He was born and raised in Edinburgh and was an exceptional athlete. He played professional rugby for the London Harlequins and even had two international caps for Scotland. Injury cut his sports career short. He turned to finance and, through grit and hard work, climbed the corporate ladder. He was a likable guy; the sort you would go the extra distance for.

He and his chief of staff, Owen Davis—the bank's chief administrator and Alasdair's trusted partner—were the twin architects of New York's success. Alasdair was instinct and firepower. Owen implemented his instructions with structure and scalpel.

Owen was short and narrow-shouldered, always in a perfectly pressed charcoal suit. He had close-cropped silver hair, and his wire-rimmed glasses gave him the air of a reserved academic—until he spoke. His words were sparse but precise;

his power lay in deliberate, measured action and the unwavering support from Alasdair. He was 62 years old and about five feet six inches tall. His family owned a small chain of retail stores throughout Wales, and he was the first in his family to attend university. He earned a 2.1 degree in finance at Oxford and spoke perfect Welsh, albeit with a posh English accent. Owen had never married, and everyone suspected he was a closet homosexual. If Alasdair was the spear, Owen was a loyal officer who operated with a surgeon's tool: quiet—and lethal when necessary. Together, they built something Swansea didn't understand: a lean, aggressive, profitable engine that ran on autonomy.

Swansea and the retail banking operations always followed policy and process, while New York operated on instinct and initiative. One was designed for compliance; the other, for survival.

Dmitry, my infrastructure head, had been quietly observing the friction for years. Throughout his tenure with the bank, Alasdair's aggressive pursuit of profitability and Todd's desire to avoid conflict with the head office's IT department had placed Dmitry in the middle.

One afternoon, as we debriefed yet another Swansea directive, he tossed the printout onto my desk and shook his head. "They hate us because we win, and because we don't ask 'how high' when they say 'jump.'"

Dmitry knew every inch of the place. One afternoon, he walked into my office with a smirk and a stack of printouts. He was one of the few people who could make cynicism feel like a form of intelligence. He was born in Moscow and moved with his parents to New York when he was about five years old. A product of community college, he had somehow earned a degree in computer science. His father passed away when he was 18, and that forced Dmitry to become the head of the household. With his mother and younger sister, he lived in

Brighton Beach. He talked little about his family, but I once overheard him on the phone with his mother. Gentle. Patient. It was the only time I saw the armor drop. He was unmarried and did not appear to have any outside interests. He was all about work.

"You want to understand this place?" he asked. "Ignore the company organization chart. Follow the tension."

He was right. Dmitry's cynicism wasn't background noise; it was radar. If he got twitchy, it meant something was coming. If he started pacing, you knew a storm was already closing in.

In every meeting, every vendor call, every budget review, there was a pattern. The teams in New York talked about Swansea's orders. But they pushed my team to build side systems. Duplicating data, while creating an illusion with Swansea that we were following their rules. In reality, the New York technologists had built a series of systems that hid underneath. The systems were crude, but functional.

We were a financial institution on the surface, but beneath it, we were a resistance cell with custom trading applications and Bloomberg data terminals. We didn't have a motto, but if we did, it would've been *keep the lights on, make money, keep Swansea out*.

No drama, no heroes. Just survivors.

And yet, we delivered. Month after month, New York hit its numbers. Agricultural finance, including loans for renewable energy projects in Oklahoma, meant multi-party leasebacks and tax-equity flips. The financing of cannabis farms in California involved multi-currency hedging, asset depreciation layers, and time-charter triggers. Hedging for European private equity shops meant building synthetic exposures that no spreadsheet in Wales could model. These were financial instruments entirely foreign to the operational teams in Wales, who were more accustomed to managing local mortgages, personal loans, and branch-level retail banking. Our business wasn't just different; it was unrecognizable to them.

Back in Wales, things were wobbling. Rising costs. Bad press. Missed quarters. And here we were: just 2 percent of the headcount, but 60 percent of the profit. They didn't celebrate us. They resented us. They couldn't copy us, so they tried to contain us.

But beneath the camaraderie and quiet cynicism, the tension was tightening. I sensed a reckoning was coming. And though I didn't want to admit it, part of me wondered if it would also engulf me.

Six weeks in, I got the note. Not an email. Not a meeting request. A single sheet of paper slid under my office door:

Sushi Yasuda. Thursday. 12:30 p.m. Alasdair. Owen. Carolyn. Erica. You.

No greeting. No signature.

The restaurant was discreet. Pale wood, no music. Precision everywhere, from the knives behind the counter to the cadence of the servers' feet. The sharp tang of rice vinegar lingered in the air. Knives clinked softly against lacquered boards. Even the servers' footsteps seemed rehearsed. The diners had already seated themselves.

Owen gave a slight nod. Alasdair didn't look up. Erica smiled and pointed at the seat next to her. I sat between her and Carolyn.

"You're late," Erica said.

"I'm early."

"Then you're learning."

We ordered. Or rather, they ordered for me. The food arrived in silence. Not awkward, just economical.

Then Alasdair leaned in.

Something flickered in his eyes then, grief, maybe, or resignation. He wasn't just a soldier taking orders. He seemed to be a man counting the days until they finally came for him. I was struggling to understand why. Part of me admired his defiance. Another part feared being drawn into something I didn't fully understand.

"You've read the memos."

"I have."

"And?"

"They're retail-grade systems designed by people who've never seen a complex financing deal. Implementing them would wreck your books in six months. It would eliminate our ability to manage risk. We'd be trading blind."

He smiled.

Owen spoke next. "David, we didn't bring you here to be a caretaker. We brought you here because we need a chief technology officer who knows technology and, more importantly, knows how to fight."

Erica added, her voice soft but eyes sharp, "And one who knows when not to ask for permission." Carolyn nodded in agreement.

There was a long pause. "We won't protect you," Owen said. "But we'll back you."

I felt the weight of what they were asking. It wasn't just about systems anymore. It was about choosing a side, maybe the losing one.

I wasn't sure if that made me feel brave or more expendable.

Alasdair raised his glass. "Are you in?"

I looked at each of them in turn. I hesitated. Not long, but enough to wonder what kind of war I was walking into. Enough to wonder whether this was loyalty or suicide.

"I'm in."

CHAPTER 5
THE FORTRESS

One of my first tasks after arriving at the bank was to review the data security infrastructure, technology designed to protect the branch from external cyberattacks.

I was shocked by what I found. Our cybersecurity protection was practically nonexistent. There were no effective protocols in place, no firewalls worth mentioning, and no one managing the ongoing maintenance. When asked who the data security manager was, everyone drew a blank. Worse still, I couldn't find anyone in leadership who seemed remotely concerned.

If something went wrong, it wouldn't just be the systems that crashed; it would be my reputation, my career that plummeted. It might even mean prison.

I discussed this with Dmitry at length. He informed me he had raised this issue with Todd on numerous occasions. However, Todd had neither an appreciation for the risk nor any desire to ask for the budget to implement a remedy. Todd had convinced Alasdair that all was fine, and the IT team in Swansea handled all matters related to data security.

When I delved into the details, it became clear that there was no technical segmentation between us and Swansea.

Meaning we were one extensive network. They could reach into our systems *at will.*

They justified this vulnerability by saying they needed live access to our financials, daily profit-and-loss statements, risk profiles, and month-end close data. But from my perspective, we were one click away from catastrophe. Looking back, it was only because the bank operated under most people's radar that we had escaped being compromised.

I realized we needed to improve. I did not want any sort of cyber breach on my watch.

I envisioned a network where we controlled the flow, not them. We would build a secure platform, pushing only the necessary data to Swansea when needed, on our terms, rather than letting them pull unfiltered raw data from our systems. It wasn't just about protection; it was about reclaiming control.

Over the next few weeks, my inbox became a Warzone. Group IT sent follow-ups. Then reminders. Then escalation notices. I responded to no one. Instead, I built a shadow plan with Dmitry and two trusted developers. We mapped what we needed to comply with on paper, just enough to make things look official, and what we would continue to run off-grid on a local network, controlled only by us. It was risk management through subterfuge. Sometimes rebellion looks like silence. Sometimes, it's just choosing not to reply.

The trick wasn't in saying *no.* It was saying *yes* slowly, vaguely, and with layers of plausible deniability.

When Swansea demanded we adopt their document management system, Dmitry found an old test server in our disaster recovery site and installed it there. It didn't connect to anything, but as far as central IT was concerned, the New York branch was now "fully integrated."

We weren't rebels for the sake of rebellion. We were defending something: efficiency, profit, independence. We weren't just managing risk; we were managing identity, defending a culture Swansea never bothered to understand.

We developed the plans to increase technical security and autonomy, and I immersed myself in the tech details. Frankly, having been an executive for over 20 years, this was not something I was used to. But I rallied the IT team and impressed upon them the importance and urgency of this project. They fully embraced it.

I observed that the New York team differed significantly from other bank offices in which I had previously worked. Most of us weren't from elite schools. We weren't polished business school graduates. Being immigrants, strivers, and hard-nosed New Yorkers, we could smell bullshit a mile away. We didn't need permission to do our jobs; we just needed space.

And that made us dangerous.

A week after the sushi lunch, Carolyn invited me for drinks after work. We met at a quiet bar in Midtown, with mahogany booths and a telling lack of TVs—this place had been around for a while. The air was heavy with the scent of citrus peel and old varnish. A jazz trio played low in the back, just out of sight. She ordered gin. I went with a beer.

She slid a napkin across the table. "Your bonus formula," she said.

I raised an eyebrow.

"Unofficial, of course. But Alasdair had me draft it. If you make it to year-end and we stay in the black, you're looking at something between $500 and $700k. Maybe more if Swansea stays out of our way."

"That's generous."

"It's a bribe," she said. "To stay in the trench."

I took a long sip.

"Who else is in the trench?" I asked.

She smiled. But something in her eyes held back. "Everyone who matters."

There was a flicker of something, uncertainty? Weariness? But it was gone just as quickly.

I left the bar with a buzz, not from the beer, but from the clarity. I had walked into a war, yes. But I wasn't alone. And now I had a side. Moreover, the potential rewards were significant.

That night, over dinner with Sue, we talked about the bonus. By now, we were in a decent place financially, no longer burdened by debt or uncertainty.

Sue rarely got involved in the finer points of our finances, but she had an instinct I had learned to trust. She could sense when something was off, even if I couldn't explain it yet. She said less these days, but her silences had become heavier, watchful, almost waiting for me to face something I was trying to ignore.

That night, she leaned in across the kitchen table and looked at me, not just as my wife, but as the person who had weathered every storm by my side. Her calm, steady presence reminded me what was really at stake: she *trusted me* to handle those storms, and the thought of her losing that trust was unbearable. But that evening, she leaned in with quiet conviction, and we agreed: we'd use the bonus to make one of our shared dreams a reality, a second home in Florida.

It felt as if we were finally building something lasting. Something beyond just surviving.

The next morning, I drafted my first genuine act of rebellion: a budget request disguised as a disaster recovery project. Inside was an architecture that would not only protect the branch from external threats of cyberattacks, but it would also result in us becoming segmented from the head office, meaning we would be operating on a New York-specific network.

We filled it with redundant servers, encrypted data sets, leading-edge firewalls, and monitoring tools, all isolated from Group IT's reach. It would cost money, but we'd bury it where no one would find it. When Erica saw it, she didn't even blink.

"I'll pass it off to the accounting team; they'll make it disappear," she said, almost too quickly. "You know, David, this kind of autonomy only lasts until someone notices," she added, more thoughtfully this time. "Swansea's not blind, they're just slow."

I nodded, but something twisted in my gut. If this went wrong, I wouldn't just be out of a job; I might be the one they blamed when the dust settled. And worse, I wouldn't be able to say I hadn't seen it coming.

Dmitry and I spent nights mapping it out, our own digital fortress. A setup that, in straightforward English, meant we could survive a cyberattack, hide in plain sight, and keep our enemies at bay. Firewalls, encrypted backups, isolated networks, all the things that sounded like overkill until you needed them. We called it *Project Fortress Manhattan*.

Besides installing the latest data security protection, the project required hiring a local New York-based data security manager. If Project Fortress Manhattan was paranoia, it was also preparation. We were done hoping that everything would be okay.

Over the next few days, I prepared a detailed management presentation outlining the project's goals, risks, and strategic benefits, along with a comprehensive budget. Given the urgency, I presented it to the New York executive team at the earliest opportunity.

Alasdair visibly paled as I outlined the current setup and the risks we were running. Before I even reached the budget slide, he cut me off. "Approved," he said sharply. "Get this installed. Immediately."

A few days later, as we packed up for the night, Dmitry looked at me with an air of vague concern. "You know, when Swansea finds out about Fortress Manhattan, they are going to be pissed," he said. "They'll come for Alasdair. Eventually."

I nodded. "Then we make sure he's not alone."

Two days later, Swansea called an all-hands video meeting. The invite came from Group IT but was labeled as a "collaborative alignment session." Everyone knew what that meant.

We gathered in the main conference room. I sat at the end of the table, flanked by Dmitry and Erica. Owen sat in the room, just outside the camera's view. The overhead lights flickered slightly. The room was quiet except for the soft hum of the projector fan.

Across the screen, five unfamiliar faces appeared, corporate uniforms, monotone voices, and that tight-lipped Welsh efficiency. The individual in the center introduced himself as Peter Vogler, group head of technology strategy, reporting directly to the group chief information officer, who was a member of the board. He had the blank-eyed confidence of someone used to compliance by default, not by merit.

"Today," he began, "we will discuss progress on further harmonizing infrastructure and data compliance across all branches."

He clicked on a slide. There came a flowchart of dependencies and deadlines—boxes, arrows, acronyms, all stitched together in a way that defied logic. It looked like something designed to confuse rather than clarify, an instruction manual for madness.

"New York is behind," he said flatly.

I leaned forward.

"Behind ... what?"

Vogler blinked. "The roadmap."

"From what I have been told, we never agreed to that roadmap," I replied.

"Months ago, we sent it to Todd Smith, and he assured us he and Alasdair had agreed," he responded.

A murmur ran down our side of the room. Erica crossed her arms.

Vogler raised a hand.

"You're expected to comply."

"With what, exactly? A storage protocol that doesn't scale. An authentication model built for retail banking?"

"These are our group standards," he replied. "Global best practice."

"No," I said. "They're generic. And this isn't a generic branch." I was not loud, but my tone was firm.

I could see him flinch. He was not used to getting pushback from the IT team in New York.

There was silence. Then Owen's voice, off camera.

"We're done here."

The screen froze. The meeting ended. We sat in silence for a moment before Erica let out a laugh.

"That went well."

I chuckled, but the adrenaline still flowed. My hands were still slightly trembling. That call had felt like a line in the sand, and we'd just stepped over it.

No one ever mentioned Project Fortress Manhattan.

CHAPTER 6
THE LINE

Later that evening, Owen knocked on my office door. No fanfare, no entourage. Just Owen, in his usual perfectly pressed suit, holding a folder. Erica, who was standing outside my office, lingered a moment too long before leaving. It was as if she wanted to say something, but didn't. Her eyes scanned the folder in Owen's hand before flicking to me. Curious, calculating. Then gone. He closed the door behind him and sat opposite me.

"You handled that well," he whispered. "Peter Vogler reports directly to the group CEO. He will now paint a target on you."

I nodded. "I figured. In fact, I've already taken a couple of very stern phone calls from his junior managers."

He leaned forward. "The bureaucrats in Swansea want us to fail. Not just miss targets, but *fail*. Publicly. So they can dismantle this office, reassign the clients, and claim the strategy was flawed from the start."

"Why?" I asked. "We're making most of the money."

"Outside of the CEO, the executive board in Swansea firmly believes that the risk we're running in New York will ultimately lead to the group's demise."

"And Alasdair?"

"He's the only reason they haven't already pulled the trigger."

Owen paused, then opened the folder. Inside, there were handwritten notes and a Swansea internal memo, redacted with black marker. I scanned it. It was a draft plan to migrate our book of business to Singapore within 18 months. The memo was a warning disguised as a forecast.

"They never intended this for our eyes," Owen said.

"Someone on the inside sent it anonymously."

"Do we have a mole?" I asked.

"No," he said quietly. "Not a mole. A patriot."

I stepped out of the office to clear my head and found Erica standing by the printer. She looked up, gave a half-smile, and tapped the display panel.

"Funny how these things always jam right after a Group IT call," she said, casually. "That Vogler guy, does he really report to the CEO?"

"Direct line," I said.

She nodded slowly. "Power is shifting. It always pays to know where the center of gravity is."

She left before I could respond.

That night I didn't sleep. I lay awake staring at the ceiling, reviewing everything: the videoconference, the memo, Project Fortress Manhattan, the lines I had crossed.

I thought about Sue and the kids. About the life we'd built in the US, about what would happen if this all came crashing down.

Should I play it safe and follow in Todd's footsteps, or stick to my principles?

At breakfast that morning, the smell of fresh coffee mingled with buttered toast. Morning light spilled through the kitchen window, catching the edge of Sue's cheek as she reached across the table. Sue asked what had kept me awake. I gave her the details, and without giving it a second thought, she advised me to do what I thought was right.

"We'll be fine," she said, her fingers wrapping around mine. "We always are."

As always, she was the foundation and support that kept me going.

Decision made. I'd stick to my guns. But a voice inside me, quiet, persistent, kept asking: *How long before the guns turned on me?*

That day, Dmitry found me in the data center. I was triple-checking the switch configurations, paranoia, maybe, but something told me one of those days was coming.

He leaned against the server rack.

"Did I ever tell you why I left Solomon Brothers, my previous job?"

I shook my head.

He took a deep breath. "I was part of a team running its global telecommunications network. Good job. Family was proud. Then one day, corporate sends in these new guys, consultants. Their job was to centralize everything. Make it more efficient. Within six months, the entire local team was gone. They outsourced us to a vendor two blocks away. Same building. Lower pay. No pension."

He looked up at me.

"That's why I've stayed here so long. This place under Alasdair—it's different. It feels as if we actually matter."

"You do," I said.

Dmitry smiled, but there was sadness in it.

"Don't let them turn us into another line item. Not like last time."

I nodded and clapped him on the shoulder.

"Not on my watch."

With the budget for Project Fortress Manhattan approved, we set out to implement it as soon as we could. I knew I had to play politics with Swansea. So I reached out to the technology executives at the head office and informed them that the US Federal Reserve had recently completed a full technology audit of the New York branch. Before they issued a formal report, they had given us the opportunity to fix our data security weaknesses.

This was only partly true, but it gave us the cover we needed to move forward. Reluctantly, and without me going into the details, they had acknowledged the project.

Over the next few months, my team worked every available hour to implement the project. By the time we completed it, we had created a fully redundant, highly secure data security infrastructure: hidden logs enabled, a mirrored shadow of our environment—ready to run autonomously—and dual internal and external firewalls. It wasn't just about survival anymore; it had become an act of defiance. We weren't just shielding infrastructure; we were protecting a culture, a set of values Swansea would never understand. Every keystroke felt like a stand. Every line of code, a line in the sand.

Our team operated like a restaurant kitchen during dinner rush, controlled chaos with a shared sense of urgency and pride.

As part of this project, I made my first hire—the branch's first data security manager. Sanjay Patel started a few weeks after the team interviewed him. I had found him through a recommendation from an industry friend. The recommendation described him as brilliant at his job but also mentioned some baggage. Dmitry, Carolyn, and I interviewed him. We all agreed that he knew his stuff, but his flamboyance was atypical for someone who had chosen a career in data security.

He was 50 years old and of Indian descent. His Eton and Oxford education demonstrated that he came from money. He was loud and expressive and clearly relished making people slightly uncomfortable. Not that it mattered, but I assumed he was homosexual. He lived in downtown Manhattan, just a short distance from the office. He also had a habit of vanishing for long lunches. I'd later learn that most of them involved a drink.

But what struck me most was that Sanjay wasn't just brilliant; he was painstakingly meticulous. He treated vulnerabilities as personal insults. When he spoke about intrusion detection, it was with the precision of a surgeon and the flair of a playwright. He wanted to prove something. Maybe to us, maybe to himself.

By the time he formally initiated projects that we had been quietly planning while designing Project Fortress Manhattan, he had already established a set of protocols that, coupled with the new data security technology, ensured the branch was protected.

One evening, I stood alone in the server room, watching the status lights blink. A pulse, steady and silent. Beneath my feet, the hum of the backup generator. Above my head, a tangle of cable trays and fire-suppression ducts. In that room, beneath the blinking lights and humming fans, it wasn't just circuits and fiber. It was New York's heartbeat. And now it was strong. Two days earlier, Dmitry flagged a strange log entry—a minor issue, a mistimed login from a non-routable IP address—but it was enough to raise our pulses. We scrubbed everything and found no breach, but the silence afterward felt loaded, as if someone had knocked but not entered.

Outside, New York pulsed with its usual contradictions, steam rising from sewer hole covers, the smell of roasted peanuts and hot asphalt, horns blaring while pedestrians jaywalked with impunity. In a city built on pressure and reinvention, our little server room had become a fortress.

In the office, we were ready.

Let them come.

This wasn't just defense anymore. It was a declaration.

CHAPTER 7

THE CHRISTMAS PARTY

W e weren't trying to create friction for its own sake. We were *defending*—efficiency, profit, independence.

As 2007 ended, profits were spectacular, the best the branch had ever produced. Alasdair and Owen wanted the team's performance to be celebrated, so they commissioned a Christmas party that would go down in history. For reasons known only to himself, Sanjay had enthusiastically volunteered to plan and manage the party. They gave him a generous budget, but I'm sure he overspent.

The venue was the Rainbow Room at the top of Rockefeller Center. It was more than extravagant; it was operatic. Floor-to-ceiling windows looked out across Manhattan. A live jazz band played standards near the bar while a string quartet performed near the dessert tables. There were jugglers, stilt-walkers, and walking magicians drifting between tables. Champagne flowed like water. Gold balloons hung from the ceiling. Laughter rose in overlapping waves, punctuated by the clink of cutlery and the low hum of the jazz band. The air was thick with competing aromas: truffle oil, briny oysters, singed citrus from cocktail garnishes. The room grew warm as more bodies filled the space; coats were shrugged off, silk and velvet brushing against shoulders in passing.

All downtown office staff and their partners received an invitation from the company, which put the executive team up at the Ritz-Carlton for the night. There was no expense spared.

The food? Unbelievable. Sushi stations manned by chefs flown in from Tokyo. A raw bar with oysters from three continents. A carving station serving wagyu beef and truffle-roasted duck. And a dessert buffet that looked more like a jewel case than a pastry spread.

Midway through the evening, a professional tarot reader told fortunes on a large desk near one of the enormous windows, while servers in tuxedos offered miniature crème brûlée and espresso martinis on silver trays. No speech, no PowerPoint slides, just quiet nods of appreciation from Alasdair and Owen as they worked the room, shaking hands, sharing a few jokes, making sure everyone felt seen.

It felt surreal, like a dream we knew couldn't last. The higher the celebration, the sharper the fall.

As the party buzzed, I spotted Carolyn alone by the drinks table, with the same poised elegance and that knowing glance we'd exchanged during my interview. She slipped into Alasdair's inner circle with ease, reinforcing her role as a steady presence among the leadership, a quiet counterbalance to Erica's sharper edge.

For one night, the stress lifted. People laughed without glancing at their phones. I saw teams from finance *clinking* glasses with operations; IT staffers were chatting with traders. Dmitry even danced briefly with one of the compliance officers. It was the first time I'd seen him loosen up. Normally stoic, he smiled freely and even danced, letting the tension slide off his shoulders just for a few hours. Sanjay, like a headwaiter, charmed everyone as if he were already the star. Beneath the flamboyance, though, was a hunger to be respected.

That night, I caught him standing alone near the window, dressed in a flamboyant red silk smoking jacket, watching the skyline. He didn't notice me. His shoulders sagged, and his mask had fallen. For just a second, he looked tired. Lonely, even. Then he turned, saw me, and the grin snapped back into place like armor. He was back to his old self, making sure no one left without a gift bag.

It was totally over the top. I remember talking briefly with Alasdair and asking him, "If Swansea finds out, are they going to be pissed?"

"Fuck them," he said, his words slightly slurred. "We're the ones keeping the lights on. Let them throw a party in Swansea, if they can afford one."

As we were leaving, I saw Sanjay deep in conversation with Erica. His animated expression and hand gestures suggested he was pitching something. She nodded occasionally, her face unreadable. It crossed my mind as strange, just for a second. Then I dropped the thought. Sanjay always wanted to be taken seriously. Behind the theatrics and lunchtime gossip, there was ambition. He craved a seat at the adult table, even if he didn't quite know how to ask for it.

Later that night, back at the hotel, Sue reflected on how ostentatious the whole thing was. "That must have cost north of a million dollars," she remarked, still in disbelief as she kicked off her heels.

I laughed. "Sanjay's budget was five hundred thousand."

"So he treated the overage like a rounding error?"

"Pretty much."

Back in Swansea, word of the party reached the group board by the following week. Photos circulated, as did the rumors about the cost. Alasdair didn't flinch. When questioned, he shrugged and said, "We performed. This was recognition, not excess."

But the tone had changed.

That party became a legend in the downtown office, but it also lit a fuse. Swansea saw it as arrogance. We saw it as proof: we were doing something right, and something worth defending.

That Christmas, for the first time since I'd joined, I felt pride. Not just in the numbers, or the architecture we'd built, but in the people. The defiance. The unity. We weren't just fighting for autonomy anymore. We were fighting for each other. And that made it worth everything.

CHAPTER 8
THE INNER CIRCLE

That sushi lunch a few weeks ago marked a shift I hadn't anticipated. I went from outsider to operative. The change wasn't declared; it unfolded subtly. It came in glances, calendar invites, hallway nods from people who once dodged eye contact. Suddenly, I was in meetings that weren't on the official calendar. Emails came with blind copies. People lowered their voices when I walked by, not because I was a threat, but because I was now part of the machinery—trusted, yes. But also implicated.

There's a moment in every political machine when your role changes without warning. One day, you're proving yourself; the next, you're a cog that's already been installed. Still valued, but now instrumental. That was the shift I felt. Not promotion. Not recognition. *Deployment*. And with that deployment came pressure, the kind you carry in your chest like a ticking clock. A quiet internal rattle of urgency that never fully fades.

One morning near the elevators, a junior compliance officer, someone I'd never spoken to, stopped me mid-step. "Quick one," he said, eyes too eager. "The network change you approved last Thursday, was that intended to isolate your backups from group view?"

I blinked. He shouldn't have known that detail. "It's part of the resilience policy," I said, keeping my voice even. He nodded, tapped a note into his phone, and walked away as if it were nothing. That's when I knew. They didn't fully trust me yet. I was under review.

That afternoon in the corridor outside the boardroom, Alasdair pulled me aside. "Keep your head clear," he said, almost under his breath. "They're watching how we respond, not what we say. You get that, right?" I nodded, unsure if I had. He smiled slightly. "Good. I knew you would."

What followed was a club governed by function, not fraternity. Its currency was competence, not camaraderie. If you delivered, if you stood your ground when Swansea pushed, you stayed in the room. But if you flinched, played it safe, or tried to hedge your bets, you were done. There were no training wheels, no handrails, and no second chances.

Alasdair built his circle like an engineer assembles a machine with only function in mind—no place for theatrics, no tolerance for vanity hires. If you got results, you were in.

Erica, head of back-office operations; Carolyn, head of HR; and I, chief technology officer, covered all the major operational activities and had formed a solid bond. It felt like I was part of an excellent team. And as Alasdair built his team, I did the same with mine. Dmitry, my lead technologist, and Sanjay, our data security manager, formed the core.

I had always taken pride in building teams based on excellence. Both men were technically brilliant. Dmitry was a real high-tech geek, methodical and stable. But behind his reserved exterior, I sometimes sensed a quiet anxiety, as if he knew how fragile our systems—and our position—really were. Sanjay was more of a thinker; he could spot vulnerabilities others missed and had a sixth sense for risk. But he was also volatile, known to drink during lunch more days than not, and gossiped as if it were a competitive sport. Somehow, he always knew what you'd done before you had.

One busy afternoon, Sanjay knocked lightly on my office door and stepped in, holding a printed report.

"I think someone's fishing," he said.

I looked up. "Meaning?"

"Two log-ins from Wales this week. Odd times. Wrong credentials. They didn't get in, but they weren't using the standard admin path either."

"Could it have been a mistake?"

"Maybe," he said, not convinced. "But it felt deliberate. Like someone testing fences, seeing where they sag."

I studied him. Sanjay was usually irreverent, sometimes too much so. But not today. Today, he looked sharp. Focused.

"Thanks," I said. "Good catch."

He nodded and turned to leave. "You asked us to build a fortress. I'm just keeping watch."

And for the first time, I realized he wasn't just the guy who joked through status meetings. He was one of the people I'd started to rely on.

Erica had also changed. She spoke little in group settings, but when she did, it was always precise and rehearsed. She had a habit of asking questions that sounded helpful but often revealed more than they concealed. At the time, I took it as a sign of keen thinking. In hindsight, it feels more like reconnaissance.

Owen had built his own set of disciples, which consisted of a few senior underwriters, the senior loan officer, and Reginald Blaine, who was responsible for business development. Reggie: too polished to be trusted, too smooth to pin down, floated between alliances like a man who knew which side of the boat to lean toward without getting wet. You never quite knew whether he was bluffing or betting. I once watched him share an elevator ride with two executives from opposing factions. By the time we reached the lobby, both thought he was on their side.

He was dangerous in the way a smile can be a disguise. He was officially the head of business development. To me, he was the classic gray American banker. He wore affability like a uniform, impeccably dressed in an American-cut suit, always ready. One moment, he'd charm Swansea with textbook deference; the next, he'd crack jokes in Alasdair's office as if they were old friends. He was the only person I knew who could make both sides feel seen without ever revealing which side he was on. It was unsettling. Useful. And deeply calculated. He was never careless until, of course, he was.

Sometimes I wondered if Reggie was playing a long game, whether he was hedging his bets between Alasdair, Owen, and Swansea, waiting to see who would survive. His neutrality wasn't just diplomatic; it was tactical.

We were just months away from the financial collapse of 2008, though the signs were still shadows. Markets twitched, headlines speculated, but business hadn't yet seized up. In New York, we were in full stride. Our specialty—structured project finance—looked pedestrian to Wall Street's highfliers, but it was the right horse in the wrong race: steady, collateralized, and grounded in reality. It didn't dazzle, but it delivered.

The irony wasn't lost on us. While synthetic returns and fragile derivatives seduced the big investment banks, we stuck to fundamentals, lending money against physical assets, turbines, tractors, steel in the ground. It wasn't glamorous. But it was real. The kind of transaction you could audit with checklists and clipboards, not spreadsheets. In the end, it was the least admired strategy, until it was the only one left standing.

Our other business interests included funding for large data center projects, solar grids, and agriculture infrastructure anchored by government backing and locked into long-term contracts. These were capital-intensive, horizon-bound plays, slow to build but near-guaranteed in return. Swansea had no patience with them. They certainly had no appreciation of the reliability of the income streams these products generated. Our steady gains looked like a challenge to their worldview. Worse, it came from the branch they had dismissed as parochial, and they never forgot it. That stung.

Back in Wales, Cambria was faltering. They had sunk capital into bloated home mortgage portfolios and an overambitious retail expansion that outpaced demand. They were building a brick-and-mortar branch network when everyone else was turning to digital banking. Margins were thin, risk assessments stale, and morale teetering.

Meanwhile, in New York, we were outperforming expectations. Our top-line revenue was strong, but it was the bottom line that rattled them. Despite our cost base, we consistently delivered excellent net profits. We didn't just stand apart; we exposed their inefficiencies. And that made us dangerous.

The Manhattan office occupied three floors in the new Freedom Tower. The middle floor, our heartbeat, was all glass and glare. The trading room, framed in transparent offices, offered no privacy but made power visible. Welsh flags hung from the ceiling, although none of the traders came from Wales. Sales and trading teams filled one side with tension and momentum; back-office operations on the other side ran the silent choreography that kept us compliant.

One level down sat the dealmakers and our data center, partitioned behind smart glass that turned opaque at the tap of a badge. And above that, on the top floor, was the brain. It held the boardroom with its panoramic downtown Manhattan view, two video conference suites built for high-stakes calls, and the unblinking presence of HR and Group Legal—always watching, always nearby.

The data center in particular became a fortress within a fortress. It wasn't just about firewalls or authentication layers; it was about presence and control. Physical keys, biometric access, locally mirrored logs, protocols—all technical components that kept Swansea at arm's length away. We now controlled every inch. Now, they didn't just lack visibility; they lacked jurisdiction. It was our stronghold, and everyone knew it.

Alasdair held the big corner office. From the floor-to-ceiling glass windows, you could see down to the charging chaos of Wall Street: briefcases, cigarette smoke, a blur of ambition. But up here, above it all, the calm was eerie. A sealed aquarium of power, where silence carried more weight than shouts.

The so-called process optimization team showed up on a Wednesday—three of them. One took photos of whiteboards when she thought no one was looking. Another hovered too long over Sanjay's console. "Is this script part of the group standard?" She asked, tapping the screen. Sanjay glanced at me, then nodded. "Of course." She smiled, barely. "Just checking."

The next day, I found a Post-it on my desk. No name, just a system path I didn't recognize and a timestamp from midnight. I tried to find out exactly what it was and ran the audit logs twice. Nothing stood out. But it was enough to keep me awake that night.

I started getting subtle signals. Swansea began copying unnecessary recipients: compliance officers, legal officers, people from departments with no stake in the discussion. And the names weren't junior. They were senior enough to stall things without explanation. Project approvals slowed to a crawl. Vendor contracts that once took a week now lingered for six. When we asked why, the replies came back frosted with vague authority, or worse, outright condescension. It wasn't an oversight. It was orchestration.

"Your local deviations are under strategic review," one message read. "Please reconfigure systems in alignment with group architecture and submit updated compliance documentation within the prescribed window."

Translation: *Your independence is inconvenient. Quietly comply, or we will methodically sideline you.*

Inside New York, though, the mood was electric. Deals closed. Bonuses landed. Headcount grew. For once, the IT team wasn't an afterthought. We were integral. I'd restructured the group, let a few people go, elevated a few dark horses, and recruited a couple of high-caliber reinforcements who knew how to deliver under pressure. The result was a unit that could run lean and hit every target. No excuses. No drama. Just precision.

I'd barely wrapped one project rollout before the next was already on the roadmap. Dmitry and I were building a purpose-built, hardened, traceable network infrastructure from the ground up. No shortcuts. No borrowed code. It wasn't just robust; it was defensible, which in that environment meant everything.

One night, as I packed up for the day, laptop bag slung over one shoulder, I saw a glow from Sanjay's office. Most of the floor had gone dark, but his door was half-open, the flicker of a security dashboard dancing across his glasses.

He didn't look up when I knocked gently and leaned in.

"Still here?" I asked.

"I live here now," he said, dry as a martini. "The nightlife in firewall logs is truly sensational."

I chuckled and stepped inside. His screen showed a cluster of login attempts, timestamps clustered tighter than they should've been.

"What am I looking at?" I asked.

"Someone in Swansea pushed a credential injection against our backup server," he said. "Twice, actually. Failed both times. It was sloppy, looked automated. But it pinged me."

I frowned. "Testing us?"

"Or testing what we can see," he replied.

He tapped a few keys and isolated the originating IP.

"Not Group IT's usual sandbox. This came from the admin segment. That's not routine maintenance."

I felt a slow burn behind my eyes. "Did you flag it with Dmitry?"

"Not yet," Sanjay said. "Wanted your read on it first. We can ignore it, of course. But I've archived the logs. Air-gapped, offline. Just in case."

I stared at the screen. There was nothing overtly damning. But the intention was obvious enough: reach, poke, observe.

"Good work," I said. "Keep watching. But let's not go wide with this yet."

He nodded, then looked up at me, and for the first time since he'd joined, his confidence faltered just a little.

"David ... do you ever wonder if we're the bad guys in their story?"

I paused. "All the time."

He smiled faintly, then turned back to the screen. "Then we might as well be competent villains."

I headed home, eager to leave the cares of credential injections behind.

"You just flinched when the cutlery clinked," Sue said.

I set down my fork. "Just tired."

"No, this is something else." I opened my mouth, then closed it. "They're watching you, aren't they?" she asked. I hesitated, then nodded. She didn't speak again. Just cleared the plates with a kind of quiet that stung more than any argument.

Then came word of an *offsite*. We had heard whispers from Swansea that some of the group divisional leaders were planning a leadership alignment weekend in the United States. Nothing formal yet. When he felt it was more fact than rumor, Alasdair called the management team together for a meeting in our large boardroom. He informed us that this offsite was likely to happen, then delivered a powerful speech, which was aimed at preparation.

"Wales will never admit it," he said. "But without us, this whole thing collapses." He looked around the room. "Make sure that at the offsite, you act like it."

The mood changed after that.

This appealed to something deep within me. I wasn't just building systems; I was building permanence. Proof that I could shape something that ignorance or hierarchy couldn't dismantle. And I wanted to believe that being needed meant being safe.

"Does our system log who accesses admin controls, like who changes permissions or edits config files?" Erica asked during a routine update meeting.

I paused. "Yes. With some customization." She nodded, scribbled a note, and changed the subject.

Later, Dmitry leaned over. "Why would she need that?" I didn't have an appropriate answer. But the hair on my neck stayed up for the rest of the day.

It felt as if we were preparing for a trial we hadn't been told we were part of.

CHAPTER 9
THE OFFSITE

The invitation came wrapped in charm: a weekend offsite in the Catskills—senior leadership, fresh air, no agenda, just time to relax and reconnect. On paper, it looked benign. In reality, it felt like a trap.

Sue was skeptical from the start.

"They want you out of your element," she said. "Watch what happens when you stop moving."

She wasn't wrong. They manicured the resort, making it antiseptic. Every surface radiated synthetic sincerity: pine-scented air, soft jazz in the lobby, fresh fruit at every turn. The air was too clean. Their smiles were overly rehearsed. Nothing spontaneous. Nothing real. Just curated calm, designed to lower defenses.

They told us to leave our laptops behind. They discouraged phones.

"We want a presence," the event coordinator chirped. *Presence.* What they meant was *control.*

At least 20 senior executives were flown in from Wales. These were the ones leading the meetings and events.

We had name tags, breakout sessions, and fire pit gatherings. There were no formal presentations, but plenty of quiet conversations. Erica, always composed, navigated the weekend like a diplomat, smiling, listening, observing. You couldn't tell what she believed. Her stillness wasn't just restraint; it was strategy.

Owen kept to himself, disappearing on long walks. Alasdair was visible but guarded, his usual charisma dulled to something more functional. He looked tired. More than that, he looked boxed in.

I tried to play along. Participated in the group hike. Nodded during the mindfulness exercise. Even laughed once or twice. But I couldn't shake the feeling that we were being measured. Not just for performance. For loyalty.

Then came the real agenda on day two.

A closed-door "feedback" session. Someone brought each of us in alone. The questions weren't about cohesion. They were about governance. Data access. Compensation structure. Influence. Alasdair endured 90 minutes of questioning. When he emerged, he looked pale.

"I need a smoke," he muttered.

He didn't smoke.

When it was my turn, I kept my answers vague.

"Do you believe Group IT aligns with the branch's strategic priorities?"

"Yes, wherever possible."

"Has Alasdair Stewart ever asked you to circumvent group policies?"

"I act in the best interest of the bank."

"Do you feel comfortable reporting concerns anonymously?"

"I prefer clarity."

Afterward, I found Dmitry alone on the deck, arms folded, staring out into the trees.

"This isn't a workshop," he whispered, his voice low and deliberate. "It's a loyalty test."

His tone wasn't bitter; it was surgical. A diagnosis. And we all knew it wasn't just Alasdair. We were all under a microscope.

That Saturday night, they held a "reflection circle." Each of us was asked to share one thing we'd learned about ourselves that year. Most gave the expected answers: gratitude, resilience, balance. When it was my turn, I hesitated.

"I learned that trust is fragile," I said. "Hard to earn. Easy to lose."

There was silence. Then polite applause. But I saw Erica watching me—not smiling, not frowning, just watching. Calculating. As if she were logging it away.

That Sunday morning, the facilitator encouraged us to write letters to our future selves. A facilitator handed us some plain paper and pens.

"You'll get them back in a year," she said.

I wrote mine in silence. Three lines. Folded it twice. Sealed it:

Remember who you are. Remember why you stayed. Remember who you can't become.

The ride back to the city was quiet. No one spoke much. The air in the van was heavy, not with exhaustion, but with realization. Whatever had happened up there hadn't brought us closer. It had confirmed what most of us already suspected: the walls were closing in.

That night, I told Sue about the weekend offsite: structured sessions for breakout, the bland food, the HR-led "empathy exercises" that felt more like a rehearsal than a retreat.

She listened, arms folded. "That wasn't team building," she said.

"What do you mean?"

"I've seen this before," she said, brushing her hair back. "When I worked in real estate. Before a layoff or takeover, they gather everyone. Pretend it's about connection, but they're watching. Seeing who complains. Who cliques together. Who doesn't clap at the right time."

I paused. "You really think it was surveillance?"

She gave a half-shrug. "I think it was a loyalty test. And I think you just passed, which means someone else didn't."

The following Monday, Alasdair called us in early. His face was gray. Not tired, but hollow. He didn't sit.

"Someone's trying to break into this office," he said.

He didn't name names. Didn't have to. We knew. The offsite hadn't been about bonding; it had been reconnaissance. Someone had returned to Swansea with ammunition.

Erica remained unreadable. She nodded at the right moments, furrowed her brow when appropriate. Her notes were meticulous. Her questions, neutral. Later that morning, she handed me a folder with updated governance protocols.

"I thought you'd want these on file," she said.

Helpful. Efficient. As if she'd expected the question before I even asked it.

In that moment, I felt a brief surge of gratitude; she was looking out for me, or so I believed. That's the thing about trust, it doesn't shatter all at once. It chips. And that file folder, with its immaculate formatting and preemptive relevance, was the first chip.

Sue noticed the change in me before I did. One evening, I stood by the sink, staring at nothing. She touched my arm.

"You're bracing for impact," she said.

I nodded.

I didn't have the words for it then, but she was right.

I'd stopped sleeping properly. I couldn't tell if I was worried about the firm, or about what I was becoming inside it.

She didn't try to fix it. Just stayed close. Made sure I ate. Slept. I didn't ask questions I wasn't ready to answer. Without her, I would've cracked. She was my ballast, silent, steady, always there.

"There is always a silence before people disappear," she said one morning over coffee.

The next few weeks passed in a fog of process changes and HR directives. The company issued a new code of conduct. Updated ethics training modules arrived. We were subjected to a full systems audit, not by an external examiner, but by the head office data security function.

It felt like a prostate exam.

Sanjay kept his head down, muttering about redundancies and "paper tigers." For all his bravado, I could see the edge creeping in; his jokes had become sharper, more frequent, as if to mask unease. Dmitry became almost fanatical, triple-checking everything, running simulations late into the night. He had bloodshot eyes from fatigue, but he wouldn't stop.

"Paranoia is a survival skill," he said once. I didn't argue.

Meanwhile, our work slowed to a crawl. Deals stalled. Vendor payments required double approval. It wasn't sabotage; it was suffocation.

One morning, Alasdair called us in again, before sunrise. No coffee. No preamble. Just pacing.

"They will not stop," he said. "We've embarrassed them too many times. Now they need a fall guy."

He turned to me. "They'll come for you first. Then me."

"Why?"

"You're new. You don't have institutional protection. And you built a system they can't control."

I swallowed hard.

Erica handed me another folder.

"We've documented everything. Paper trails. Timelines, sign-offs. You're covered. But start planning exit ramps."

"I've got the backups stored off-site," Dmitry added. "If they pull anything forensic, we'll know."

It had the weight of the final planning meeting before a coup—or a funeral.

Still, the work didn't stop. The New York business units kept closing deals. The branch continued to report earnings, and my technology team kept the place running, maintaining system uptime and meeting our internal service level agreements—contracts between our technology and the businesses we support. Every day, I wondered when the hammer would fall. But we weren't just reacting anymore. We were watching them, too. And we were ready.

One Saturday, I went for a run, my usual route into our local town center, then over to the park, but I couldn't shake the sense that we were heading for a cliff. The early spring air was damp, tinged with the scent of wet concrete and thawing leaves.

I remembered something Alasdair once told me early on, when I first joined the bank. We'd grabbed a beer after hours, and I'd asked why he'd chosen to work at Cambria instead of a Wall Street powerhouse.

"They needed me," he said simply. "And I needed the space to build something. I don't like being micromanaged."

He had joined the bank in 2002, when our US office was little more than a satellite. Within two years, he'd doubled its headcount and restructured its credit committees. He had a vision, and he executed it with precision. That was what made him a threat to Swansea. He didn't just protect turf; he expanded it.

After that conversation, I started asking around. Everyone had a story about Alasdair stepping in to close a deal, fix a mess, or back an employee others would have written off. He was no saint; his temper could cut steel, but he was loyal, and he expected the same in return. And now, the vultures were circling.

The following week, an email arrived from Group Legal. It was innocuous on the surface, an invitation to a compliance training. But the fine print gave it away: *attendance mandatory for all staff with administrative access to systems.*

That meant me, Dmitry, and about five others. The timing was deliberate. I forwarded it to Erica. Her reply came quickly. "They're building a case. Watch your step."

I closed the email and stared at my screen for a long moment. Outside my office window, the Manhattan skyline glinted in the morning sun. From up here, the city looked invincible. But I knew better. Somewhere out there, another request was being drafted. Another search was underway. Another thread was being pulled. The actual battles did not take place in boardrooms. They unfolded in shadows, steered by paranoia, enforced through silence, and waged through control. Whispers, memos, audit trails—these were the battle-grounds now. And we were in the middle of one. But we weren't going down quietly.

What made us a target was never incompetence. It was *performance*. Back in Wales, the bank was flailing, overextended, under-capitalized, desperate for wins. New York wasn't just surviving. We were excelling. And that made us a threat. Not just to egos, but to survival. If the narrative became that a foreign satellite could outperform the mother ship, the entire power structure risked collapse. So instead of celebrating us, they came for us. They had to.

There were even whispers in the market that one of the large Swiss banks had made a discreet approach to acquire our New York operation. The offer, though informal, was serious, and the board flatly declined it. That only deepened the rift. From Swansea's perspective, New York wasn't just an outper-forming division. It had become a self-sufficient asset that others wanted. That kind of attention was risky. It made us look like the prize, not the problem.

And someone in Wales would not let that stand.

CHAPTER 10
THE TRUSTED ALLY

B y mid-2008, I had become fully established in my role. The team I had inherited, or more accurately, rebuilt from the ground up, was finally humming. We had the right mix of developers, infrastructure engineers, and support personnel. These weren't box-tickers or clock-watchers. They were responsive, engaged, and critically aligned with the demands of an investment banking environment.

The team implemented major components of the technology security infrastructure, or as we knew it, Fortress Manhattan. We had established a certain amount of protection against cyberattacks. It also meant that Swansea could no longer access our network. We had closed the loop.

The day we went live with the last of the components and data filters, the user community complained that our network was slow. Our new security tools gave us the opportunity to investigate exactly what was happening. Upon inspection, we found that 60 percent of our network was being eaten up by personal activity. Employees accessing ESPN videos proved to be the most frequently visited site on our network. There were other personal uses, including a significant number of people visiting dating apps.

We turned on our whitelist filter, which allowed only work-related activity to be accessed. This, in an instant, blocked all access to personal websites for every member of staff. There were no exceptions. The uproar was loud, but after a few days, this soon subsided, and the performance of our network improved. From then on, no personal surfing would be allowed. Our new system blocked it.

By then, I had gotten used to the pace, pressure, and fire drills that came with supporting this business and its high-stakes trading operation. This was my professional comfort zone. For the first time in months, I felt something dangerously close to satisfaction.

I finally started sleeping properly—no more insomnia. One night, I slept past my 5:30 a.m. alarm and missed my train. This was possibly the first time that had ever happened. Sue noticed, of course. I actually found it shocking, and I told myself it was temporary, that I was just tired.

But peace in a place like Cambria's New York office was always temporary. Just as our internal dynamics had stabilized, pressure from Swansea began to build, but slowly at first, like distant tremors before an earthquake. It started with emails. Then came the conference calls. Then, inevitably, the mandatory group-wide video meetings beamed in from a lifeless boardroom in Wales, where senior IT managers droned on about "standardization," and "compliance," and "alignment with group strategy." All code, of course, for one thing: do it our way, or else.

The boardroom itself matched the tone, dim fluorescents humming overhead, a dull gray conference table scarred with coffee rings, and linoleum floors that squeaked with every movement. It looked less like a seat of strategy and more like a forgotten back office from another decade.

But the message was unmistakable: Head Office hated that the Manhattan branch was operating independently, especially after we implemented Project Fortress Manhattan. They no longer had unrestricted access to our systems or data. That alone made us a problem.

Our team had designed tools and platforms that worked for our New York-based employees. Real-world trading needs. Fast, responsive, tailored. In contrast, Swansea was pushing a one-size-fits-all setup, clunky and outdated, built for bureaucracy rather than business.

They didn't like our systems because they couldn't understand them, and worse, they couldn't control them. We had installed safeguards that they couldn't override without permission. We even kept a separate set of logs to monitor what they were trying to access. That wasn't defiance. That was survival.

What we didn't see, at least not clearly, was that Swansea itself was under pressure. Group Compliance had flagged their outdated infrastructure. European regulators were circling. Some at HQ saw our success not as a threat, but as a benchmark they couldn't meet.

Their systems were slow, old, and completely out of step with the way we worked. We didn't just build new tools; we built a wall. We ensured that no one could tamper with our setup unless we permitted it.

It wasn't about being secretive. It was about staying in control and staying safe.

I didn't hide my disdain on the calls with the group technology team in Swansea. I was never much into corporate theater.

"I understand the group strategy," I said during one particularly heated session. "But your platform doesn't support the kind of trading books we run here. You're trying to fit a square peg into a round hole."

The Welsh head of enterprise systems, a smug, angular man named Jones Ritter, leaned forward in his chair with a mechanical smile.

"That may be," he said, his heavy Welsh accent sharpening with condescension, "but integration is not optional. We are *one* bank."

That phrase, "we are one bank", became a kind of corporate curse. I heard it endlessly over the months that followed, often accompanied by veiled threats: audits, escalations, compliance reviews. It was bureaucracy masquerading as leadership.

But I wasn't entirely alone. Alasdair, whose political weight inside the bank had been growing steadily, was fiercely protective of our autonomy. He didn't trust Swansea, and that mistrust was mutual.

By that point, Alasdair and I had developed a solid rapport. We weren't friends in the traditional sense, but there was mutual respect. He appreciated that I didn't sugarcoat things, that I always told him the truth. I appreciated that he didn't pretend to understand the intricacies of technology. Once a week, without fail, he'd wave me into his glass-walled office.

"David," he'd say, motioning to the chair across from him. "Tell me what nonsense they're pushing on us this week."

And I would. I'd vent; he'd listen. Sometimes he'd chuckle; sometimes, he'd scowl and jot something in his leather notebook.

"Leave it with me," he'd say. And more often than not, he'd make the problem go away.

These conversations frequently involved Erica. She had by now become one of my most trusted allies. Her bullshit radar was even better than mine, and when push came to shove, she had a way of making the numbers talk.

Owen also sat in on many of the conversations. Where Alasdair was blunt and combustible, Owen was all polish and poise. An articulate man who never raised his voice but somehow commanded every room he entered. Owen had always walked a careful line. Too Welsh for the Americans, too American for the Welsh. That had once made him a perfect bridge; now it made him suspect to both sides. Swansea didn't trust his loyalty. Alasdair doubted his restraint. And I ... I wondered how long he could keep both masks intact.

Even as the global banking system started showing early signs of distress, we remained profitable and just. Our foreign exchange desk was still printing money. Less than before, but still in the green. Our transportation finance book,—aircraft, shipping, rail—was stable. We were seeing some transactions perform poorly, but the portfolio was okay. From a branch-level perspective, we were holding our ground. The group in Swansea, on the other hand, was showing signs of serious distress.

The pressure mounted slowly at first. People dropped hints on calls. They questioned our access to funding sources. At first, I dismissed them. Curiosity, perhaps. But over time, the questions became more pointed. They wanted to know if we could help with liquidity. Although they never said it, I sensed the bank was running out of cash. If we had options, they didn't.

At that stage, accessing the Federal Reserve's discount window wasn't on the table, not seriously. It was still too early. The wider markets hadn't yet tipped into crisis. But you could sense it building. And you could sense that Swansea already feared where things were heading.

The Welsh and English financial press had speculated about Cambria's viability. British Colonial and the Royal Bank of Wales were hoarding capital. Our peers were ducking for cover. In New York, we were still running lean and sharp, and from the outside, maybe even smug.

Even external analysts had noticed. A minor article on Bloomberg News that week called us "the most stable nerve center in a shaking system." The visibility, once a shield, was becoming a spotlight. It painted a target on our backs—one they couldn't ignore. The spotlight made us a potential target for a cyberattack, yet I felt comfortable that our IT security platform, Fortress Manhattan, would protect us.

But just as we thought we had a handle on the resistance, the shape of the threat shifted.

It started with a quiet arrival. A new face. A "strategy consultant" sent by Head Office to help us "align processes" across regional hubs. Rhys Bennett. Mid-thirties, tan suit, impeccable manners. The kind of polished presence who spoke in frameworks and balanced scorecards.

"He's here for three weeks," Erica told me, passing the itinerary across my desk without sitting. "Technically embedded with ops, but he's already spent an hour in the server room asking about our access logs."

"He's a spy," I said flatly.

She didn't disagree.

I watched him over the next few days as he worked the floor. He asked soft questions with hard intent:

"Who approves firewall changes?"

"How are incident reports escalated?"

"Why do we store our logs locally instead of mirroring them to HQ?"

Innocuous on the surface. But he was assembling a map, not of our systems, but of our loyalties.

On Thursday, Dmitry walked into my office, unusually quiet.

"You okay?" I asked.

"They called me," he said. "Swansea. Jones Ritter and one VP."

I straightened in my chair. "About what?"

"A job," he said. "Permanent role. Head of enterprise infrastructure, in head office."

That hit me harder than I expected. "Are you thinking about it?"

He met my eyes. They offered a housing allowance, a company car, and even a travel allowance.

I said nothing.

He paused. "But they don't understand what we have built here," he added. "I'm not going. I have family responsibilities. My mother and sister need me."

Relief washed over me, but it didn't last. The message was clear: They weren't just trying to hobble us from Wales. They were trying to hollow us out from within.

"They know Fortress Manhattan works," Dmitry said, rising to leave. "They can't beat it. So they'll try to dismantle it."

First came the new global project office, based in Newport, Wales. Every technology initiative, no matter how small, now had to be registered, reviewed, and rubber-stamped. Management froze the budgets. Hardware orders stalled. Approvals disappeared into the ether.

Then came the infrastructure rejections. Routine upgrades blocked. Storage expansions denied. Firewall renewals flagged for "additional scrutiny." When I pushed back, Swansea escalated to Alasdair. When he pushed back, they escalated to the group chief operating officer. And round and round we went.

Looking back, maybe it had been weeks in the making. The subtle uptick in duplicate audit requests. The delays in standard reporting lines. It had all been groundwork. Now the strike was landing.

Midstream, our data encryption overhaul project came to a halt during one particularly maddening week. Swansea said they hadn't included it in the budget, even though we had approvals signed the previous year. It went beyond just obstruction; it was sabotage.

I stormed into Erica's office, rejection email in hand.

"They're putting client data at risk to make a point," I snapped. "This isn't politics. It's security."

She read the note, jaw tightening. Then, without a word, she picked up her phone.

"Alasdair," she said. "You need to come down here."

Erica's actions reflected no panic, no drama. Just movement. In that moment, I saw what made her so threatening to the people upstairs. She didn't escalate; she activated.

Five minutes later, he arrived, read the email, and sat down without saying a word. The silence stretched.

Finally, he looked at me. "Move forward with the project," he said. "If they want to fire someone, they can start with me."

My stomach dropped. It was the right call, the only call, but it was also a line in the sand. We had just taken a stand, and I knew instinctively that from this moment forward, there was no going back.

CHAPTER 11
THE WATCH

The cracks in the relationship with Head Office were no longer hairline fractures. They were widening fissures, and everyone could see them. Swansea saw them. So did we. Sue remained the one part of my life that hadn't tilted sideways. She didn't push, but she watched. But when I started sleeping with my laptop in the bedroom, she spoke up.

"You need to find a way to turn this off, even just for a night."

She was right. She usually was. I didn't tell her everything, but I didn't have to. She could see the fight I was in, even if she didn't know the battlefield.

"I'm proud of you, you know," she said one evening. "Even if you don't tell me what's happening."

That almost undid me. She was the one thing in my life I wasn't defending against.

Back in the office, Sanjay was coming apart. Within days, he received a formal caution from the security team in Swansea about undocumented security protocols, an absurd charge. He fumed, then disappeared for lunch for nearly two hours. Again.

I found him one day at a bar off Lexington, swirling ice in a half-finished whiskey.

"You've got to stop," I said quietly.

He looked up, eyes ringed with fatigue. "Stop what? Being smarter than them?"

That afternoon, Alasdair caught me outside the lift. "Get your guy under control," he said. "If they smell disorder, they'll pounce."

I nodded. But I wasn't sure what control even looked like anymore.

Sanjay had always been brilliant but volatile. He thrived under pressure, but he also wore his emotions like a flag. The gossip, the drinking, and the refusal to play politics made him vulnerable—and a target. I had brought him into this world, and now I wasn't sure I could protect him from it.

Meanwhile, Erica flagged a string of HR issues. Minor stuff like overlapping vacation requests and conflicting shift notes, most of which had already been resolved. She placed a folder on my desk before I'd even asked.

"Already flagged the duplicates and looped in Carolyn," she said. I flipped through. The formatting matched the head office's template, not ours.

"You preempted them," I said.

She smiled. "Isn't that what we're supposed to do?"

She had a past she rarely discussed, a stint in corporate restructuring that ended after a whistleblower incident. I didn't know the details, but sometimes I wondered if that experience was why she stayed two steps ahead. She read subtext faster than anyone I'd ever worked with.

Owen called a meeting. "This isn't about firing people," he said. "It's about building a paper trail. They're documenting everything. Lateness. Minor mistakes. Anything they can log."

I asked if anyone in Swansea had actually said who was on their radar.

"They don't need to," he replied. "The goal is erosion—of morale, of trust. Just enough to make people question themselves and each other. Then they'll act. Not because the business is failing, but because they want control."

New York, once an exotic outpost, was becoming a power center. We had the money, the access, and the initiative. And in Alasdair, we had a leader who wouldn't back down. His influence had grown too visible, too fast, and in a group that valued control over competence, that made him a threat. But even as we rallied, something in the air shifted. There was an unease I couldn't name.

Word came that Edward Thomas, the group CEO, was under increasing pressure. That weakened Alasdair's position. We'd been on the front foot, but now I couldn't shake the feeling that something was coming. Compliance checklists appeared overnight. Legal queries with no obvious target. Silence when we asked for clarification.

One afternoon, Erica stepped into my office and closed the door. "Have you noticed the spike in audit trail requests?"

"Yeah," I said. "They're fishing. But I don't think it's about us."

She nodded slowly. "I hope you're right."

A week later, a junior in finance mentioned, casually, that Swansea had requested a full breakdown of Alasdair's travel expenses for the last 18 months. That got my attention. Nobody asked for expense reports unless they were building a case.

When I raised it with Alasdair, he waved it off. "Let them dig," he said. "I've got nothing to hide." But his eyes gave him away—a flicker of doubt. Maybe even fear.

It wasn't déjà vu; It was pattern recognition. The same quiet buildup I'd seen before back in London. Late-night queries. Sudden freezes. A personnel file request. Back then, they hadn't fired the executive. They discredited him. Slowly. Efficiently.

Two days later, Carolyn received a call from her Swansea counterpart asking for a copy of Alasdair's personnel file.

Highly unusual for someone at his level. She flagged it for Erica, who called me immediately.

"They're circling," she said. "It's not noise anymore."

Owen suggested we meet off-site. "Neutral ground," he said. "No glass walls. No metadata."

We chose a pub in the East Village, narrow, loud, and forgettable. Perfect.

Dmitry showed up late, breathless, and scanned the pub as if he expected a tail. "They're still watching," he said. "I disabled two ghost profiles this morning. One of them pinged our internal DNS server." He slid a napkin across the table. On it, a web of login spikes, timestamps, and IP clusters. "They're tracking behavior. Not breaches, habits. They're building a case on patterns."

I looked at Owen. He already knew.

Erica, silent until then, finally spoke. "How do we react?"

"We tighten outbound filters," Sanjay answered. "Clean routing logs daily. No shadows. No noise."

All technical jargon, but Erica nodded. "Perfect," she said, calmly. Like she'd practiced.

I should have questioned it then, how smoothly she pivoted, how well she understood the threat. But in that moment, I was grateful. We needed people who were ready.

The truth was, I was tired. Each morning, as I climbed the subway stairs, the dread pressed harder. I felt it in my gut: something was closing in, and no amount of preparation would stop it.

By the end of the month, we had a fortress. Not elegant, but dense. Redundant layers. Encrypted decoys. Noise traps.

We'd stopped the bleeding.

But we hadn't stopped the hunt.

They weren't probing anymore.

They were preparing.

CHAPTER 12
THE CRACKDOWN

The fault lines weren't forming. They were already there. And we were standing right on top of them.

The following week, Group Risk unexpectedly upgraded an internal IT audit planned for our branch to an "emergency review." They didn't call it an investigation. They called it a review. Three people arrived unannounced from Swansea, all with neutral suits and unreadable expressions. One of them had been in HR for 15 years. Another used to run compliance out of Newport, Wales. The third said little.

Alasdair greeted them personally. Shook hands. Offered coffee. His smile didn't reach his eyes. They didn't ask where to sit; they took chairs. One unpacked a slimline ThinkPad and began typing within seconds. Another glanced around the room as if he were assessing a crime scene. I noticed one of them had a ring binder pre-tabbed with sections: *Privilege Escalation*, *Network Topology*, and *Chain of Custody*.

They weren't there to ask questions; they were there to confirm a predetermined verdict. A formal request for access logs, transaction workflows, and internal control procedures had been emailed to every department head by noon. They wanted the last six months. No exceptions. It didn't feel like an audit. It felt like a raid in slow motion.

"I want full cooperation," Alasdair told us in the executive huddle. "Don't obstruct. Don't editorialize. Just give them what they ask for."

He looked tired, but not defeated. Just resigned.

"I've seen this before," he added. "This isn't about controls. It's about *control*."

Owen nodded quietly. Erica took notes.

The office felt colder than usual that week, as if someone had turned down the thermostat just enough to notice. The hum of the fluorescent lights seemed louder. Coffee sat untouched in the breakroom, stale and burnt-smelling. Even the elevators moved more slowly, groaning under the weight of anxiety. People walked in whispers.

That night at home, Sue sensed it before I told her. She met me at the door with a look.

"They're here, aren't they?"

I didn't ask how she knew. She just knew.

"What are they trying to achieve?" she asked.

"No idea. Owen thinks it might be about job cuts, but that makes little sense to me. We're profitable, maybe the only branch in the group that is. Why target us?"

Sue sat down beside me and thought for a long time before speaking.

"Maybe it's not just about cuts," she said. "Maybe they want to dismantle what you built ... because they couldn't build it themselves. It's easier to tear something down than admit you couldn't make it work."

We made dinner, poured some beers, and sat in silence while I decompressed. In a world of politics and pretense, her presence was the only thing that didn't feel conditional.

"I feel like we're about to lose control," I told her eventually.

For a while, she said nothing. "Do you think it's time to look for another job?" she asked after a pause.

My answer was unconvincing. "No, not yet. I think I can manage through this."

The truth was, we had built something rare in New York. We weren't bloated or bureaucratic. We ran lean, took calculated risks, and kept close to the market. Alasdair had brought in people who thought like owners, not caretakers. Our FX desk had outperformed every quarter since I arrived. Our transport business was stable and profitable. Even our back office had one of the lowest error rates in the group.

But none of that mattered now. Success without obedience was disloyalty.

Back in the office, I noticed Sanjay had started coming in late and leaving early. His mood had darkened. He wasn't saying much, which was unusual in itself, but the tension rolled off him like heat. I kept meaning to pull him aside, but there was always something more urgent. And besides, part of me didn't want to know. If I knew, I might have to act.

That week, people whispered. First, about the files being requested. Then, about who was being questioned.

"They've asked for internal emails. Watch your tone. Assume visibility," Owen texted me one night.

Dmitry caught up with me at the coffee machine.

"They spent two hours with Craig yesterday," he said quietly, referring to one of our database administrators. "They were asking about system admin overrides—what we log, how often we check."

"Did he give them anything?"

"Nothing they didn't already know technically," Dmitry replied. "But it felt as if they were rehearsing a narrative. As if they already had a script and just needed voices to fit it."

They weren't gathering evidence. They were staging a case.

Dmitry glanced around before continuing. "I've been logging their access trails. Quietly. If they're making copies, we'll know."

I raised an eyebrow. "And if they find out you're tracking them?"

"Then I'll be in the room next to you when it all blows up."

It was gallows humor, but I appreciated it. We'd crossed from engineers to insurgents. I nodded slowly. That sounded about right.

Erica stood nearby, offering clarifications when asked, never overstepping, but always available. I realized later that they seemed to know her by name. I also noticed that one auditor, the quiet one, spent a lot of time near Erica's desk. At first, I dismissed it, but later that afternoon, I caught them in a quiet exchange by the printer. It could have been nothing. Or it could have been everything.

That evening, I found Sanjay still at his desk, alone, staring blankly at his screen. I asked him if everything was all right.

He looked up, uneasy. "They pulled me into a room today. Said someone from Head Office wanted to speak with me. One-on-one."

"About what?"

"Swansea. They called it a development opportunity. A chance to join a task force back at the head office. Said it would be 'a good fit for someone with a fresh perspective.' Then they asked about the leadership here."

I cringed.

"They wanted me to speak off the record," he continued. "Said I'd be helping the bank, bringing transparency. But it didn't feel right."

"You think they're testing you?"

"Maybe. Or using me to test someone else."

I placed a hand on his shoulder. "You don't owe them

anything except your work. Not your loyalties. Not your silence. Not your complicity."

My actions would mean choosing sides before the battle lines were officially drawn.

CHAPTER 13
THE BREACH

Three days into the review, Dmitry knocked on my door with a printout in hand and a look I hadn't seen before: tight, almost angry.

"We've had a breach," he said. "Or something that looks like one."

The document detailed a new network profile tied to a device out of our Swansea office. Someone had granted it backend permissions usually reserved for internal infrastructure work. The access trail was clean, almost too clean.

"Who created this?" I asked.

Dmitry hesitated. "Sanjay's credentials. Time-stamped last Tuesday. Just after lunch."

My stomach sank. That was the same afternoon he vanished for nearly two hours, came back late, distracted, breath faint with whiskey. I'd made a mental note but hadn't followed up.

We launched an internal investigation within the hour. The access had allowed someone in Swansea to pull all of our operating accounts from the past six months. It was data we provided to Head Office anyway, but usually in summarized data sets. What they took was everything. But it wasn't what they took, it was how they took it. No summary reports, no request trail—just raw access, as if we'd handed over the keys.

Erica flagged that detail. Calm, efficient, almost too efficient. "They'll claim it was a technical miscommunication," she said, already drafting a sanitized summary.

I asked Sanjay directly if he had created a network account for someone in Swansea without approval.

He looked offended. "Absolutely not," he said. "Why would I do that? You think I'm that careless? They're setting me up. You know I wouldn't do that."

I wanted to believe him. But the evidence was tight.

The pressure from my peers in New York was immediate. Alasdair didn't say it outright, but the implication was clear: someone had to take the fall.

It was a Tuesday afternoon when the HR directive arrived, cold, curt, and final. Sanjay was to be terminated immediately "for cause," following an internal compliance review triggered by a network breach traceable to credentials he allegedly provisioned. The official language was clinical:

"... unauthorized profile creation ..."

"... failure to follow security protocols ..."

"... negligence with privileged access ..."

But the facts didn't sit right. The profile in question had been generated from a Swansea IP. The logs were incomplete. And Sanjay, for all his quirks, was fanatical about access control.

I called him into my office, hoping for a simple explanation. He walked in with his usual defiant energy, but the moment I gestured to the chair, he looked wary. Defensive.

"Is this about the breach?" he asked, cutting straight to it.

I nodded. "They're saying you created the profile. That it was handed to someone in Wales. Do you know anything about it?"

His eyes narrowed. "Of course not. I'd never hand off credentials without dual authority. And I log every profile, *every single one*, David."

I believed him. However, I was unable to do anything. Compliance was already involved. Carolyn had forwarded the HR packet. There was no room left for discretion.

"They're not asking questions," I said. "They've already decided."

He sank back in the chair, stunned. "So that's it? After all I've done?"

I didn't speak. I couldn't.

His face twisted, not in rage, but disbelief. "I caught their first intrusion attempt. I flagged it. You remember that. I *protected* this place."

"I know."

He stood slowly. "Then why do I feel as if I have already been erased?"

I handed him the envelope. He took it, then stared at it for a long moment.

"I thought you were different," he said quietly. "I thought we all were."

I wanted to say something, anything. But what could I say? That I agreed? That I was just as helpless? He walked out without another word. No theatrics. No slammed doors. Just a long silence that hung in the air long after he'd gone.

Later that night, I sat alone in my office replaying the conversation. I opened the network logs myself, hoping I'd missed something, some clue that would clear his name. But I found that someone had already archived and sealed the audit trail. And for the first time in this entire war, I wondered if *we* had become the thing we feared most: a system that devoured its own.

The office felt different afterward. His desk sat empty, a coffee mug still there, half-washed. The air smelled faintly of old aftershave and plastic keyboard covers. Conversations lowered when people passed his chair.

Erica said little. Just forwarded me a one-line email: "Clean documentation. Important we close this loop."

Her tone was neutral. But her timing was perfect. Too perfect.

I called Sanjay the following Monday. No answer. Sent a text, "Let me know you're okay." But the message sat unread.

A week later, I tried again. This time, someone had disconnected the number.

And just like that, he was gone.

It was Erica who had asked Sanjay to create the profile. It was Erica who passed the credentials to the head office. And it was Erica who let me think I'd made the right call.

Later that afternoon, I received an encrypted email from Swansea. Subject line: *Immediate Risk Review Follow-Up*. The body was brief. Formal. Clinical. They were requesting a complete archive of server logs, backup snapshots, and historical email traffic for three individuals: myself, Dmitry, and Alasdair.

It didn't say why. It didn't have to.

I walked the printout to Erica's office, closed the door, and dropped it on her desk. The paper felt warm from the printer but cold in meaning. She didn't seem surprised to see me. If anything, it felt as if she'd been expecting it.

I caught her glance before she dialed, sharp, calculating, and laced with dread. Not confusion. Not concern. More like someone realizing a plan had accelerated without her sign-off.

She read it, lips thinning, then picked up her handset and dialed a number from memory.

"Alasdair, come down."

He appeared five minutes later, still in his jacket, as if he'd sensed this moment was coming. When he read the request, his expression barely flickered. He didn't sit. Just stood silently for a few seconds.

"So it's begun," he said.

"What do you want to do?" I asked.

Alasdair looked at the two of us. "Give them what they asked for. Clean. Full compliance. Let them think they're winning."

"You're not going to push back?" Erica asked.

"Not yet." He exhaled. "But I need time to move a few things. As long as the current CEO is in place, the board still sees me as an asset, not a threat. This feels like a local power play out of Swansea. But if the wind changes at the top, that protection disappears. And we all know it."

He didn't look at us when he said it. Just stared out the window at downtown traffic like a man watching something drift out of reach. It wasn't fear exactly; it was calculation. He was working the angles, even now. But something in his posture said he knew the game had changed. This was no longer a simple turf war; it was a deliberate effort to discredit and dismantle everything we had built.

It was the most vulnerable I had ever seen him. And that scared me more than anything else.

Erica caught me in the hallway before I could slip out.

"You okay?" she asked.

I hesitated. "Not really."

She exhaled slowly. "They're moving faster than I thought," she said, almost to herself. "I've seen this before, in another job."

There was something in her voice, less shock than recognition, as if she were syncing to a playbook she'd memorized.

"Well, what happens next?" I asked.

"They rewrite the history books."

For the first time, I wondered which side Erica would be on when the initial shots rang out. She didn't seem surprised. She was already ahead of this. I told myself she was just being proactive. That she was helping. But a part of me, even then, knew something didn't sit right.

I walked to the data center and sat there for a while. The hum of the server fans filled the silence like static. I could smell ozone from the UPS room and stale vending machine coffee left over from the afternoon.

I sat there for a few minutes, lost in my own thoughts. I then decided to run and archive the backup tape program. Nobody asked for it, and nobody needed it. But I ran it anyway, just in case. I wasn't sure if I was preparing for war or digging my own grave.

But I knew one thing: The fight had come to our doorstep, and Swansea would not stop until the ground gave way beneath us.

CHAPTER 14
THE EYE OF THE STORM

In September 2008, the world changed. We watched the news in disbelief as Lehman Brothers collapsed. Bank of America swallowed Merrill Lynch. AIG teetered on the edge. The US government granted Goldman and Morgan emergency access to convert into bank holding companies. Even the titans were suddenly fragile. The mood on Wall Street turned somber, subdued in a way I'd never seen before.

Within our branch, the atmosphere was tense but calm. There was fear, yes, but it wasn't panic. We were lean and agile compared with the lumbering giants of the New York financial markets, and more importantly, we weren't sitting on a pile of toxic mortgage-backed assets.

Alasdair had long distrusted the subprime market. He thought the yield and advertised upsides were phony, and the models were rigged. Alasdair vetoed several attempts by traders to push us into complicated, structured credit transactions. At the time, some called him overly cautious. Now, they were calling him a prophet.

The Monday after Lehman collapsed, the calls started coming in. Not panicked, exactly, but quiet voices asking whether we had capacity. Whether we could move quickly.

Whether our balance sheet was "still intact." We hadn't changed our risk appetite. But suddenly, that made us a rare commodity. Alasdair called an emergency strategy session. Owen, Carolyn, Erica, and I sat around the boardroom table with coffee going cold. He didn't pace. He didn't raise his voice.

"There's blood in the water," he said flatly. "We're one of the few boats still floating. Let's fish."

Erica frowned. "There's opportunity, but it's coming from pain. Clients are desperate. Counterparties are collapsing."

Alasdair didn't blink. "Which is why *we* set our terms. High yield, tight covenants. We're not here to make friends. We're here to survive."

That month, we closed three emergency refinancing deals, each more aggressive than the last. We called them "liquidity bridges." But they were lifelines, offered at terms that would've been laughable six months ago.

One of the senior traders raised concerns. "This pace isn't sustainable," he said. "We're taking on more exposure while onboarding new credit models. We don't even know if some of these clients will last the quarter."

But the deals kept coming. Our fees soared. Our risk team worked weekends. I remember walking past Dimitry one evening, long after most had gone home. He was slumped over his monitor, red circles under his eyes.

"We're the only unscorched house in a burning city," he said, not looking up. "Feels wrong to profit from the smoke."

I didn't answer. I didn't have one.

The events in early October paralyzed the markets. Liquidity evaporated. Interbank lending stalled. The financial markets were essentially gridlocked. Clients who used to answer emails in seconds were now unreachable for days. One deal with a midsize municipal utility fell through hours before signing—our counterpart simply vanished. Another client asked to pause a transportation lease indefinitely, citing "unquantifiable exposure."

Inside the office, Alasdair convened an all-hands meeting in the trading room, a rare move. "Nobody leaves a question unanswered," he said. "Our calm will be our edge." It felt as if the entire financial system had frozen mid-inhale, uncertain whether it would breathe again.

Yet amid the chaos, our New York branch remained active. In fact, we were still trading and, from what I could tell, still making a profit. Our FX desk continued to thrive. Volatility was a trader's best friend, at least for those who knew what they were doing. Our transportation finance portfolio remained solid; we had been conservative with our credit profiles. Alasdair and Owen's caution, once questioned, now looked visionary.

At the group level, the need for our branch to provide liquidity became critical. Although I was not directly involved in the funding strategy, the signals were unmistakable: desperate conference calls, sudden reporting requests, panicked emails sent at odd hours. Our principal contribution to the group became our access to the Fed's discount window— an opening that allows financial institutions to borrow directly from the Federal Reserve, typically at reasonable rates, and when no one else will. It's a last-resort lifeline, rarely granted to foreign banks, but we were among a handful that were afforded that privilege.

You didn't just walk into the Fed and ask for a lifeline; you had to prove you deserved one. Demonstrating control, compliance, and liquidity wasn't optional; it was everything. We had all three.

Years earlier, Alasdair had fought relentlessly to secure that privilege, understanding it could one day be our lifeline. Now, with Europe on the brink and the British government scrambling to stabilize its major banks, Swansea finally understood the value of what they had in us. We were the oxygen masks.

Head office, which had been trying to cut our legs out from under us just months earlier—even calling our systems "unmanageable" during one of their infamous calls—was now clinging to us for survival. The contradiction was obvious to everyone, especially Alasdair, who once joked that if we'd been any more "noncompliant," Swansea might've sent in tanks instead of auditors.

Their tone changed overnight. Gone were the lectures about group integration. Now it was, "Can you run the numbers on how much liquidity you could access from the Fed this week?"

I remember walking into Alasdair's office late one evening in mid-October. He was sitting with Owen, both looking unusually relaxed for men presiding over a global meltdown. They had a bottle of red wine open between them. French, and expensive. Two glasses already poured.

"David," Alasdair said, waving me in. "Come drink. We may be the only bank in Europe not on life support."

I smiled, but I didn't sit. The laughter in the room felt surreal. I couldn't shake the disconnect, how the world outside was disintegrating while we toasted another win. My nerves were fraying beneath the surface.

"We've had three calls from Swansea today," I said. "They want daily updates on our liquidity pool, our counterparty exposure, and our access to the repo market. They've also asked for direct access to our trade capture systems."

Owen laughed softly. "Of course they have. They want what we have, but without admitting they need us."

Alasdair stood, walked over to his glass wall, and stared out at the downtown skyline. "Let them have their reports," he said. "But not our systems. Not those under our control."

I took a seat, and for a moment, the three of us just looked at one another. No words. Just the unspoken understanding that something had changed, not just in the markets, but in the power structure of the bank. We weren't a rogue outpost anymore. We were at the center.

And Head Office hated it.

You could hear it in their voices during the Monday calls. Cordial greetings and formal language masked an underlying tone of resentment. Their empire was sinking, and we were their life jacket.

That fall, the dynamic flipped entirely. Swansea stopped giving instructions. They started asking for favors. Could we hold off drawing more from the Fed so it wouldn't raise red flags? Could we share our compliance documentation so they could show the British regulators how robust their US unit was?

It was galling.

But Alasdair, to his credit, played it smart. He didn't gloat or taunt. Quietly, ruthlessly, and always one step ahead, he continued to execute. He began shifting capital between New York legal entities, optimizing regulatory treatment and freeing up liquidity. The result was dramatic: we doubled down on profitable aircraft leasing and renewable energy projects while others retreated.

One of our senior relationship managers told me about a call with a major pension fund manager. "They practically begged us to keep the deal open another week," he said. "Same guy wouldn't take my call six months ago."

Owen had heard the same. Prestige was now secondary to survival.

They cautiously allowed me to expand the technology team, a strange luxury, as firms all around us were laying people off. One developer, who had survived a brutal layoff at Lehman, confided over drinks that he kept a packed box under his desk, "just in case." We brought in new support engineers.

Upgraded our disaster recovery site from New Jersey to a hardened data bunker in Pennsylvania. I implemented new monitoring systems and hired a new cybersecurity analyst to replace Sanjay, whose departure had raised eyebrows across the team.

But the reaction within the team was mixed. Some saw the new hires as a sign of strength; others, like Erica, called it "a gamble we'd be blamed for later." She cornered me one evening in the hallway, eyes sharp.

"You know they'll spin this," she said. "They'll call it empire-building. Mark my words."

She didn't say it out of malice. She was detached and spoke as if she had seen this before and knew how the narrative would eventually unfold. I didn't push back. Part of me agreed with her.

Even Swansea's silence on the upgrades carried weight. They didn't approve of it, but they didn't stop it either. They couldn't afford to. For the first time, our decisions weren't being questioned; they were being watched.

One of the new hires, a junior systems analyst, asked me in the hallway, "Why are we expanding when everyone else is cutting?" I shrugged. "Because we still can." He didn't look reassured. Neither was I.

Cambria's European operations continued to unravel. Rumors of exposure to Lehman's debt and derivative bets circulated widely. In mid-November, a London-based financial blog published a scathing article questioning the bank's solvency. Swansea issued a terse denial. The markets barely reacted. Nobody believed them anymore.

Our US client base, however, remained loyal and continued to grow. With market liquidity drying up, institutional borrowers were desperate for capital. Our focus on infrastructure and clean energy gave us credibility. Clients who had once overlooked us were now knocking on the door. We saw an uptick in new deal inquiries, especially small renewable energy projects that had stalled because of the crisis. Owen saw the opportunity immediately.

"Move fast," he told the team. "While the others freeze, we act."

At one point, I asked him whether he was concerned we were becoming overextended. His answer was telling.

"This moment won't last," he said. "If we don't grab market share now, we'll regret it for years."

The world was flooding, and we were safely buoyant, floating on a liferaft built from caution and diligence. It was surreal. A peer bank had just announced another thousand layoffs while we were wiring signing bonuses. One client, a West Coast utility, called us directly to say, "You're the only ones still answering the phone." Word was getting out. We were not only surviving; we were the exception. And everyone, including our own team, knew it wouldn't last forever.

But even as the numbers remained positive, so did the unease. We were very visible. Too successful. And too foreign. You could sense it on the Monday calls. The words were polite. The tone was not. One senior manager from Swansea ended a liquidity update with, "We appreciate your ... resilience." It wasn't a compliment.

One night in December, I sat in the kitchen with Sue, sipping tea. I'd been quiet all evening. She asked what was wrong.

"I don't trust what's happening," I said. "It's all too good. Too fast. Swansea needs us now, but what happens when they don't?"

She looked at me, eyes steady. "Then they'll come for you. Not because you failed, but because you made them look weak."

She was right.

Sue had always seen these things before I did. She noticed tension in their voices, a hint of danger in their timing. I remembered a dinner we had back in 2001, just after I'd praised a telecom CEO for his confidence. I'd actually met him while working at British Colonial, but at that time, we were watching him give an interview on Bloomberg TV.

She had looked up from her plate. "He's sweating through his collar," she said. "That's not confidence." A few months later, the company imploded, but I had already moved my pension. At the time, I thought it was luck. I don't anymore. That realization settled over me like frost. Our success had made us visible, enviable, and vulnerable. We were living on borrowed time. And someone inside would be the one to open the door.

That night, as I was locking up my office, I saw Erica through the glass wall, still at her desk. She was just staring at her screen. One hand rested on a folder I hadn't seen before, marked "Internal Authorizations, Privileged Systems" in neat print.

She didn't look up, but I saw her fingers tighten slightly on the folder's edge.

I turned off the light and walked out. The image of Erica at her desk stayed with me.

The door wasn't open yet, but someone had found the key.

CHAPTER 15
THE GATHERING

The new year approached with a muted celebration—no champagne in the office, no toasts at desks, just quiet nods and cautious handshakes. A few people from the FX team went for drinks across the street, but even they seemed subdued.

The global financial storm still raged at the same time our value to the group had eroded. We had hit a barrier with the Federal Reserve and were having a tough time borrowing more money through its discount window.

In the branch, I noticed a change. It wasn't just fatigue; it was anticipation. Everyone could feel it in the air, like the dry tension before a storm breaks. We all sensed that the real reckoning hadn't passed; it had merely changed shape. Somewhere in the walls, or in a server log no one had noticed yet, the next move was already taking form.

In January, Alasdair called a meeting with just six of us, his tightest circle. We met in the small conference room with no windows, no recording system, and reinforced glass walls that muffled the outside sound. Phones off. Notebooks closed. Even our watches were left on the table by the door. Alasdair wanted nothing that could transmit data in the room. It was *that* kind of meeting. I was sensing his paranoia and struggled to understand where it was coming from.

"They're going to try to pull something," he said, his tone lower than usual. "I don't know when or how, but the mood has changed. The emails are colder. Requests are more frequent and pointed. I feel it in the way they ask questions now. Less curiosity. More calculation."

Owen nodded. "We have had three deal approvals rescinded with no explanation. They're clipping our wings slowly."

"Compliance has asked for shadow reports of my metrics," Erica added. "That's not normal." She said it as a warning, not a complaint. I remember thinking how calm she seemed, too calm, given what she'd just admitted.

We all sat in silence for a beat.

"Whatever happens," Alasdair said, "I want to make sure the branch survives. If they remove me, you all need to stay in place. Keep the operation steady."

It was the first time he'd spoken about being removed. I left that meeting with a genuine sense of foreboding.

That night, I took a walk through Battery Park to clear my head. It was cold and nearly deserted, just the way I liked it. The city, even in crisis, had a rhythm. But my mind was on Swansea. On what exactly, I didn't know. I thought about the systems we'd built, the people who depended on us, the clients who trusted us, and the possibility that everything could be dismantled in weeks.

I'd spent years building this career. After London, after arriving in New York, I began anew, and, despite the challenges, I created a successful career. I couldn't let them take it from me.

When I got home, Sue was asleep. I sat on the edge of the bed and whispered, "I think they're going to make their move." She didn't stir, but I knew she felt it, too. The sense of it had settled deep, unshakable and cold. And I wasn't ready. Not yet.

The next morning, I arrived at the office before sunrise. The air in downtown was frigid, with a strong wind coming off the water; the pavement was slick with black ice. Traffic lights blinked across empty intersections, casting red and green reflections on glass towers that loomed like silent sentries. It felt as if the city had stopped to hold its breath.

I walked onto the floor in near-darkness, passing dimly lit desks and empty chairs. The glow from a single monitor at the far end caught my eye. Dmitry, already logged in, headphones on, immersed in server logs.

"Morning," I said, startling him.

"Didn't sleep," he replied without removing his headphones. "I've been watching the logs. There was a remote session from Swansea at 3:04 a.m. into the staging environment."

"Credentials?"

"Senior audit override," he said, his voice flat. "They didn't even try to hide it."

It was brazen—a message, not a mistake.

As part of Project Fortress Manhattan, we had to agree that at least one department outside of New York could have administrative access to our systems. We all agreed that it would be the group's audit team. This ensured the audit team could independently conduct reviews and audit-related monitoring outside of New York operations. We certainly never expected that they would use these privileges for anything other than official audits.

I closed my eyes. They were probing, testing our defenses, or worse, laying the groundwork for what came next. If our core directory were to go down, trades would freeze. Client trust would vanish.

"Keep a record. Mirror everything. And don't tell anyone else, not yet," I said.

Dmitry nodded. We both knew what was happening. They were already inside the walls.

By midday, Swansea sent another request, this one dressed up as a compliance formality. They wanted full administrative rights over our primary directory servers, citing "centralized oversight requirements." I forwarded the request to Alasdair without commentary.

He called within minutes. "Don't respond. Stall. We'll talk tonight."

That evening, we met in his office after hours. He dimmed the lights, cloaking the cityscape behind him in shadow.

"I want you to prepare a backup telecoms server," he said. "Off-site. Something they won't think to monitor."

"For what?"

"If they cut us off, I want to be able to reach the team."

It felt like overkill, but then again, maybe overkill was all that stood between us and annihilation.

"We've got at most a few weeks," he added. "Maybe less."

"What's the trigger?" I asked.

"When they stop asking questions and start issuing orders again."

Back at my desk, I emailed Dmitry and instructed him to provision the backup system. A third-party data center in New Jersey housed it, technically unrelated to the bank. I asked him to set it up under a fake project name and conceal it within a regular maintenance plan, something no one would look twice at. We kept the login details on a secure USB stick I carried with me at all times. It wasn't sophisticated, but it gave us something simple and private, just in case everything else got shut down. I wanted to be sure we could still communicate, even if the worst happened.

For the rest of the week, the mood continued to shift. People whispered in the hallways. Lunches were shorter. Jokes were less frequent. The traders, normally cocky and sharp-tongued, were suddenly subdued. I overheard one say, "Feels like we're being watched." He wasn't wrong.

Erica called me into her office on Thursday morning. I noticed she didn't seem rattled. Just composed. Almost rehearsed. As if she already knew how this would play out.

"I heard from Carolyn. HR has been told to prepare contingency files for all managing directors in New York."

"Termination packets?"

"Complete files. Histories. Red flags. Likely payout calculations. It's coordinated."

"Are they including you?"

She nodded. "Everyone. Including you." She watched me closely as she said it, as if she were taking mental notes.

I sat back, the weight of it settling over me. "So, we're past the surveillance stage."

"We've entered the execution phase," she replied.

By Friday, Alasdair summoned the core team again. This time, he didn't sit.

"They'll make their move in March," he said flatly. "Maybe sooner. My guess is they've already drafted the press release."

He had become a man full of paranoia, or he knew something and was not telling us.

"Do we go quietly?" Owen asked.

"No," Alasdair said. "We go with clarity and conviction. We document everything. Assume they'll distort the record. Make it harder. We keep our own records. If they're going to fabricate anything, we make sure they have to work twice as hard, and that we're three steps ahead."

He looked at me. "Make sure the logs can't be tampered with. Use layered encryption. Create immutable snapshots, time-stamped and cross-verified. Store them off-site, somewhere air-gapped, somewhere Swansea can't touch."

I nodded. Later that day, I received an email from a former colleague at another European bank, someone I trusted, someone who'd been through a similar battle. We hadn't spoken in years, but the message was unmistakable. Just one sentence: *This happened to us, too.*

And that was all I needed to know.

We weren't just victims of bureaucracy.

We were targets.

And someone inside the room wasn't just watching; they were helping draw the battle lines.

I replayed every closed-door meeting, every side glance, every change in tone. Had I missed something? Or worse, had I let it happen, piece by piece, because I didn't want to see it clearly?

CHAPTER 16
THE MATHEMATICIAN

The bank had survived the financial crisis, but not without scars, and not without cost. Global markets had buckled. Institutions once deemed too big to fail had collapsed or merged in desperation.

In New York, we were fortunate to remain standing, but even that felt like a miracle of timing, strategy, and luck. Although we had managed to produce a small profit the previous year, the pipeline for new deals had slowed to a trickle. Distressed assets now dotted our portfolio like landmines, and the mood had shifted once again. It wasn't panic. It was something quieter, more ominous: not just fatigue but resigned, smoldering dread.

Some of us had tracked the news obsessively, watching other banks fall like dominoes, wondering if we'd be next. One morning, someone pinned a *Wall Street Journal* article to the break room corkboard with the headline circled in red: "Next in Line?" It was meant as a joke. It wasn't funny. The building itself seemed more brittle in those weeks. Conversations were shorter. Meetings opened with silent glances.

By the start of 2009, a false sense of normalcy began to creep in. Bank CEOs were back on CNBC, the Fed had calmed the system, and the champagne flutes were quietly returning to conference receptions. Analysts started speaking in hopeful tones. Some dared to forecast a recovery. But inside Cambria, it was anything but normal. Behind closed doors, decision-making was delayed, tempers flared, and department heads conferred in hushed tones. There was no celebration, only the tightening of ranks. The party might have resumed in Davos and DC, but in our corner of Manhattan, the music never started.

The board abruptly removed Edward Thomas, the group CEO in Swansea, from his post. There was no press conference, no farewell memo, just a short, sterile email: "Edward Thomas has stepped down to spend more time with his family." In Wales, there was no public acknowledgment at all. For a man who had served for over 30 years, it was a humiliating erasure. There were whispers about a boardroom coup. Some suggested a rift between Edward Thomas and the supervisory board over the bank's exposure to US assets. Others hinted at a personal scandal, though no one ever substantiated it.

What struck me most was the speed. One week, he was on the year-end call with stakeholders; the next, his name was erased from the website. Even his internal biography vanished. It was like watching someone vanish mid-sentence, erased, not replaced.

Edward Thomas had enjoyed the respect of his senior colleagues in New York. He was what people called a "lifer," having joined the bank straight out of university. He had climbed the ranks methodically, without flamboyance, and under his guidance, the bank had grown from a modest Welsh regional into a player with a real international footprint.

It was Edward Thomas who had supported the decision to build the New York branch from scratch rather than buy an American firm. That had been a bold move, and one that many in Swansea had quietly opposed. For us, it was a declaration of independence. For them, it was insubordination masked as strategy. We weren't blind to the irony; his global ambition might have been his downfall. His legacy, once celebrated, was being systematically erased, and we couldn't help but wonder if we were next.

When the email landed, there was a brief, stunned silence on our floor. Then came the whispered calls, the instant messages, the closed-door chats. You could feel the oxygen shift. People suddenly remembered unfinished projects, questionable memos, and unguarded comments. Alasdair said little, but the look on his face said everything. Owen pulled me aside and muttered, "This isn't just a reshuffle. Someone's cleaning house."

"Brace yourself," Erica more bluntly said. "The next guy will not be one of us."

One thing I knew for sure. Without Edward Thomas's support, the business in New York would become totally exposed to the political ambitions of the management team in Swansea. Unless, as we hoped, Alasdair received that promotion.

Then, a few days later, the second email came: "Effective immediately, Dr. Cadwgan Rhun will assume the role of group chief executive officer." The message was terse, but its weight was enormous. Within minutes, the entire floor seemed to freeze. It wasn't just the arrival of a new CEO; it was the sense that an entirely new era had begun, and none of us knew what rules it would follow.

The name Cadwgan Rhun meant nothing to most of us. A few quiet inquiries to contacts in Swansea yielded more confusion than clarity.

He wasn't a banker, they said. He was a mathematician. A theorist. A professor who had been teaching economics at King's College Oxford. He appeared to have some advisory experience, but no visible profit-and-loss track record.

One source described him as "elegant and chilling."

Another simply said, "Be careful."

Someone else claimed he'd once advised NATO on cyber-warfare simulations, a whisper that seemed too strange to be false. No photos surfaced in the internal directories. No interviews. He was a name, a credential, an icy wind blowing through the executive ranks before anyone had met the man.

Alasdair, hearing the news, was ... livid. He believed he'd earned the job. After years of leading the only part of the bank still turning a profit, after orchestrating that Fed lifeline in 2008, the promotion felt like his by right. Instead, the board handed the reins to Rhun, someone new, someone safe.

There was more to it than a professional blow. It was personal. Alasdair never said much, not out loud. But I remember the way his eyes narrowed when I talked to him about it. His shoulders tightened. He wasn't just disappointed. The experience humiliated him, and he wouldn't forget it.

From that moment on, the dynamics were forever altered. Rhun didn't just replace Edward Thomas; he marked a new era, one defined by control rather than collaboration. And Alasdair? He bristled, but he was already planning his response.

Suddenly, the halls felt colder, as if the HVAC had overcorrected. Fluorescent lights buzzed just a bit louder. Even the carpeted silence of the executive floor seemed more oppressive, every footstep a whisper of uncertainty.

The political reality in New York changed instantly. Edward Thomas's willingness to back our team in New York felt like vindication for our ambition and vision. With him gone, I felt like a man suddenly aware of the trapdoor beneath his feet.

CHAPTER 17
THE VISITOR

As Rhun settled into his new position, the culture evolved in subtle but unmistakable ways. The tone of the senior leadership changed dramatically. Our earlier meetings with Edward Thomas, while formal, had always carried an undercurrent of mutual respect, even warmth. That disappeared overnight. Collaboration gave way to caution. People chose their words more carefully, avoided eye contact longer, and checked over their shoulders more often. It wasn't just the hierarchy that changed; it was the atmosphere. Decisions slowed. Questions carried hidden meanings. Trust receded.

Not that Rhun barked orders or stormed through the halls. He didn't need to. His presence alone changed the temperature in the room. Meetings grew more formal, and every email from Swansea carried the weight of courtroom testimony. Alasdair's authority remained, technically. But in practice, everything was now filtered through an invisible gatekeeper.

There was no overt conflict, no televised showdown. But signals were everywhere: Rhun's clipped responses in strategy sessions, the curt nods he gave when Alasdair spoke, the subtle reallocation of committee authority away from Alasdair, always in private, never public.

Shortly after Rhun's appointment, the board called Alasdair to Swansea for a face-to-face meeting. It was unannounced. I assumed it was to settle him down after he didn't get the promotion to CEO. When he returned, something about him had changed. He was quieter, more guarded. Whatever was said in those meetings had left a mark. In subsequent video calls with Rhun, the tension between them increased even more. There was no shouting, no overt hostility, just an icy formality that felt even more dangerous. Rhun spoke to Alasdair with clipped precision, and Alasdair responded with the strained politeness of someone deeply insulted but unwilling to show it.

I assumed the friction came down to one thing: Rhun saw Alasdair as a threat. And Alasdair knew it. Rhun wasn't punishing Alasdair for failure. He was eliminating a threat. Behind the calm professionalism lay a deliberate recalibration of power, and Alasdair was the first obstacle.

Alasdair spoke little in the next few senior management meetings after Rhun's appointment. But his silence wasn't calm. It was tense, brittle, and magnetic. Everyone around the table noticed it, especially Cross.

"He's jumpy," Erica whispered to me during one Tuesday session, her voice low and grim.

Over coffee a few days later, I asked if she'd ever come across Rhun before.

"Not directly," she said. "But a former intern of ours had once studied under Rhun at Oxford. Said Rhun had a reputation, brilliant but nasty. Vindictive, even." She stirred her coffee slowly. "People like him don't rise alone," she added, almost offhand.

"What do you mean?"

"They get help from the inside. Usually from someone everyone trusts. Someone overlooked. Invisible until it's too late."

That seemed like a vague, throwaway comment. But in hindsight, it felt rehearsed.

The real bombshell came two weeks later: Rhun had plans to visit New York.

The email we received painted it as routine. "... a familiarization tour to engage with regional leaders and understand local market dynamics."

No one believed that.

The mood in the office shifted immediately. Carolyn began assembling welcome packets with nauseating enthusiasm. Warren Blake, who headed the legal department, brushed off the compliance decks as if he were preparing for a trial. Alasdair instructed me to create a 45-minute presentation on our tech infrastructure, focusing on system integration, strategic upgrades, and cost forecasting. Alasdair and Owen had to present the branch strategy, performance trends, and 12-month projections.

What followed was a tightly choreographed two-week scramble. We subjected all our materials to review, revision, and re-review. Alasdair held two full practice runs. At one point, I overheard him rehearsing in the mirror of the men's restroom.

"This is not a man you can bluff," he muttered. "He already knows the answer before you open your mouth."

People began working later, tempers were shorter, and no one dared miss a meeting. I overheard someone joke, "Is this a bank or a Soviet tribunal?"

On the morning of the visit, the building hummed with nervous urgency. Artisanal pastries and three kinds of mineral water filled the massive oak table in our large boardroom. Alasdair wore a tailored navy suit with no tie, an understated and deliberate choice. Owen looked like a man preparing to defend his PhD. Rhun arrived just past 10 a.m. with a small entourage: a personal assistant, someone from Group Risk, and a junior analyst from Strategic Planning. Rhun was very tall, at least six feet five, with a long, angular frame and short, jet-black hair slicked back like lacquer. His face was sharp, his voice quiet and clear, and his eyes … scanned everything. He reminded me of the Child Catcher in the film Chitty Chitty Bang Bang; if he wore bespoke suits and advised hedge funds.

He shook hands precisely and offered a slight nod of acknowledgment, but there was no warmth. He wasn't rude, just efficient. As he moved through the trading floor, he paused. "Where's the systems monitoring console?" he asked.

I pointed it out. He walked over and began asking questions. Deep technical questions.

"Is this server isolated from your branch's core systems?"

"What audit controls are built into the interface?"

"What's the fail over time to Swansea?"

He wasn't showing off. He was genuinely curious and frighteningly competent. As a technologist, I found it very unnerving to be questioned in such detail by the CEO. Most I had previously encountered had trouble navigating their personal computers. After spending the morning meeting with various department heads, it was my turn. His assistant ushered me into a small side conference room where Rhun waited alone. I brought my laptop with the slide deck, but he waved it off.

"No slides," he said. "Talk to me."

I blinked, laptop still in hand. This wasn't a briefing. It was an interrogation.

As I waited to begin, I felt the sweat pooling under my collar. My thoughts scrambled to recall the essentials, striking a balance between clarity and caution. I shut the door. No one else was in the room. It felt less like a meeting and more like a quiet indictment. He was polite, but utterly joyless. Not a trace of curiosity about me as a person.

"You've built a network with no integration with group architecture," he said. "Why?"

I took a breath. "We've optimized the group systems for standard commercial banking," I said. "We're a purpose-built merchant banking branch. Our systems reflect that. They work."

"And what if I told you Head Office IT was offering you your own development budget, fully funded, autonomous, but required alignment with group platforms?"

I paused, considering what he'd just said. Was I being lured into a trap, or worse, being bribed by the group CEO?

"I don't resist funding," I replied. "I resist using the wrong tool for the wrong job."

He stared. Then nodded—slightly.

"Thank you," he said. "That will be all."

I stepped into the hallway and exhaled. Alasdair was waiting at the far end, hands in his pockets, eyes fixed on the carpet. When he saw me, he nodded once. No words. Only a flicker of acknowledgment, and I understood its meaning: the verdict wasn't in, but the judgment was quietly underway. I returned to my office and sat there for a while. Through the glass window, I saw Erica walk past. I followed her with my eyes. She didn't walk straight back to her office. She paused by the window, watching the street below for a moment too long, as if considering something unspoken. Erica never wasted a movement. That stillness felt deliberate.

I packed up, turned off my PC, and left for the evening. A rare early night. As I walked down the corridor, the air smelled faintly of lemon polish and burnt coffee. The floor was too quiet, punctuated only by the soft click of shoes across tile. Even the elevators seemed slower, as if reluctant to deliver anyone to judgment. I'd spent decades building systems and teams at various financial companies.

Wherever I worked, I had made it my goal to know every junction point, every potential failure. But beyond the wiring, I'd always thought that I had built something else, a belief that competence could shield you from politics. That if you did the work well enough, no one could take it apart. In the first weeks under Rhun, I realized how naive that had been.

CHAPTER 18
THE FALLOUT

The next day, something was different. Pressure hung in the office like static—anticipation, dread, or both. In the weeks that followed, the mood darkened. Two key FX traders resigned within days, sending a ripple of panic through the trading floor. Word spread that others were interviewing with competitors, quietly updating résumés and taking discreet calls in stairwells. This was strange timing, as we were approaching the bonus period. There was a sense that the branch was in danger of unraveling. People kept their heads down. Desks emptied early. Team leads went silent.

Then came the bonus email. It had been looming in the background, a dreaded certainty no one wanted to speak aloud. Every employee understood that the group had not made a profit; worse, it had incurred a significant loss, and the guidance from the board was to expect further losses in the coming years. When it finally arrived, it confirmed everyone's worst fears.

It hit mid-morning, just after the first round of espresso runs and before the traders had fully settled into their screens. A chime, a blink, and then silence. People opened the message almost in unison, the tension rippling across the floor. One assistant gasped audibly. A junior in capital markets dropped his cup.

It was terse: "In light of the group's overall financial performance, there will be no performance bonuses issued this year."

It read like a footnote but struck with bureaucratic force.

The message applied across the entire group: Head Office, London, and New York. The pain, it seemed, was to be shared equally. But that framing ignored a critical truth: at the time, New York was the only profitable unit within the entire bank. And the compensation model here differed from the rest of the group.

The reaction at the Manhattan office was volcanic. Traders shouted openly across the floor, venting rage at anyone who would listen. Senior managers slammed office doors and held impromptu meetings that ended in shouting matches. One VP in Infrastructure punched a filing cabinet so hard, his knuckles bled.

It wasn't just anger; it was disbelief. The New York branch had been profitable. Bonuses were not just expected; they were relied upon. Some staff had maxed out credit cards, planned home renovations, and put down deposits on vacation homes. One analyst quietly called her spouse from the stairwell and broke down in tears.

I remember the exact moment it hit my floor—9:08 a.m. A risk analyst read the email aloud, voice cracking, and then just sat down at her desk and stared at the screen. Phones rang unanswered. People stood around in stunned silence, unsure whether to scream or laugh. Some did both. The news hit harder because we had not only survived the storm, but we had *outperformed*. We had made money when others hadn't. We had done our part and then some. For New York, this wasn't just a policy decision; it felt like a betrayal of trust, a punishment disguised as fairness. Things started to settle down slightly after about a week, but the damage was done.

Then, out of nowhere, Alasdair's assistant pulled me aside. He wanted to meet for lunch: his usual spot, the steakhouse near Fulton Street. I assumed it would be just the two of us. When I arrived, though, there were already four of his direct reports seated, and Owen was on the far side of a large round table. The mood was formal, quiet. Plates of french fries were untouched.

After some polite small talk, Alasdair put down his fork and spoke.

"I'm going to do something," he said. "They won't like it in Swansea, but I'm doing it anyway."

He told us plainly and without ceremony that he was going to pay out bonuses to the top ten performers in the branch. This was against direct orders from group HQ, but he had shielded a previously approved discretionary pool from Swansea's oversight. The recipients were the five of us at that table, plus six from the trading room.

Owen had looked pale that afternoon, as if the weight of what Alasdair had shared settled on him differently. I caught his eye during the meal. He didn't nod or speak. But something in his expression told me he knew exactly how dangerous this was. No one said anything; I believe we were all in shock. But Alasdair was firm. They would pay bonuses to some. It wasn't a declaration. It was a confession. And a warning.

That evening after the steak lunch, I told Sue what had happened. I explained Alasdair had secretly decided to pay bonuses to only ten people in the branch, and that I was among them, the "chosen" few. She said nothing at first. Just sat back, arms folded, brow furrowed, studying me the way she did when she was thinking several moves ahead. I could tell she was uneasy.

"You can't tell anyone," I said.

She blinked. "Not even the kids?"

"Especially not the kids."

At first, I struggled with it. Within my own team alone, several top performers had worked themselves to the bone through the crisis. Why me and not them?

We didn't discuss numbers at that point. It was early March, and all Alasdair told us was that we were on the list. Nothing more, no details, just confirmation and a quiet nod of inclusion, and the weight of what it might mean.

Weeks later, he called each of us into his office individually. When it was my turn, he handed me a sealed envelope with my name typed on it. Inside was a letter outlining the payment. He looked up at me, nodded once, and said, "You earned this. Quietly, and completely."

There was pride in his voice. But also fatigue. Like someone expecting the blowback he knew was coming.

The bonus was substantial, $750,000, far more than I had anticipated. But given the circumstances, it felt obscene. Instead of the usual joy, it brought a tightness in my chest I couldn't shake. The number on the page felt unreal, and the weight of what it meant settled in fast. It wasn't happiness. It was something closer to dread.

I was deeply concerned that the appearance of a bonus, especially at a time when much of Wall Street had received little or nothing, would draw the wrong kind of attention. I was sure that when the executive board in Swansea found out, it would cause a political firestorm. The optics locally in the branch were also risky, and I worried someone would notice. April's payday came and went without bonuses for the majority. Morale dropped even further.

The night the funds landed in our account, Sue and I discussed it quietly over dinner. We agreed not to spend any of it immediately. No lifestyle changes. Nothing that would draw attention. We agreed it had to be invisible. Still, we sat in silence for a long time, each turning over what it meant. Part of me felt as if I'd betrayed my colleagues, people I respected, who were now grappling with shock and anger.

The guilt sat heavily in my gut. People throughout the office remained devastated. The situation eroded trust. I avoided the break room. Erica and I began taking our coffees outside at a local coffee shop, walking two blocks to a little park bench across from a bakery neither of us had ever entered. We spoke in low tones, watching the passersby.

One day, as we sipped our coffee in tense silence, she finally spoke.

"Do you think it was a mistake? Taking it?"

"I don't know," I admitted. "Maybe." I paused. "Honestly, it never even occurred to me that refusing it was an option."

She looked over at me. "You know this changes everything, right?"

I nodded. "We crossed a line."

"No," she said, voice low. "Alasdair crossed it. We followed."

She said nothing more, but her silence pressed against my chest harder than words. We walked back in silence, each step weighted with unease. The office felt colder now. Something was shifting; we just didn't know what.

At the end of the month, we submitted our accounts to Head Office, which was the standard procedure. Three days later, Erica summoned me into her office.

"Swansea has asked questions about the bonus payments," she said.

I looked at her, concerned. "I suspect Alasdair is going to be in deep shit," I replied.

"They're not asking Alasdair, they're asking me—I don't know what to say."

"Tell them it was a special entry allowed by Alasdair and advise them to call him," I replied.

About an hour later, I was sitting at my desk when I suddenly heard Alasdair's raised voice. I looked up as he was closing his office door. For an hour, I could hear him shouting. He finally put the phone down and came storming out of his office, walking straight into Erica's and closing the door behind him.

Later that afternoon, Erica told me that all hell had broken loose. Rhun had summoned Alasdair to Swansea. He was to fly that night.

He was already back in New York on Friday. Although he never told me the reason for his visit, I was sure they reprimanded him about the bonus payouts. Looking back, I now see that pressure had been mounting for weeks after the bonuses were paid. I had assumed that word of it reached the executive board in Swansea. Although Alasdair never mentioned it, the signals were there.

It began quietly. Invitations omitted from critical conversations. Shadow audits of projects Alasdair backed. Strategic roadmaps delayed inexplicably. Rhun never spoke Alasdair's name in criticism, but his influence was everywhere. I remember waiting for Alasdair in the hallway one afternoon. He was late for a meeting with compliance, and his expression was grim. He said little, but the message was clear: he was being contained.

That night, his office was unusually empty. No lights, no sounds. It felt final. And although no one had said anything, it was clear that the campaign to isolate him was underway.

In hindsight, the bonus payouts provided Rhun with exactly what he needed. They confirmed the story he wanted to tell the board: Alasdair was undisciplined and unmanageable, and that New York thought itself above the group. The narrative didn't have to be true. It just had to be plausible.

Alasdair was once again summoned to Head Office. Upon his return, he looked like a broken man. Erica told me the board had warned him that this was his last chance. He no longer had the authority to spend the bank's money this way. All future bonuses and pay increases now required Rhun's approval.

I pressed Erica to tell me how she knew this. Her response was vague. Unconvincing.

CHAPTER 19
THE VANISHING

I t felt like a typical Thursday morning; quiet, cold, and humming with the low thrum of fluorescent lighting. I arrived at the office just after 7:30 a.m., earlier than usual, hoping to get a jump on the latest batch of emails from Swansea.

The American branch had felt heavier in recent weeks, as if the air itself was weighed down by something unsaid—a static pressure that settled over everything.

There was more to it than the usual post-holiday lull or pre-bonus anxiety. Something deeper had taken root. The management team in Swansea had become much more assertive. There had been an uptick in random "compliance reviews," strange requests for access logs, and unexplained questions about system architecture.

Alasdair had grown increasingly terse in meetings, and Erica, never one to be rattled, had asked me privately if he was okay. It was subtle, but unmistakable: Was someone quietly turning the screws? She asked in a concerned tone, but the consistency of it started to feel rehearsed, as if she were building a case, not expressing genuine worry. Something was very off with her, but I could not put my finger on it.

She also began volunteering information more freely than usual, offering technical insights about systems she hadn't touched in months, sending me articles on cybersecurity best practices, and once casually asking me if I thought our audit trails could be externally manipulated. At the time, I thought she was just being thorough. Now, I wonder. Once, I caught her on the phone late, speaking Welsh in hushed tones. She ended the call the moment she saw me.

Within the branch, the rumor mill was in full swing. Much of the gossip centered on potential job losses and business restructuring. Then there was noise, when, out of nowhere, Erica had to make an emergency trip to Wales. This even seemed to spook Alasdair. All the staff seemed to be engaged in some form of conspiracy theory. Even the cleaning staff had appeared more cautious, more alert.

One cold morning, I paused briefly in the lobby before heading up. I watched the revolving doors cycle endlessly, as if ushering in change with every rotation. The wind outside had left a faint chill in the air, and static clung to my coat as I walked toward the elevator. Something was shifting. Something inevitable. Still, I reached my office on the 29th floor, powered up my terminal, and wrapped my hands around the comfort of a black Dunkin' Donuts coffee, then began sorting through the flood of overnight requests. Even before Alasdair had called me into his office mid-morning, the day had carried an undercurrent of unease.

In his office, his blinds were drawn, and his desk was unusually bare. The door closed behind me with a click.

He didn't look up. "I want a full sweep of the building. You will need to be discreet. I think my calls are being monitored."

I let out a short laugh. "Alasdair, seriously? Are you sure you're not overreacting?"

He looked up sharply. "Do I look like I'm overreacting? Something isn't right. I want to know who's listening."

I hesitated. "You think someone here planted surveillance equipment? In this building?"

"I don't know," he said, his tone clipped. "But we're being watched, and we are being listened to. And I want to know from where."

"What on earth makes you think that?" I asked.

"I was on a call with Ewan Jones, the global head of foreign exchange trading, last night. He brought up a subject that only two people—Owen and I—knew about."

"And you are sure Owen has said nothing to anyone, one of his traders, maybe?"

He smirked and replied, "Absolutely not." "I think someone has bugged either my phone or my office," he said.

He didn't elaborate. He didn't have to. The look in his eyes wasn't nervous; it was fear.

"I'll make some calls," I said. "Quiet ones."

"Good. And David ... put nothing in writing."

That afternoon, I began searching for firms that handled corporate espionage countermeasures. After a few discreet inquiries, I found a small company in New Jersey that specialized in TSCM, technical surveillance countermeasures. We arranged for them to come in over the weekend. The only people who knew about the sweep were Alasdair, Dmitry, and I. I assumed Alasdair had informed Owen, but I was never sure.

The following Saturday, I arrived at the office at 7 a.m. Dmitry showed up at about 7:30 a.m., rumpled but focused. He was loyal, but I always wondered how much he really knew.

With the rest of the building empty, we met the two-man TSCM team in the loading bay at 8:00 a.m. sharp. They wore plain clothes and carried their equipment in unmarked wheeled cases. Alasdair didn't show. That didn't surprise me.

Over the next 12 hours, the team swept every inch of the executive floor. Conference rooms, private offices, telepresence hubs, phone closets, even inside ceiling tiles and ductwork.

They found nothing. Just layers of dust and the faint buzz of badly grounded wiring.

On Wednesday morning, I walked into Alasdair's office with the full report in hand. It was clean. Thorough. They'd logged every scan, every frequency, every anomaly, and confirmed nothing suspicious.

Alasdair read it in silence. Halfway through, he pushed it aside. "Then we missed something," he said flatly.

"Alasdair," I replied, "this is the most comprehensive sweep money can buy. If there was anything ... they would have found it."

"I know they're listening," he cut in. "I can feel it. The quiet is too perfect. The timing is wrong. This doesn't prove we're safe. It proves they're better than we thought."

His certainty chilled me. The results didn't ease his fears; they intensified them.

A week later, Alasdair had asked me to step into his office after hours. Most of the staff had already left, and the floor had taken on an eerie quiet that only comes late in the day. He was sitting behind his desk, unusually quiet and contemplative. He had dimmed the overhead lights to near-darkness, casting stretched shadows across the room. A single monitor glowed behind him, the light low and flickering, illuminating his face like the fading glow of a dying ember. He didn't speak right away, just stared at the screen for a long beat before finally turning to me with an almost distracted air.

"Tell me something," he'd said casually. "If someone wanted to really bury something in our systems, hide it so deep no one would find it, how would they do it?"

I laughed at first. Thought it was some kind of test.

"Seriously," he pressed. "Which is harder, planting something secretly or scrubbing it completely?"

"You can scrub data, but metadata always leaves a trail," I remember answering. "Planting's harder. You'd need root access, time, and tools most people don't even know exist. Why?"

He didn't respond. Just nodded slightly and turned back to his monitor.

I then reminded him that since implementing Fortress Manhattan, the only remote access to our systems in New York was a single technical account held in a safe by the group audit team in Swansea. And if they ever used it, it would trigger alarms we would catch. He snorted, but did not seem convinced. I left his office that night with an uneasiness that clung to me for days. But I never brought it up again.

A few days later, I had arrived at the office early, after picking up my usual hazelnut Dunkin' Donuts coffee. I passed Carolyn's office on my way in. She didn't see me, but I saw her, standing, tense, one hand pressed to the glass.

"Yes, I understand," she was saying into the phone. "But if this gets traced back to me, they'll unseal everything. You know what's in that file."

A pause. Then quieter: "Just tell him it's a group-level restructuring. Don't get into the why."

Her voice shook, just slightly. She caught sight of me and hung up mid-sentence.

Then, 30 minutes later, I saw him—Alasdair. I could hear his rapid, clipped steps echoing sharply down the hall long before he ever reached my office door. As he passed, our eyes briefly met, but neither of us spoke. His usual precision and calm had vanished. He was unraveling. He was broken. He was defeated. His gaze fell, and he turned for Owen's office. Another brief pause, but this time, he handed Owen something small—what appeared to be a flash drive. Alasdair whispered something, then turned for the elevators.

I thought about stepping out to stop him, to ask what was wrong, but something about the way he moved froze me in place. It was like watching a structure collapse in slow motion. His reflection briefly caught in the steel elevator doors before they slid open and swallowed him whole. I should've moved. Should've asked. But I didn't. I just stood there, watching the elevator doors close around him like a vault. He was gone.

I stepped into the hallway, slowly, cautiously. The corridor was mostly empty, just a junior legal associate swearing at a jammed printer, and one intern frozen mid-step, clutching a stack of printouts like a life preserver. Even they seemed to sense it, that charged stillness in the air that makes people lower their voices and glance over their shoulders.

I checked the time, 8:42 a.m. A knot formed in my stomach. Alasdair always remained composed—maintained control. But what I'd just seen wasn't Alasdair. His face had the look of a man whose world was tilting beneath him, whose final foundation had just crumbled. Whatever this was, it wasn't ordinary. It was a flare. And I hadn't moved fast enough to catch it.

Still, I returned to my desk and tried to focus. I told myself it was probably a client emergency, something high-stakes but explainable. Or maybe a personal issue, a family crisis. But the image of him stayed with me, his wild eyes, his clenched jaw, the desperate cadence of his steps. It gnawed at me, persistent and loud in the back of my mind, like an alarm that hadn't finished sounding, stuck halfway between silence and catastrophe.

By 11:00 a.m., people had begun actively searching for Alasdair. He had missed two key meetings, one with a major client that had taken weeks to schedule. His absence wasn't just inconvenient; it was disruptive. The usual excuses didn't hold. His assistant looked visibly anxious, and even the senior staff began exchanging nervous glances. With no explanation, speculation filled the vacuum. The gossip started slowly, then picked up the pace like a current pulling everything downstream: rumors of illness, a resignation, even a quiet dismissal.

No one had facts, but everyone sensed something was deeply wrong.

At one point, I passed Erica in the hallway. She stood at the printer, watching pages feed through but not reading them. Her expression was unreadable. I asked if she'd heard anything. She shook her head too quickly.

"No clue," she said. "But something's definitely not right." Her eyes avoided mine, and her pace as she walked away felt just a shade too measured. Her fingers twitched slightly at her side, barely perceptible unless you were looking. I was.

By early afternoon, the excuses had collapsed under the weight of silence. Alasdair's assistant was no longer masking her worry. She'd tried him repeatedly. Calls, texts, even checked with building security. He'd also missed a crucial funding call with the trading desk. A private session with Owen had been canceled without explanation. His office door remained locked from the inside.

Someone from accounting tapped politely, then again harder. No answer. An executive from compliance whispered to facilities staff near the hallway junction. Even compliance had poked its head around the corner. The tension was no longer subtle. It buzzed beneath the surface like overloaded wiring.

I tried calling him. His office line went straight to voicemail. His mobile didn't even ring. I fired off a quick text, then another. No response. This wasn't just unusual; it was impossible. Alasdair was always online and reachable. The silence now was total.

I drifted toward the break area and caught sight of his assistant pacing near the elevators. Her heels tapped a frantic rhythm on the tile floor. Her eyes were red-rimmed. When she noticed me, she offered only a tight glance, jaw clenched.

"He never just vanishes," she muttered, more to herself than to me. "Not without a word. Never."

Just before 4:00 p.m., my desk phone rang. It was Carolyn.

"David, can you come down to my office, please? There are two gentlemen here from Swansea. They say they're here on behalf of Dr. Rhun and require access to the technology infrastructure."

Her voice was clipped and formal, sounding as if someone were reading from a hastily written script. It wasn't an invitation. It was a summons.

I paused for a moment, her words hanging in the air like dust motes in the light. Around me, colleagues still feigned focus, but no one was truly working. The atmosphere had shifted. Whatever normal had been, it was gone.

Somewhere nearby, a printer jammed and beeped its distress into the silence. No one moved to fix it. No one looked up. And in that stillness, I felt something break loose, subtle and irreversible, the moment just before a levee breaks.

My gut told me this wasn't another audit. It wasn't even about Alasdair anymore. It was the next move in a game I hadn't realized we were playing.

And I was about to find myself at the center of the board.

CHAPTER 20
THE ENVELOPE
ALASDAIR STEWART

I had arrived early again that day. The office was still half-dark, lights flickering on as the sensors caught my footsteps. I liked it that way, quiet, neutral, untouched, before the watchers took their places.

But something felt wrong. Not visibly. Not obviously. But the stillness wasn't comforting; it was expectant. The kind of silence that waits for a blow.

At 7:42 a.m., there was a knock at my door.

Carolyn.

She didn't ask to come in, just stepped inside and closed the door behind her. Her face was blank; her posture rigid. In her hand was a sealed envelope.

"This isn't how I wanted to do it," she hissed.

I already knew. Somewhere in my gut, I had known for weeks.

She placed the envelope on my desk. "Effective immediately. There's a copy for your records. Group HR will be in touch."

I didn't reach for it. Not at first. I looked at her, really looked at her, and saw something behind the professionalism, regret, maybe. Or shame.

I nodded once.

She turned and left. No hug. No handshake. No explanation.

I picked up the envelope, tucked it under my arm, and walked out without a word. I didn't clear my desk. Didn't log out. On the way to the elevator, I passed Wallace's office. He saw me. I saw him. Neither of us spoke.

As I passed Owen's office, I handed him a small thumb drive, smiled, and said, "insurance." He sat there stunned, taking the drive without a word.

Downstairs, I didn't call a car. I walked.

Three blocks away, I ducked into a coffee shop on 43rd, ordered a black coffee, and took a seat near the window. Only then did I open the envelope.

Termination for cause. Breach of internal controls. Subject to review.

It wasn't just a dismissal. It was a burial.

I stared at the letter, then at nothing. Minutes passed. Maybe an hour.

I had built that business. From nothing. Brought in capital when no one else could. Landed flagship deals. Lifted group profitability year after year, and through our access to inexpensive Fed money, saved the group from collapse.

And yes, I threw a Christmas party. An extravagant one. Because we'd earned it. I'd paid discretionary bonuses the next year, against the group's advice. I thought rewarding loyalty would earn me the same.

I'd been wrong.

The board summoned me to Swansea the following April. The room had been cold, wood-paneled, severe. They talked about optics. Discipline. Alignment. Not once did they mention performance.

Rhun was already in the building, and I wasn't being considered for the group CEO position anymore. I already knew that. That door had closed the moment the board had hired Rhun. Once onboard, he told them I was unmanageable. The bonuses were just his proof.

I was supposed to be the group CEO. He should not even have been there. But that had flipped. Quietly. Permanently.

And now I was here, sitting in a Midtown coffee shop, terminated by *envelope*.

How do you break the news to your wife that all your efforts have been undone by a single meeting?

I folded the papers neatly. Put them back in the envelope. Took a sip of coffee. Watched the city move around me as if I no longer belonged to it. I hadn't answered any calls since I left the building. The phone buzzed constantly in my pocket. I didn't even look.

Truthfully, I was embarrassed. Shocked. Not just in the way it happened, but by how utterly final it felt. I didn't know what I was supposed to do next. Go home? Pretend it was all a misunderstanding? There was no script for this.

And worse, I had let them down. My team. The people who built that office beside me, who trusted me to keep them safe from the politics and the purges. I'd promised them something better. And now I was gone. No explanation. No warning. Just a vanishing act in a suit.

Somewhere between the ambition and the arrogance, I had missed something. A shift. A betrayal. Just beyond the edge of my certainty, a storm forms.

How had it gone so wrong?

Maybe the answer was already hidden in decisions I didn't challenge, in alliances I didn't question, and in the silences I mistook for loyalty.

Or maybe the mistake was thinking I was still in control.

CHAPTER 21
THE PURGE

After Carolyn's summons, I arrived to find her flanked by two unfamiliar men. Both wore identical black suits, ties, and shoes polished to a near-mirrored gleam—shoes that looked as though they'd never touched pavement. One was tall and angular; the other short and broad.

They stood motionless, posture rigid, like mannequins awaiting activation.

At their feet sat four matte-black cases stacked with military precision. Their eyes remained unblinking. They didn't speak. They simply stared.

"These men are from Wales," Carolyn said, her voice taut, reluctant. "They represent Dr. Rhun and require full administrative access to all core technology systems immediately."

My first instinct was disbelief. "You've got to be pulling my pisser," I said, letting my guard down by reverting to Cockney slang. Half-laughing, searching their faces for some flicker of humanity.

Nothing.

The tall one blinked once. The short one remained inert. Carolyn looked uncomfortable, like someone who had rehearsed for this moment but now wished she hadn't.

"David, this comes directly from Swansea," she said, gesturing subtly to the cases. "Please cooperate. It's not optional."

I turned toward her. "I don't know who these people are. I'm not handing over access to the system that processes the bank's entire dollar-based transactional load without Alasdair's express sign-off."

Her expression shifted almost imperceptibly into a wince. It disappeared quickly, as if she were fighting back something close to doubt, guilt, or fear.

"Alasdair is no longer with the bank."

"What?"

"Effective this morning."

"That's not possible. I saw him this morning."

"I'm asking you not to obstruct this process," she stated firmly, but her voice caught slightly.

"Obstruct? I'm responsible for uptime, security, continuity. My data center and the servers within it route billions. Giving strangers root access without clearance isn't just irregular, it's insane. If anything fails—"

"Nothing will fail," she snapped, sharper than I'd ever heard her.

I stared at the two operatives. "You want access? Then, produce formal authorization from Rhun, signed and printed. On Cambria letterhead. Until then, nobody's touching a terminal."

The short one finally spoke. His voice was low, deliberate, antiseptic, with a very strong Welsh accent. "You will receive documentation shortly."

"Carolyn," I said, calm but cold, "if you push this through and it explodes, your name leads the report."

Her jaw tightened. "Point taken."

During my time at the bank, I had never seen Carolyn this rattled. She was clearly very uncomfortable. Gone was her typical poise. Her haunted eyes suggested she'd spent all night trying to justify this to herself. She didn't look like an accomplice. She looked like someone trying to survive.

They left together. Carolyn was stiff with tension, and the Welshmen trailed behind her like shadows. Once outside the room, I followed them with my eyes as Carolyn glanced over her shoulder, catching my gaze for the briefest moment, then looking away.

Five minutes later, my desk phone rang. Swansea HQ lit up the LED.

"This is Professor Dr. Cadwgan Rhun."

His tone was razor sharp, each word honed and bloodless.

"You are to grant my representative's full administrative access. Without delay. Without exception."

"With respect, sir, I need that in writing," I said. My voice held steady, but my pulse did not. I could feel my blood pressure rising.

"You are overreaching, Mr. Wallace."

"And you're asking me to violate the global compliance policy via a verbal order? That's not overreach; it's negligence. I won't do it. Not without written authority."

Silence.

"You'll have the documentation," he said coldly. "I suggest, for future reference, you recall your place in the chain of command."

Click.

Fifteen minutes later, Carolyn returned with a sealed letter. She did not say a word, just dropped the envelope on my desk, turned, and left. I watched her walk away, her spine rigid, but her shoulders sagging ever so slightly, as if the weight of her choices had settled.

After reading it, I called Dmitry.

"Set them up in isolation. In a ring-fenced, sandboxed network on virtual machines, nothing physical and no access to production. Mirror everything. Full logging and make sure we have a video stream to see what they are doing."

"Got it. It will take about an hour."

Once we had set it up, we escorted them to the data center. They entered. The door locked behind them. For the first time since I had worked here, I had been physically locked out of our own core systems.

Twenty minutes later, they emerged. Angry.

"You've sandboxed us. We need full access," the tall one said, tone cutting.

"You've received what the letter allowed. If you need anything more, I will need further authorization from Rhun."

Five minutes later, another call. Rhun again, his voice darker.

"You were told full access."

"Your document allows access to production data. That is exactly what they have been given, via a mirrored configuration. If that's insufficient, reissue it explicitly."

"Expect it shortly. And next time, don't play God."

Ten minutes later, it came. A detailed letter, clearly written by a technologist. Someone who knew our systems.

We gave them what they wanted. Dmitry adjusted the environment. The logging we implemented continued, allowing us to maintain an audit trail of their activities. But from a technical perspective, they held the key to the vault.

We watched via our network monitor as they cloned systems, not sampled, not audited. *Cloned.* They weren't reviewing. They were cleansing.

"They're targeting directories," Dmitry said. "Access logs. Admin trails."

I nodded slowly. "They're not tracing history. They're deleting it."

I went back to my office and grabbed a legal pad. Over the next half hour, I recorded everything that had happened that day: who entered, what was accessed, and for how long. I even captured the events with Alasdair earlier that morning. This was not something I would typically have done. But Sue had once told me: "Document everything."

I didn't trust digital records. Not anymore.

I left the office at about 5 p.m. and went for a walk. I needed to clear my head. Before returning to my desk, I walked straight to Carolyn's office. Her door was open, but she looked startled when I entered. I closed the door behind me.

"Carolyn, off the record, do you know what's really happening here?"

She looked down at her desk, then up at me. Her eyes were glassy. "I know enough."

"And Alasdair?"

She shook her head. "I haven't heard from him since this morning. The men from Swansea had given me his dismissal notice and a set of instructions to fire him. I set it on his desk. He appeared to know it was coming, but I didn't see him take it. He just nodded, and I left. I wanted to get out of there. I think Rhun believed Alasdair was in the way."

"In the way of what?

"Rhun has plans. Structural changes. Clean breaks. They need clean records to go with them."

"And you? Why go along with this?"

She swallowed hard. "Because I have a daughter in college, and a mortgage, and ... because I don't want to disappear too."

It was the first time I had ever seen her truly afraid. I said nothing more, just nodded and left.

Later, I tried Alasdair's numbers again. Still nothing. Eventually, I called his wife, Claudia.

"Hello?"

"Claudia, it's David Wallace. I'm sorry to call out of the blue."

"Oh, David, hi. Are you all right?"

A pause. Clinks of silverware. A dog barked faintly in the background, and I could hear one of her children singing.

"Is something wrong?" she asked.

"I've been trying to reach Alasdair all day. He left abruptly this morning. No one's heard from him. I thought maybe he had come home." I didn't have the heart to tell her that he had been let go. It was Alasdair's right to tell his own wife.

A beat. Then, her tone changed.

"He had left early for work this morning. He said it would be a long day. I haven't heard anything from him since. David ... is something wrong?"

"He missed meetings. His office is locked. People from Swansea are here. I just want to make sure everything is all right."

"Do you think he is okay?"

"I don't know. But this doesn't feel right."

She hesitated. Then, barely above a whisper: "He wouldn't vanish. He wouldn't just go dark, not like this. He always has access to his phone."

Her voice broke just slightly on the last word. I imagined her standing in their Riverside kitchen, with marble counters, an over-polished floor, sunlight slanting in through French windows.

Claudia Stewart was stunning, 15 years younger than Alasdair, German, with shoulder-length blond hair and a bone structure that still turned heads. She had been a flight attendant for Lufthansa before meeting Alasdair on a flight to London. A life filled with travel, freedom, and independence. But something about Alasdair had made her pause, made her believe in the possibility of a shared future abroad. When she gave it all up, her career, her country, and the comfort of familiarity, it wasn't out of blind love, but a calculated leap of faith in the man she believed Alasdair was. He had punched well above his weight.

She was Alasdair's second wife. His first marriage had produced two older children, twins, both now teenagers, living with their mother in Scotland. Meanwhile, Claudia had stepped away from her own career and was now a full-time mother to their two young children in Brooklyn.

"I'm sorry," I said quietly. "If I hear anything, anything at all, I'll let you know. When he returns home, can you please ask him to call me?"

Her voice steadied, but only just. "Yes, I will. And thank you, David."

We ended the call. And for a long moment, I just stared at the phone. A weight settled over me, not just concern for Alasdair's disappearance, but the unsettling realization that I might have already crossed some invisible line by calling Claudia. Despite everything, he had been more than a boss. He was a confidant, an ally, and a mentor. And now, he was gone. Something about her tone, the confusion, the fear, had shaken me more than I expected.

I stayed in the office long after the others had left. The lights dimmed around me, and the clatter of keyboards and inaudible murmur of traders gave way to silence. I watched the access logs tick by on my screen. Each entry confirmed the Welsh were still inside the data center, crawling through the bones of our systems. By then, they had stopped being cautious. They weren't just focused on Alasdair anymore. The access logs showed them mirroring directories tied to Erica Cross, Reginald Blaine, Owen Davis, even me.

It was no longer a surgical operation.

Dmitry stuck his head in the door around 7 p.m., his usually relaxed posture now taut, eyes scanning me for clues. He had been a steady presence through many operational fires, the colleague who never panicked even when things went sideways. Seeing him uneasy only deepened the pit in my stomach.

"They're still going. I logged another five terabytes of outbound clones."

"Let them keep digging," I said flatly. "Just keep logging."

He nodded, hesitated, then asked, "Do you think Alasdair's okay?"

I didn't answer. I didn't know.

After Dmitry left, I sat back and let my eyes drift to the dark window beside my desk. My reflection stared back at me, older than I remembered, eyes bloodshot, tie loosened, collar askew. Gone, at least for today, was the smart "mod" look. The city glittered below, indifferent and eternal. Somewhere out there, Alasdair was either hiding, running, or already crushed under something too big to fight.

The feeling that had started in my gut that morning had settled now, heavy and absolute. This wasn't just a personnel issue or a quiet dismissal. This was something darker. Something planned.

I reached into my drawer, pulled out my small notepad, the same one I had used earlier, and wrote the last pieces of the day. The call with Claudia. The fact that the two Welshmen were still inside the data center. I didn't know why I was writing it all down. It was instinct, I suppose. An urge to record the moment while it was still mine.

I ended the entry with a single line:

"They didn't come to find the truth. They came to erase it."

I tore the page out and slipped it into my jacket pocket. I shut down the monitors, packed up, and walked out into the Manhattan night.

But I didn't go home. Not right away. I walked for blocks without any sense of direction, letting the sharp city air work its way into my lungs. My phone buzzed twice in my pocket, but I ignored it. I needed silence—not the absence of sound, but the kind of mental stillness that let me feel something real through the fog.

The streets blurred around me. Neon reflected off the wet pavement. Steam hissed from manholes, as if the city were exhaling something toxic. I watched people on their phones, laughing in bars, honking cabs, and I felt as if I were underwater. Moving, breathing, but separate from it all.

Eventually, I found myself at a diner on the edge of Greenwich Village—one of those places that never closes, where the waitresses are always refilling coffee before you ask. I took a booth in the back and slid the notepad paper from my pocket onto the table. I reread the line I had scrawled.

They didn't come to find the truth. They came to erase it.

I thought about crossing it out. Adding to it. But I didn't. It said enough. It said everything.

When the waitress came by, I ordered coffee and nothing else. She poured it silently, as if she knew not to ask. I wrapped my hands around the mug and stared out the window at the flickering world.

Somewhere, someone was rewriting our story—line by line. Log by log. And if I didn't hold onto the truth, even just a thread of it, it would be gone. Just like Alasdair. Just like the trail behind him. I had no idea where this was going. But I knew one thing: whatever came next, I couldn't pretend anymore. I was in it now, whether I liked it or not.

Erica told me weeks later that Alasdair had handed Owen a small black USB stick on his way out. No label. No explanation.

"Insurance," he'd said.

Nobody plugged it in. Maybe nobody wanted to know.

CHAPTER 22

THE CALCULATION
ERICA CROSS

I stood by the 14th-floor window, watching the late winter sunlight bounce off the steel ribs of the building across the street. In the open-plan office behind me, low conversations murmured beneath the hum of wavering lights. Another round of policy shifts had just come through from the group. More "streamlining." More "alignment." I didn't need a translator. I knew exactly what it meant.

Rhun was consolidating power.

Not officially, not yet, but everyone could feel it. Executives were repositioning. Messaging was becoming more centralized. Directives started bypassing New York altogether. Even Alasdair's voice in leadership calls had begun to sound muffled, interrupted. There were signs, subtle ones, but if you knew how to read them, they were everywhere. And I did.

I stepped away from the glass, crossed to my desk, and unlocked my machine. A secure email session auto-launched. A draft note waited on my screen, already half-composed.

Subject: *Follow-up, Regional Integration Queries.*

"As discussed, I will continue monitoring the New York branch's integration resilience and data traceability. Additional reports to follow under separate cover."

I didn't send it right away. I let the words sit there, loaded and waiting.

This wasn't betrayal. It was timing.

Owen, Carolyn, and David—all loyal. But loyalty isn't a strategy. Alasdair, brilliant, yes, but he was playing an old game. Defiance. Innovation. Performance. That might have worked once, but no longer. Not under a regime that valued control over courage, obedience over originality. And Rhun? Rhun knew how to win. Quietly. Permanently. I understood something most of them didn't: survival isn't about merit. It's about proximity to power. And power was shifting.

I closed the draft, encrypted the session, and leaned back in my chair. My reflection on the darkened monitor looked sharper than usual. More angular. More ... defined.

Rhun would remember who helped him consolidate control. And when the dust settled, after my peers burned out and Alasdair was removed, a vacuum would exist. The only question would be: Why not me?

It had started much earlier. I had to return to Swansea for a two-day working session on global back-office alignment. The jargon-heavy, spreadsheet-laden event that usually came with a boxed lunch and a dull headache. What I hadn't expected was a dinner invitation.

It came late, slipped in after the second day's last session. A discreet message from Rhun's assistant: *Private dinner, 7:30 p.m., The Grove. Business attire.*

I stared at it longer than I should have. There was no agenda attached. No list of other attendees. Just my name.

He was already waiting when I arrived. Polished. Cordial. Dangerous.

The conversation started with small talk but quickly turned. He praised my "composure under complexity." My "systems-level thinking." Complimented how I'd managed the tension between global and regional expectations. Then he asked how I felt about the current leadership dynamics in New York.

I was careful with my answer, cautious but honest. I said there were inefficiencies. Misalignments. I believed in the mission, but clarity was lacking.

He nodded slowly, as if confirming a private diagnosis.

Then he said it: "There will come a time when certain loyalties become liabilities. When that happens, those who've shown foresight will have a role in shaping the next phase."

It wasn't a threat. It felt like a job interview. I left the restaurant with the quiet certainty that Rhun had drawn a line, and I had already crossed it.

Did I owe Alasdair? Probably. He'd hired me when others wouldn't. When others saw failure, he saw potential. But gratitude doesn't pay your severance when a regime falls. And Alasdair's was falling. Fast.

Besides, he hadn't seen it. Not really. The shift. The inevitability of it all. He still believed performance would protect him. I knew better. So when the request came, subtle but unmistakable, I didn't hesitate.

Earlier, I'd asked Sanjay to set up temporary access credentials for a group diagnostic. I'd implied that Group Legal had cleared it. I'd said it was minor. He resisted at first. Then, after some pressure, he relented. This Sanjay thing had started months earlier. Before Rhun. Before dinner. I'd told myself it was harmless, just a temporary access profile for a group diagnostic. And when the audit trail came under review, he took the fall. I hadn't lied. I had forged nothing. But I'd shaped the story. Just enough to let gravity do the rest.

But that wasn't the real betrayal. That came later.

After Rhun. After the dinner. After the promise.

When the two men from Swansea arrived under the guise of "infrastructure harmonization," I knew what they were really there for.

They didn't say it directly. But the way they asked to be "escorted" into Alasdair's office after hours? The way they already had device IDs preloaded into their toolkit?

That morning, when I had seen Alasdair leaving the office and hand Owen what appeared to be a thumb drive, I didn't think much of it at the time. But it stuck with me.

I didn't ask questions. I stayed well out of the limelight when they were on-site.

And when they were done, I wiped the meeting room camera logs and reported back to Rhun.

Alasdair had once championed me. But champions fall. And I'd made my choice.

That night, as I filed my final report and encrypted it to group systems, I didn't feel guilt.

I felt clarity.

CHAPTER 23
THE SUMMONS

That weekend, I couldn't sleep. Not really. After granting access to the two Swansea operatives, after watching them vanish into our data center for two days, after witnessing Alasdair disappear without a trace, I was unraveling. My mind looped in endless circuits, replaying moments that felt wrong, things I'd missed, or hadn't wanted to see. They'd returned to Wales, but the damage lingered.

Sue noticed, of course. "David, are you okay?" she asked Saturday night as we sat in front of the muted television. Her hand rested gently on my forearm, trying to pull me back from wherever I'd gone.

"Still thinking about the office," I muttered, eyes fixed somewhere far past the screen.

But it wasn't just work stuff. It was a frequency humming under my skin, one I couldn't tune out. I started waking up on sweat-soaked sheets. My wife quietly changed them, her concern etched into every silent movement. She didn't press. That made it worse.

By Sunday night, I was dreading Monday like a man awaiting sentencing. I arrived at the office early and went straight to Carolyn's office, slamming the door behind me.

"What the hell is going on?"

She flinched, visibly shaken. Her blouse was wrinkled; her hair was unkempt. I'd never seen her this off-balance.

"To be honest, I have no more information than you do," she said, wearily. "As I told you before, I got a call from the global head of HR telling me I had to fire Alasdair. Then Rhun called to echo that order. And those two guys from Swansea, they handed me a letter and told me to deliver it to him. I got the sense that he was expecting it."

I believed her. Whatever corporate game involved her, she seemingly hadn't learned her lines. But that belief brought no comfort. We were all marionettes now. And no one seemed to know who was pulling the strings.

Later that morning, I discussed the events at an unscheduled coffee meeting with Erica.

"Do we know whether anything was left behind? From Alasdair?" I asked her.

Erica's glance was cool. "There was a drive. Given to Owen. He never opened it."

"Where is it now?"

"I have no idea. Owen must still have it."

The weeks dragged. Head Office provided no explanation. No press release. No interim leader.

Alasdair's office remained sealed, his name quietly scrubbed from internal emails. We kept the business alive through habit and guesswork, but leadership was gone. The heartbeat had stopped.

I tried calling him. I tried Claudia. Nothing. Not even a ringtone. It was as if they'd both fallen off the edge of the world.

Without Alasdair, the business decayed. New transactions slowed to a trickle. The trading floor lost its usual tension, replaced by a strange hush. Even Dmitry stopped cracking jokes. Erica grew distant, her eyes scanning the rooms as if she were searching for exits.

A year passed in that state. *A year.* A limbo of unanswered questions and increasingly robotic routines. Then, one morning, my phone rang.

It was a Friday. I had taken the day off. Sue and I had flown to South Carolina to watch our son compete in a college swim meet. We'd just finished breakfast at the hotel and were pulling out of the parking lot when the call came in.

Warren Blake.

The name on my screen froze me. Head of legal in New York. The kind of man who never called you unless your day was about to implode. We tolerated each other. Barely.

My stomach dropped.

I pulled the car over. "What the hell could this be about?"

Sue looked at me, alarmed. I gave her a helpless shrug as I answered the call.

"What can I do for you?" I asked. "You know I'm on vacation?"

"I'm aware," Warren said. "But this is urgent. The Manhattan District Attorney's office would like to speak with you."

My mouth went dry. "For what?"

"I'm not at liberty to say."

I said the first thing that came into my mind. "Am I under investigation?"

"No. Not to my knowledge. But they have questions. Just answer honestly. Don't speculate."

"Do I need a lawyer?"

"That's your call. They haven't subpoenaed you. And the bank will not be sending legal representation. Be at 80 Centre Street. Monday. 10 a.m."

Click.

I stared at the phone. Sue was already watching me.

"Well?" she asked.

"They want to talk. No charges. Just questions."

"Who?" she asked.

"The Manhattan District Attorney,"

Her face paled. "That doesn't sound good."

It didn't. My heart thumped like a slow drumbeat. My mind raced, replaying every decision I'd made at that firm. Every exception I'd granted. Every gray area I'd tiptoed around. Was this about the Swansea team? The server logs? A whistle-blower? Or something worse, something I didn't even know had happened under my watch?

All weekend, I unraveled. I tried to fake it for our son, smiling for the camera and cheering at his races, but I was somewhere else. Sue kept one eye on me. She said nothing, but I knew that fear gripped her. She changed our hotel sheets again after another night of sweat-soaked sleep. It was our unspoken ritual now.

On Saturday, we were invited as guests of the university to watch the football game, and that evening, we had dinner with our son, Christopher. At one point, he pulled Sue aside and asked if I was okay. She told him it was a work problem. I got the sense from him that he realized that this was a big deal, but he said nothing directly to me.

That night, I lay in bed staring at the ceiling, trying to rehearse answers to questions I hadn't seen yet. Sue placed a hand on my chest.

"Whatever happens," she said softly, "we deal with it together."

I nodded. I didn't trust my voice.

The rest of the weekend was a blur.

I left home early that Monday morning. After arriving at Penn Station, I found a coffee bar and sat there for an hour. At 9 a.m., I left. At 9:15 a.m., I arrived at 80 Centre Street. It loomed like a monument to anxiety. Towering limestone. Brass-trimmed doors. A building built to make you feel small. I cleared security, and someone escorted me to a fifth-floor interview room. Windowless, fluorescent-lit. The air was stale and institutional.

Six people waited around a metal conference table.

Two NYPD detectives, one balding, the other with a barrel chest. Two women in gray suits, assistant DAs. And two men in dark jackets with the posture and stillness of cybersecurity experts.

No one smiled.

"Mr. Wallace," one prosecutor said, "we appreciate your cooperation. This conversation is being recorded. You are not under arrest. You are not being charged. You are here voluntarily. Understood?"

I nodded. My throat felt like sandpaper. I imagined my wife sitting alone at home, clutching her phone, waiting for an update.

"Let's begin," they said.

And then the door clicked shut.

CHAPTER 24
THE INTERVIEW

What followed was two hours of focused surgical questioning. They started with routine IT governance: How were admin accounts provisioned? Who had access to the physical servers? Were system logs immutable? How often were backups performed? Was access reviewed quarterly? Were intrusion detection protocols in place?

Then the questions turned darker: Could a system admin plant a file without being traced? Could someone impersonate a user? Could someone forge an email's metadata? Is it possible to change logs retroactively? Was there any way to erase activity from the audit trail?

The two technical consultants in the room were very interested in Project Fortress Manhattan and how it protected the branch. I was asked at least four times if it was possible for anyone outside the branch to get into our network remotely. I repeatedly explained that only one account existed outside New York, a technical account for emergencies only, secured in an audit-function safe at the head office in Swansea. The company heavily restricted remote access privileges and accounts, limiting them to only a handful of New York employees.

They asked and re-asked. They flipped through the sequence. One ADA would ask, then a detective would pose the same question with a twist. They were probing for contradictions. I did my best, kept my answers tight, factual, emotionless. But it was draining.

At one point, one consultant opened a laptop and swiveled it toward me. On the screen was a snippet of Linux terminal code. The detective beside him slid a printout across the table.

"Do you recognize this login string?"

I studied the line. My stomach clenched. It was a command-line invocation, a remote login. Alasdair's user ID was part of the path.

"Yes," I said cautiously. "It's a remote session. Looks like someone signed into the system. But ... Alasdair had never used the command line."

"Explain," said the balding detective.

"He didn't have the technical skills to do that himself. Whenever he needed remote access, one of my guys had to guide him over the phone. He hated the terminal. Didn't even like right-clicking. This command is precise. Structured. Not his style."

They showed me another string, and this time it was from Owen's machine. My answer was the same. Over the next half hour, they asked the same questions about several senior staff members.

The ADA leaned forward. "So, someone else could have used these credentials?"

"Yes. If they had either the passwords or if they had access to their machines."

"Could these machines have been left unattended after hours?"

I thought back. "It's possible. But we had motion sensors. Badge logs. I'd need to check." My first thought was that the cleaners went into offices all the time, often late at night, and no one ever questioned it.

She scribbled something in her notebook.

The questions resumed. I lost track of time. There were moments when my thoughts jammed; technical details I'd known for years now felt slippery, as if I were seeing them through fog.

One of the assistant district attorneys kept narrowing her eyes slightly every time I hesitated. The cybersecurity consultants never looked away. At the end, I was pale, drenched in sweat, and trembling slightly.

They thanked me. Told me not to discuss the meeting, and just like that, it was over.

As I walked out, my mind spiraled. I'd convinced myself that someone inside the branch had committed a major financial crime. And that maybe, somehow, I'd missed it. Or worse, helped cover it up without realizing.

There had only been one question about Alasdair, and that was technical, but the same questions were asked about Owen, and he was still with the bank. There was no mention of Alasdair's disappearance, nor of his accounts. Very little had pointed to him at all—just technology infrastructure, process, and access. Everything felt clinical, detached.

I walked out of the building and stood on the sidewalk, breathing in the spring air as if my lungs were experiencing oxygen for the first time. It was cool and metallic, laced with the scent of car fumes and hot-dog water from a nearby cart. My heart still pounded. The chill did nothing to calm me. My hands were clammy. I wiped them on the sides of my trousers.

The first thing I did was call Sue.

We went over every detail I could remember.

Like me, she immediately suspected that someone had committed a financial crime, but that is wasn't me.

"From what you've said, I don't get the impression that

you're implicated," she told me. Her voice was steady, soothing. It was exactly what I needed to hear.

Back at the office, I didn't go to my desk. I went to the 29th-floor break room, sat in a corner chair, and stared at a vending machine for ten straight minutes. I felt scraped raw. My throat was dry. My shirt clung to my back. The hum of the refrigerator was the only sound, and even that felt too loud.

When I finally returned to my office, Warren was already waiting. He stepped inside and closed the door.

"You all right?" he asked.

"No," I said. "Not even close. What the hell is going on, Warren?"

He exhaled, shifting uncomfortably. Even he looked pale. His eyes were bloodshot, his jaw clenched, as if he'd been up all night.

"I'm not at liberty to say."

"Come on," I said, standing. "They really drilled down into our technical infrastructure. They asked about the credentials of all the senior staff. Is everyone under investigation? Has someone stolen something? Manipulated the books? What is this?"

He didn't answer. He didn't even blink.

"You know," I said. "Don't you?"

He met my gaze, expression unreadable. "I can't help you. Not yet."

Then he left. But before he did, he glanced at the door twice, as if checking we were still alone. For a brief second, I thought he was going to say more. His lips parted, his brow furrowed, but he just shook his head, turned, and walked out.

That night, I stayed late. Long after everyone else had left. I pulled historical logs. Firewall entries. Badge reader data. Looking for any anomalies. I built timelines and tried to reconstruct what might have happened. I found nothing. No matter how much I uncovered, one truth stood out like neon in the dark: they weren't speculating. They were building a case. But who was the target? Was Alasdair's firing related? At that point, I still did not know, but I suspected it was.

That realization hit me harder than I expected. I walked to the restroom, locked myself in a stall, and just sat. My hands were shaking. I could hear my breath, shallow, erratic. My pulse drummed in my ears. The artificial calm I'd tried to wear like armor was cracking.

This was the point when I actually realized that I wasn't just a bystander in this anymore, whatever "this" was. I was a witness. A loose thread in a tightly wound secret that someone, somewhere, had gone to great lengths to bury. And if I kept pulling, I didn't know what would unravel: my career, my team, maybe even my life as I knew it. My mind was in full panic mode.

Later that evening, after the cleaners had left and the office was empty apart from me, Erica returned. Usually composed, even breezy, she now looked like someone who hadn't slept for days. A quiet intensity had replaced her usual effortless calm, making my stomach tighten. Wrinkles marred her dress. She clutched a file folder too tightly in one hand, standing at the doorway of my office, expression drawn.

"Hello," she said, clearly surprised to see me still there. She looked startled. "I've been thinking about that envelope, the one with the compliance memo from last week," she said quietly, almost by accident. "About who else might've seen it before it landed in my inbox."

"What compliance memo?" I asked.

She stepped in and closed the door.

She did not respond to my question: "You know who handles compliance intake before me each morning?"

I shook my head.

"Penny Kramer. Compliance operations."

Compliance was the team that ensured all of our operational activities were undertaken within the law. Their technical tools monitored every aspect of the branch's daily business activities.

Erica continued, "She's efficient, meticulous, never misses a protocol, but she's also ... too quiet. Too observant." I asked around. She's been logging overtime hours with no documented assignments. I remembered walking past her cubicle late one night. She snapped her laptop shut the moment she saw me. I chalked it up to privacy. Now, it felt rehearsed."

Something twisted in my gut.

"What are you saying, Erica?"

She looked pale. "I think someone's watching the watchers. And Penny might be part of it. Or being used by someone who is."

I wanted to say that she was being paranoid. But after the last few weeks, paranoia felt like prudence.

My mind jumped back to the days before Alasdair's disappearance. I remembered that I'd caught fleeting glimpses of unease, random systems became inaccessible for short periods, logs disappeared and reappeared with minor differences, and patches were implemented without record. At the time, I'd dismissed them as human error. Now, they looked like pieces of something far more deliberate.

I walked home that night in a kind of trance. The city moved around me. People laughed at cafés. Car horns blared. But I couldn't feel any of it. I took the subway to Penn Station and got on the last train home. I reached my house in Chatham and stood outside the front door for a full minute before going in.

When I got home, Sue met me at the door. She already knew most of it. I'd called her after the interview, but seeing me in person told her the rest.

"Rough day?" she asked gently.

I nodded. We didn't need to say much. She just stepped aside and let me in, placing a hand on my back as I passed.

It was late, but I spent the rest of the night staring at the TV. I couldn't focus. My thoughts kept looping. Had Alasdair died? Was he hiding? Was he forced out, or part of something bigger than I could see?

When Sue went up to bed, I retreated to my home office. I told her I'd be up shortly.

I knew I wouldn't be able to sleep without a bit of digging, so I established a remote technical access link to the bank's network and began poking around, examining logs and user activity, still searching for technical clues that would help me understand what was going on.

Every corner of the network I examined felt infected, although I found nothing. Every user account of people I trusted felt like a question mark. Even Rachel from compliance, who once flagged a mistyped vendor code but had coffee with me every Friday, now seemed like a cipher. And Doug, my network guy, loyal for years, had recently asked for root access, which gave him full access to absolutely everything on a system that didn't match his project brief. I'd approved it without a thought. Now, I questioned it. I was becoming afraid, not of being wrong, but of being right. Or was I just becoming paranoid?

The following morning, Erica sent me a text: "Check your drawer. Now."

Inside my desk drawer, tucked behind a stack of NDA forms, was a small USB stick. No label. I inserted it into my offline laptop.

There was a single folder: *Echo Logs*. Inside was a second file, small, unassuming, titled *note.txt*. I opened it. Five words stared back at me: "You're looking in the wrong direction." No metadata. No author. Just a plain text warning that made my stomach turn.

Inside were five encrypted log files. The file names included timestamps, each corresponding to one of the Thursday night VPN events that Doug had previously flagged. And inside one decrypted file, which included session metadata, packets logged in raw code, and a curious directory tree structure with subfolders named things such as */audit dump/*, */mirror_archive/*, and */q4_projection/alt*.

It was technical and dense, but one thing was clear: someone had mirrored a segment of our internal finance directory onto an external node in Swansea.

The last changed file? Dated the morning Alasdair disappeared. One of the outbound logs referenced a server alias I didn't recognize: *mirror13.trident-gate.net*. It belonged to someone else. It wasn't even domestic, and looked like a technical component that resided at the head office.

I pushed back from the desk. My hands were stiff. My pulse kicked in my throat. I stared at the USB stick as if it were a live explosive.

Maybe that's exactly what it was.

How could we have missed this? I thought to myself.

What I didn't know then, what only became clear much later, was that the police had already seized Alasdair's PC from the office. They hadn't told me. They'd gone to Warren quietly, and he'd let them in after hours. I can't say I blamed him. They had a warrant. The kind that comes with consequences if ignored. Once they had imaged the machine and found what they were looking for, they arrested Alasdair at his home, more than a year after his initial disappearance.

CHAPTER 25
THE RECKONING

After that first interview with the DA's office, life at the bank settled into an eerie kind of quiet, a silence that felt less like resolution and more like the moment before a pressure valve gives. Alasdair was still gone. No updates. No announcements. No farewell. His office remained locked for weeks.

Eventually, Carolyn had it cleaned out at night by a junior HR assistant. A framed photo of his wife and two young children sat on the desk for days before it vanished. An old rugby ball, once sitting on the corner of a desk like a half-forgotten signature, was gone. For a while, the door stayed open, as if someone might still walk in. Then, without comment, it stayed shut.

It was like a chapter that no one dared to revisit.

The month after my interview, I checked the court logs, still trying to understand what all this was about. And there it was, Alasdair's name. A docket entry marked "ongoing investigation" was all that appeared—without a listed charge. My stomach turned. I assumed, like many probably did, that it was financial fraud. Misuse of internal systems. Something that fit the story we'd all quietly started telling ourselves.

I hated that I had believed that. But what else was I supposed to think?

Back in the office, Owen tried to take the reins. Technically, he was Alasdair's chief of staff. But with Alasdair gone, Owen became the de facto head of New York. The space Alasdair had left behind was cavernous, but Owen handled his new role with quiet diligence. It didn't last. Owen grew more withdrawn, arriving later, leaving earlier, eyes locked on the middle distance. One morning, I saw his office dark at 9:30. It remained that way all day. He was still in charge on paper, but in spirit, he'd already checked out. You could almost see the exact moment duty gave way to silent surrender.

We never formally discussed it, but once, in the hallway, I caught him staring at a group photo from a 2008 leadership offsite. He looked at it for a long time.

"He didn't deserve this," he said and walked away. His voice had cracked slightly. That was the last full sentence he ever said to me.

I had had no personal correspondence from Dr. Rhun for a while when Dmitry stepped into my office and whispered, "You're wanted on a Teams call. *Group*. Rhun's on it."

When the video popped up, Rhun was alone. No senior managers. No compliance backdrop. Just a dark office, a half-empty glass of water beside his keyboard, and that same dispassionate expression.

"David," he said. Not Mr. Wallace. Not chief technology officer. Just *David*.

"We've been reviewing certain decisions made by local leadership, particularly in areas of infrastructure and risk," he said. "There's no formal concern. Not yet. But ambiguity invites speculation. And speculation in times like these is a risk we can't afford."

I met his eyes through the screen. "Are you accusing me of something?"

He smiled faintly. "Not at all. This is simply ... a reminder. That visibility goes both ways."

Then he ended the call.

The business performance in New York was suffering. Gone was the swagger in the trading room. Even without seeing the numbers, it was clear we were no longer at the heart of the group. At senior management meetings, there was no talk of new business.

"How are we performing?" I asked one day after making a quick stop at Erica's office.

"It's ugly," she replied. Her voice was flat, but her eyes didn't quite meet mine. For a moment, I thought she might say more. Instead, she turned back to her screen.

Then one day, Owen was gone. No email. No farewell drinks. Just an empty office and a line through his name on the org chart. The word was that Swansea had made the call. Too quiet. Too hesitant. Too close to Alasdair. They wanted a clean break.

With Alasdair and Owen gone, our independence collapsed, and with it, what little momentum we had.

I asked Erica if she had any idea what had happened to the thumb drive Alasdair had given Owen.

"No idea," she responded, and I let the matter drop. But something about it gnawed at me.

Two months later, Swansea sent their proxy: Stephen Jones. A risk guy. Reserved. Exacting. Not there to lead, just to monitor and quietly dismantle.

There was something chilling about Jones's presence. He rarely blinked. His pen moved like a metronome. Instead of asking for context, he just took inventory. He spoke clipped, overly formal English, tinged with a faint Swabian accent. He referred to systems by ID codes instead of names, reducing everything human to mere data points.

His suits were identical, charcoal, cleanly tailored, devoid of personality. His shoes were always silent. His watch gave a single beep 58 minutes into every meeting. He never acknowledged it, but at the hour, he always stood. You felt yourself lowering your voice in his presence. He didn't seem cruel, just utterly indifferent. That was worse. He felt less like a banker and more like a silent ruler. The verdict before the sentence.

The day he arrived, the mood shifted. Erica muttered, "Another of Rhun's watchdogs." Carolyn said nothing, just sat a little stiffer. Even the junior staff sensed it. Something had budged, and no one knew yet how deep it would go. Reggie clutched his notebook like a shield and—usually talkative—became guarded. When I asked him for a status update, he handed me a printed list, eyes avoiding mine. Later in the elevator, he whispered, "They're not here to understand. They're here to erase."

Someone, probably Erica, claimed Jones had been responsible for the closure of three Eastern European branches. No press. No drama. Just shuttered doors and silence.

In Jones's second week, he asked for a meeting. Systems, staff, budgets. I walked him through everything—our infrastructure, headcount, key projects. He took notes. He didn't ask a single question.

At the end, he closed the file I'd prepared.

"I believe we can reduce staff by 40 percent," he said.

"Sorry?"

"Forty percent. The business is shrinking. You don't need this many engineers."

He wasn't wrong. Things were slowing. FX had lost two top traders. Transportation finance was treading water. The old energy, the us-against-Swansea spirit, had long since drained away. Still, I pushed back.

"These people built the systems you're still relying on. Without them, we wouldn't have made it this far."

He looked up. Calm, unwavering. "This isn't about merit. It's about cost."

A week later, I let 12 people go.

That morning, I sat motionless at my desk for an hour before calling the first name. My hand hovered over the phone. I rehearsed my lines, trying to find a tone that was honest but composed. But when Marissa from Application Support walked in, eyes already glassy, I faltered. She didn't cry. I did. Not visibly. But enough that I had to pause before I could speak. She left her badge on my desk without a word.

Some cried. Most didn't. Gary from infrastructure shook my hand and said, "Thanks for fighting."

That one landed hard. Until then, it had already been the worst day of my professional life. These weren't just colleagues. They were builders. And I believed I owed them more than a severance packet and a handshake.

The office shrank around us. Hallways quieted. Projects stalled. Emails slowed. Even the Wi-Fi seemed to carry less traffic. One afternoon, I passed the main conference room; half the chairs were gone.

The following month, we were told our disaster recovery site in Pennsylvania would be decommissioned. Swansea wanted to consolidate in Wales. "More efficient," they claimed. I wrote a detailed memo: *latency, compliance, continuity—none of it made sense.* The Fed would never sign off.

Jones replied with one line: "We will proceed as planned."

By midyear, my responsibilities had tripled. I was no longer just the CTO. I was also head of insurance, security, and premises. As roles became vacant, I quietly absorbed them. At first, I resisted. Then I just complied.

I started grinding my teeth again, something I hadn't done since my junior analyst days in London. The night sweats returned. I'd wake up soaked, heart hammering. Sue noticed the tension in my shoulders. The way I stirred coffee but never drank it.

She asked whether I wanted to talk. I said I was fine.

I wasn't.

At night, I lay awake replaying meetings, second-guessing decisions I'd already made. I felt as if I were watching everything I'd built fall apart, one thread at a time.

Sue tried to reach me. She brought me tea and asked me to go for a walk. I told her I had a deadline. The truth? I didn't know how to explain the thing I barely understood myself, that I felt as if I were fading from something I'd spent years holding together.

That week, I woke up drenched three nights in a row. Sue said nothing. She just changed the sheets and closed the window. I felt a sharp mix of guilt and gratitude.

On the third night, as she tucked the corner of the sheet beneath the mattress, she said softly, "You're not sleeping. You're not talking. I feel like you're disappearing."

I didn't respond. Not because I didn't want to. But because I didn't have the words.

But still, the unraveling continued.

Back at the office. The lights stayed on. The emails kept arriving. But someone had extinguished something essential. We weren't just being restructured. We were being erased.

And somehow, we all knew it.

CHAPTER 26
THE FIXERS

Then, without warning, Johann Meier turned up at the branch. He was the board's sharpest enforcer. He walked into the office on a Tuesday morning as if he owned the place. Security badge active. Email working. Someone had clearly expected him. He was a well-known and respected figure at the bank, but he arrived with no fanfare.

That morning, I received a calendar invite from Carolyn: *Executive Update—Conf Room 7C—10:00 a.m.*

What remained of the senior team filed into the glass-walled room on the 29th floor. Jones was already there, standing off to the side. Meier stood at the front of the room as if he were about to give a lecture.

"There are ongoing investigations into data governance, financial reporting, and network access irregularities," he said. "We will interview each of you separately, and will start today."

He looked at me. "You're first."

The interview wasn't like the one with the DA. No police. No prosecutors. Just Meier, a note taker, and a digital recorder. But it was invasive in its own way. Meier was precise. He asked about VPN logs, badge swipes, emergency overrides, and whether Alasdair had ever discussed off-grid systems. I answered each question with mechanical precision, but by the time I returned to my desk, I felt hollowed out—again.

I passed Reggie near the elevators that afternoon. He looked ... different. Paler than usual. The collar of his shirt clung damply to his neck, and he always seemed to be clutching a legal pad as if his life depended on it.

"Everything all right?" I asked.

He hesitated. "Just got out of a meeting with Meier."

That gave me pause.

"Routine?" I asked.

Reggie nodded too quickly. "Sure. Routine. Just ... clarifying reporting lines. Asking about Rhun. About the memos." He gave a tight smile. "I think I was boring enough, so the meeting ended quickly."

I watched him walk away, back stiff, steps clipped. Reggie wasn't invisible. He calculated *everything*. It was the first time I realized that survival wasn't a matter of luck. It was the discipline of leaving no edges to grab onto.

Later that day, Sue called. She sensed it before I spoke.

I gave her the basics. "I think they're circling someone," I said.

"Someone, or you?" she asked.

I didn't answer.

Then she said, "Whatever happens, keep writing down everything. It may be all you have when this ends."

I didn't respond, but I picked up my pen.

Meier was at the office for only one day. During that time, he interviewed the entire management team and a few of my technologists. The branch, once a battleground, now felt like a husk. Quiet. Slow. Dimming. But the worst part wasn't the work. It was the atmosphere. No more jokes near the coffee machine. No more casual banter in the elevator. Now there were closed doors, quick glances, and a silence that had weight to it.

On Tuesday mornings, we used to crowd around Reggie's desk as he recapped the Premier League. Now, his desk sat empty until 9:45, and no one asked why. The group chat for lunch orders hadn't lit up in weeks. Even the shared Spotify playlists had stopped. It felt like arriving late to a banquet hall after the guests had already left, napkins crumpled, music long stopped, the cleanup crew already at work.

One afternoon, I found Erica in the break room, stirring sugar into her tea with mechanical precision. She didn't look up.

"They've broken it," she said. "The spirit. It's gone."

I nodded. "They didn't even have to fire most of us. They just waited for us to give up."

"It's a much cheaper option," she said.

She finally looked at me. "You ever feel like we defended a fort just long enough to find out the rot was already in the foundations?" Her voice was soft, laced with something like disbelief. "We kept the lights on, held the walls, but it didn't matter. The collapse had already started."

There was a flicker of something in her, exhaustion, but also clarity. She had slightly rumpled her blouse, misaligning a button. She looked like someone who had stopped caring how she appeared because the pretense no longer mattered.

There were days I thought about leaving, too. I'd been in this game for a long time. Started in London as a junior analyst with a cheap suit and a hunger to matter. I'd worked 18-hour days and fought for every inch of progress. And here I was, over two decades later, watching it all unravel in silence. I worked out in my head if there was a way to walk out with a severance package, call it a good run, and leave the wreckage behind. But I couldn't. Not yet.

Part of me needed to see how it all ended. Part of me still believed I could make sense of it. And deep down, I feared that walking away then would feel like an admission of guilt, that quitting meant giving up any chance of understanding the wreckage.

I wasn't staying for the paycheck. I was staying because I couldn't look away. If this place was being dismantled from within, I needed to know who was behind it—and why. Some part of me believed that if I traced the damage to its source, I might still find a way to stop it, or at least understand it, before the lights went out for good.

And I still had the USB. Still had the logs. I had told no one, not even Sue. Part of me didn't know what to do with them. The other part feared what might happen if I did.

For now, they sat in my drawer like a loaded weapon, waiting. And so was I.

CHAPTER 27
THE SECOND INTERVIEW

Nearly a year after my first meeting with the prosecutors, the phone rang again. It was Thursday, October 7th. And with it came the cold return of something I thought I'd buried: fear.

It was Warren.

My stomach turned. It had been over a year since we last spoke, and even during our time working together, our relationship had been cold. I didn't like the man. I didn't trust him. So, seeing his name flash across my phone now felt ominous, like hearing a knock at the door in the middle of the night.

"David," he said. "They want to speak with you again. Same location. Monday. 9 a.m."

"Who?" I asked, already fearing I knew the answer.

"The New York police and the public prosecutor."

"Same people?"

"No, bigger group this time. They want to talk about the day Alasdair left. The timing. The systems access. Everything you remember."

The tone of his voice was different. Not just relaying a message, but hinting at a warning.

"Am I being subpoenaed?"

"Not officially," Warren replied.

"Then I want legal representation. Someone the bank pays for."

"That will not happen."

"You're telling me I'm expected to walk in there alone?"

"I'm advising you that it would be in your best interest to attend. That's all I can say."

I almost laughed. Warren giving legal advice? We barely tolerated each other when we worked together. Now he was pretending to be helpful. It didn't add up.

"Why are you even calling me?"

He paused. "Because someone had to. And because this time ... it's not just about Alasdair. They're circling someone else."

When I hung up, my head throbbed. My hands shook. Warren had only ever called my personal cell once before. For him to do it now, with this tone, under the guise of helpfulness? It was sinister.

That night, I didn't eat. I walked around the house like a ghost, checked locks that were already secure, stared at the same unread email for 20 minutes. Sue watched me from the kitchen. She knew better than to press. I paced the hallway. Phone still in hand. Sue stepped closer, gently took it from me, and set it on the counter.

"Talk to me," she said.

I ran a hand through my hair. "Blake told me they want to discuss Alasdair's last day. But in what context, I don't know."

She studied me. "Then we figure it out together. One step at a time. But you don't go in blind, and you don't go in alone. Not emotionally, anyway. I'm here."

But I was scared. Scared in a way I hadn't felt since Alasdair vanished. The weight settled on my shoulders like lead. That night, I couldn't sleep. I stood barefoot in the living room, drenched in sweat. Sue watched silently from the hallway. She understood silence was its own language.

"I know you said it's related to Alasdair," she said, "but it feels like it's about you now. Are you sure your team hasn't done something illegal? Could Alasdair have been the fall guy?"

The thought had been gnawing at me ever since Warren's call.

"I honestly can't think of anything that would point that way," I said.

"Just come to bed," she whispered, placing a hand on my arm.

I left the house at dawn the next day. From our home in Chatham, New Jersey, my commute into the city took an hour and a half each way. Normally, I used the time to think through the day's problems or catch up on calls. Not this time. I walked to Chatham station and boarded the Midtown Direct line, the morning still heavy with mist. My palms were slick as I gripped the rail, silently rehearsing answers, then stopping, only to start again five minutes later. When I got off the train at Penn Station, I took a very slow walk downtown. I was early by the time I reached the courthouse, so I found a quiet bench across the street and sat for some time, heart racing, watching the city move around me. I checked my phone four times. Nothing.

The courthouse lobby was cavernous and sterile. The security checkpoint beeped twice. A guard led me through cold, echoing corridors to a large conference room. They had set up the room to be like a press conference. Rows of chairs. Twenty people. Two ADAs. Three cybersecurity analysts. A forensic accountant. Four NYPD officers of senior rank. One man I didn't recognize, sitting near the end of the table, silent.

"Mr. Wallace," an ADA began, "we're focusing on the day Mr. Stewart was dismissed. We believe he may have been manipulated into actions that created irregularities, possibly without realizing it."

A chill crept up my spine.

"We're not saying he's innocent," another added quickly. "But there were anomalies. Patterns inconsistent with his behavior. Access times when he wasn't in the building. Computer sessions we can't map to any known device. Files created when he wasn't present. Network traffic we can't match to a known machine. Something was on his system that shouldn't have been there."

He continued, "We searched his PC and have completed a thorough technical investigation of all activity. We are now trying to reconcile what we found with the technical security infrastructure you have in the office and with the actions of him and other individuals the last day he was in the office."

For the first time, someone had formally linked Alasdair to a crime.

Not innocent of exactly what, I wondered.

I told them I had kept a log of that day and asked if I could reference it. Their surprise was evident. One nodded. I opened my folder, retrieved my notes, and began.

"I took notes that day. Everything I saw, heard, or inferred. At the time, I thought I was covering my back. But now it feels as if I had been documenting a crime scene in real-time."

The room shifted. Not shock, but attention. A readiness to listen.

I spoke. Told them everything. Inside, I was unraveling. My voice was calm, but it didn't feel like mine. My hands trembled. Every detail felt like a thread I was pulling, unsure if I was helping or exposing something darker.

They asked me about Erica, which surprised me. I described how Carolyn had begun quietly watching Erica. Not with distrust exactly. But close. I recalled Erica's name surfacing only subtly, in a hallway sighting, a decision bypassing protocol, a postponed audit she never pushed for again.

They asked about the two Swansea men, the data center, and the firewall port tap. I explained: we had mirrored their sessions, recorded their keystrokes, logged every action. Ryan, one of our lead network engineers, had set up a diagnostic tool, a silent observer. I informed them that Dmitry and I were monitoring everything, just in case.

As I spoke, I remembered Alasdair in the hallway, coat on his arm, meeting my gaze with a knowing look before rushing out. At the time, it meant little. Now, it echoed.

They asked about Project Fortress Manhattan. I explained that we had used a whitelist approach; only pre-approved websites and technical destinations could be accessed. It was highly restrictive, but that was the point: to eliminate vulnerability by narrowing the range of permitted activity.

Then came the question that changed everything.

"Do you believe anyone could have added anything to Mr. Stewart's machine during that period?"

I hesitated, not from doubt, but from understanding. Now I knew why I was there.

"Yes," I said. "If someone had the right permissions and, most importantly, physical access to the machine, they could add anything. Files. Registry keys. Even remote access tools."

The ADA looked around. Nods. Not surprisingly, confirmation.

This wasn't about fraud.

This was about Alasdair.

And something was done to him. Not by him.

My throat tightened. If Alasdair was a victim, what did that make me? A pawn? An enabler? I gripped the chair. My mind reeled back through every meeting, every strange silence, every time I'd missed something staring me in the face.

But my mind was especially focused on Erica. Why did they bring her up?

She had access. She'd always been in the room, above suspicion. And now, in hindsight, minor details flickered like flares. She'd once recommended postponing the backup audit. I'd overruled her. She hadn't pushed. That silence now screamed. Had she been shielding someone? Or orchestrating the whole thing? I left that room colder than I'd ever been.

Back at the office, I opened a secure file and started building a private timeline.

Then I reopened the Echo Logs. When I looked again, one folder stood out. Too clean. Too perfect. It appeared as if someone had tidied it afterward. It felt staged.

How the hell had I missed this? I asked myself.

I flagged the file: *session_hook.dll*. A dynamic-link library. Innocuous on the surface, but it could be used to spy, to control —to destroy.

Whoever did this wanted it to be found—but only after it was too late to stop what it triggered. I called Doug.

Doug was methodical. Quiet. The best.

"Run this in a sandbox," I said. "Tell me what it does."

He examined it, frowning. "This isn't malware. It's a surgical implant. Whoever wrote this knew our architecture and our blind spots. This is the kind of file that either solves everything or blows something wide open."

"In a sandbox," I repeated.

He cracked it. The shell revealed code intentionally hidden. Impossible to have passed through normal security. Someone must have planted it.

Then I remembered a conversation with a European systems architect: "Our filters would never let that traffic through without ten alerts."

The NYPD must have figured that out, too.

That explained why I was back in that room.

For a few weeks, I had wondered why Rhun's name had vanished so suddenly. We had not heard from him for a while. There were whispers coming out of Swansea that, for some reason, he was facing suspension, but there was never clarity about why.

That night, staring at the ceiling, one thought circled like a hawk: someone had planted something.

And I was thinking I'd just found the fuse, not the bomb.

CHAPTER 28
THE PLACEHOLDER

Stephen Jones, the group liaison sent from Head Office, had been quietly running the show for nearly ten months. Though he never took the New York CEO title, his authority was absolute. He attended every major meeting, reviewed all outgoing reports, and held weekly briefings with Group Compliance. Cold, composed, and fluent in the politics of control, Stephen wasn't there to inspire; he was there to document, contain, and reshape.

The one thing he did without hesitation was shrink the branch. Headcount reductions, project cancelations, balance sheet pruning—all part of the quiet dismantling. Every month, someone else disappeared. Desks were left empty. The company wound down portfolios. It was control by subtraction. We were no longer a branch of equals. We were an asset under quarantine. Through all this, our business model was collapsing. Distressed assets piled up, and while our cost base was being managed down, it was not enough to stop the rot.

Back in Swansea, the board was under enormous pressure from the shareholders. Group profits remained elusive, and although the New York office had once propped up the entire bank, it was now rapidly becoming its anchor. For me, it all came to a head the day Jones called me into his office. He wasted no time.

"You need to cut your headcount by another 50 percent," he said flatly.

I didn't flinch. "Fine," I replied. "Just tell me what the forward-looking business model is for New York, and I'll align the team accordingly."

He bristled. "You don't need to know that. Just get it done."

I held my ground. "I'm not cutting any more seasoned professionals based on a dartboard. If you want precision, I need a target."

His voice sharpened. "This isn't a negotiation. Make the cuts."

I stood. "And this isn't a factory floor. We're not assembling widgets. These are people and systems that work. You want blood? You give me the map."

By then, we were both shouting. Through the glass walls, staff had looked up from their desks. I saw Dmitry glance over. Even Erica looked startled.

Jones didn't back down. "Do your job, Mr. Wallace. Or someone else will."

I left his office without another word. But everyone had heard. And the mood on the floor shifted. Something in the facade had cracked.

Still, I did what I was told. I started a forced ranking exercise, a brutal corporate method where employees are graded against one another and ranked from top to bottom. After the first round of cuts, this was even more difficult. There's no room for nuance. No accounting for context. Just numbers. I graded everyone on performance, potential, and perceived value to the new order we were clearly being funneled into.

Then I cut the bottom 50 percent.

Letting good people go was always one of the hardest things I'd ever had to do. Not because the people I let go were irreplaceable, but because they deserved better than to be slotted into a spreadsheet and dismissed like bad inventory. But in that environment, metrics were all that mattered. And Jones got exactly what he wanted.

But I didn't just walk away. I went to bat for every single one of them. I negotiated with HR to ensure that those being let go received fair compensation and redundancy packages that respected their years of service. My actions didn't undo the pain, but they prevented it from being discarded like broken parts. If I had to make cuts, I was going to make damn sure they landed on their feet.

And yet, even as I fought for them, I felt a growing detachment. Something cold setting in. Maybe it was survival. Maybe it was resignation. Or maybe, in trying to hold everything together, I'd simply run out of things to believe in.

Not everyone went quietly. Sanjay, who'd been let go earlier in the year, filed a wrongful dismissal suit against the bank. It didn't surprise me. What had happened to him had never sat right with me, and now it was public. Legal dismissed it as nuisance litigation, but word spread. And it raised questions we couldn't answer. Questions that made people nervous.

After about ten months, Stephen Jones called a meeting of the remaining senior management team. He took two minutes to inform us he would be returning to Swansea. Someone had asked him who would take over in his place. He did not acknowledge the question and certainly did not answer it.

The meeting ended quickly, and I stood to leave the conference room.

"You know," Stephen said to me, still looking at his notes, "I once had a boss like Alasdair. Years ago. In Swansea,"

I said nothing. Just waited.

"He fought for us. Pushed back against group politics. Said he wouldn't be another yes-man." A pause. "He was gone within three months."

Finally, he looked up. "I have two kids in Cardiff. One of them starts university next year. You learn when to stand still."

Then, he closed the folder and said nothing more.

Two weeks after Jones left, we got an email from Rhun. It was the first formal communication we'd had from him in months. He announced that Reggie would be promoted to lead New York operations.

It was sudden. It was quiet. And it was strategic.

Reggie had been a mid-level manager for over a decade. Competent. Bland. Present. According to Rhun, he was there to "stabilize" the branch. But we all knew what that meant. He wasn't being promoted. He was being positioned.

The Monday after his appointment, Reggie walked in with a gray Samsonite roller and an envelope bearing the Cambria Group seal. He looked like someone on his first day at a corporate onboarding, not the new head of a global finance hub. Despite being pressed, his shirt didn't fit right. His smile was tight. His eyes said nothing.

From the moment he arrived, it was obvious: Reggie wasn't here to lead. He was here to obey. His job wasn't to fix anything. It was to keep the lights on and the questions down.

In meetings, he dodged. He deferred. He parked issues. When I raised the discovery of unexplained VPN log gaps— something I'd already spoken about with the ADA—he blinked and muttered, "Group IT is looking into overall log retention policies. Let's not overreact."

He did the same with audit alerts. With project delays. With budget freezes. He gave the appearance of responsiveness without ever making a single actual decision.

People called him "The Wallpaper." Fitting. He faded into the background, even as the branch collapsed in slow motion.

I used to fight those declines. I used to scream in meetings. Now, I just observed. There was nothing to push against. Just air.

But not everyone faded.

Erica did the opposite.

She stepped up. Quietly. Consistently. She started chairing meetings. Drafting responses. Guiding discussions. People began deferring to her. Even Reggie.

I saw it in the way she positioned herself—always two seats from Reggie. Close enough to advise. Far enough not to threaten. She didn't need the title. She had influence.

One day, I found her alone in the break room, staring at the skyline.

"Settling in?" I asked.

She turned with a polished, unreadable smile. "Just doing what needs to be done."

There was no arrogance. Just calm. A certainty I couldn't place.

I stayed late that night, scrolling through my private notes, including the timeline I'd built after that second interview. Erica's name appeared more often than I expected. Audit delays. Firewall exception sign-offs. Meeting adjournments. Quiet all the time. Always justified, enough to slide under the radar.

She hadn't taken over. She'd simply stopped waiting.

Reggie was a placeholder.

But Erica?

She was already in place.

And maybe, just maybe, this was the plan all along.

CHAPTER 29
THE FRAME

B ut then, one morning, Warren knocked on my office door. He never knocked. And the look on his face, that haunted, reluctant expression, made me feel instantly off-balance.

There was a tightness in his jaw I hadn't seen before, as if something inside him had finally broken loose, and he didn't know how to hold it back anymore.

"Got a minute?" he asked.

"Sure."

He stepped in, closed the door, and sat down without waiting to be invited. There was no hesitation in his movement, but everything about him radiated unease, his fingers tapping the armrest, his eyes refusing to settle. This wasn't a casual visit. He looked like a man about to confess, not converse.

"I'm going to tell you something," he said, lowering his voice, his tone almost breaking under the strain. "But it doesn't leave this room. This isn't gossip, David, it's a reckoning."

He waited. I nodded.

"It's about Alasdair," he said, almost wincing at the sound of the name, as if saying it aloud might summon something he wasn't ready to face.

My chest tightened. I hadn't heard his name spoken in months. The name hung in the air like a loaded weapon, familiar, but treacherous to touch. My breath caught, and for a split second, the room seemed to tilt. It was like hearing the name of someone you'd buried long ago, someone whose ghost never really left. I felt the sting of memory behind my eyes, and a tightness that had nothing to do with surprise, but everything to do with grief.

"You remember those two guys from Swansea?" Warren continued, his voice dropping into a low, almost fearful register. "The ones who accessed the systems after he left. The ones who walked in like auditors but moved like executioners?"

"I remember," I said slowly.

Warren's eyes flicked toward the hallway, as if making sure no one was listening. His entire demeanor was different, cautious, unsettled, and riddled with something close to fear. He leaned in slightly, his voice tightening as though the very walls might be listening. This wasn't just a risk; this was an exorcism.

"They didn't just pull data," he said. "They planted evidence. They uploaded a scanned document onto Alasdair's machine, an unsigned contract to arrange the murder of Rhun. A payment schedule, contact details, and anonymized usernames, all carefully constructed. They also modified his browser history to show he had accessed parts of the dark web known for connecting clients with contract killers."

He swallowed. "They even faked a cryptocurrency wallet login. Installed Tor. Buried the data in a hidden partition. They knew what they were doing."

I froze.

Warren kept going. "They made it look as if Alasdair were trying to hire a hitman to kill Rhun. It was all there: fabricated chats, scraped user threads from real forums, doctored IP logs. And they linked it all to his workstation. They left a printed version of the contract, unsigned, on his desk. Hidden under the keyboard as if it had been forgotten."

What made it unspeakable wasn't just the files or the login activity; it was the choice to tie it all to his family. They didn't just fabricate a crime; they personalized it. That photo on his desk, his wife, Claudia, and his youngest daughter at the beach, smiling, sunlit, real, had become part of the weapon, Warren told me. They wrote the credentials for the illegal site on the back of that photograph. They turned a symbol of love and pride into a grotesque prop in a story engineered to destroy him.

It was as if they wanted not only to implicate him but also to contaminate everything he cared about. This wasn't just about legal ruin. This was about the annihilation of dignity, of identity, of the right to even defend himself. And the worst part? They left it sitting on his desk as if it had always been there.

"Two weeks later," Warren said, "the Swansea team tipped off the NYPD anonymously. Said they found evidence of a murder-for-hire attempt during a routine audit. When the NYPD imaged the drive, it was all there in the logs, the chats. And documents."

I felt my stomach twist. A chill crept up my spine like an ice trickle, and my fingertips went numb as if the blood had drained from them. I tried to breathe, but the air caught in my throat. A wave of nausea hit me, sharp and unexpected. I stood up, unsure of what I was doing, whether I was about to collapse or vomit. The fluorescent lights overhead felt like interrogation lamps. My pulse thundered in my ears. I gripped the edge of my desk until my knuckles went white.

I had worked in banks my entire adult life, had seen fraud, greed, even outright corruption, but nothing like this. Nothing so vile. This was more than a scandal; it was a desecration, and it shook me to my core.

These weren't just bad actors; they were predators in suits, attacking more than bonuses or boardroom politics. This was moral rot masquerading as executive discretion. There was something so cruel about that detail, the intimacy of the frame, the brutality of its message. It was psychological warfare.

Claudia entered my mind. A few years earlier, I had met her briefly over sushi. Alasdair had insisted I join them. She was elegant, reserved, and had a laugh that mirrored his: full-bodied, unexpected, and slightly mischievous. That memory, once so light, now curdled into something unbearable. How on earth had she dealt with this?

"It was ... staged," he said. "Staged to look like a hidden compulsion. Enough to trigger law enforcement. Enough to ruin him."

I stared at him, unable to speak. The audit team in Swansea had tipped off the New York police.

"The police initially asked us to ship his computer to their office," Warren said. "We did. A week later, I noticed extra security audits on our file servers, quiet and unexplained. People from compliance were whispering in the breakroom. Someone from Group Legal suddenly started working remotely. That's when things blew up. We received a request from the NYPD to allow them to search his office. That was when they found the dark website credentials. An arrest warrant was issued shortly after. My understanding is that the NYPD went to his house. His wife answered the door."

I remembered standing in Alasdair's office that last Friday. The blinds were half-drawn. As always, notes, phone chargers, and a photo of his youngest in a baby's tennis outfit cluttered his desk.

He'd said, "You know, David, they don't care about the truth, just the version they can file."

I sat back in my chair.

"They destroyed him," I said. It wasn't just about Alasdair. It was a message to everyone. A warning stitched into silence.

Warren nodded. He looked me in the eye, not accusing, just tired. Part of me wondered why he was telling me this now. Guilt? Self-preservation? Maybe he saw what was coming. Maybe he wanted off the hook before it snapped. Whatever the reason, it didn't feel like altruism. It felt like a man emptying his pockets before a storm.

"And they used you to do it. You gave them access."

I looked at him, horrified. My mouth went dry. The floor felt uneven beneath me, as if truth had unmoored gravity. I had heard shocking things in my time, but nothing like this, nothing so intimate, so violating, so final. I could feel something tearing inside me, something I hadn't known was still intact.

"You didn't know," he added quickly. "You were doing your job. They had authorization from Rhun. You had no way of knowing."

Still, it didn't feel like enough. I saw myself at that moment, authorizing their access, shaking hands, even offering help. Back then, I felt proud to be trusted. Now, that pride felt poisoned. I was ashamed. Disoriented. If someone could weaponize trust like that, what else had I missed? Who else had I enabled?

Later that night, I would scrub my hands until the skin peeled, as if I could wash off the residue of that moment. I didn't sleep. I barely breathed.

But it didn't matter. The damage was done. I could feel it, an invisible weight pressing on my chest. My hands were trembling. My mind raced. I tried to replay that day, the morning the Swansea guys arrived. I remember pushing back against the request to give them access, but now it did not feel like enough. Now I felt sick. How could I have missed it? Was I naive, or did I just take the easy route?

"They got what they wanted," Warren said, his voice a notch lower. "Alasdair was gone. Disgraced. And the rest of us fell in line. We all saw what happened to him, what they were capable of. No one wanted to be next. So, we kept our heads down, swallowed our doubts, and went back to work as if nothing had happened."

I stared out the window for a long time after he left. In the reflection, I didn't see myself. I saw Alasdair standing at his office door, briefcase in hand, waiting for a storm he never saw coming.

He was a husband. A father. A friend. He played golf on Sundays and sent corny memes to the group chat. And now his name was buried under scandal, and I had helped shovel the dirt.

I had always known something was off. But this, this was *evil*. In that moment, a dozen memories surged to the surface: half-finished conversations, sudden changes in behavior, late-night emails that made little sense at the time. I felt a cold recognition wash over me, as if a puzzle I hadn't known I was solving had suddenly snapped into place. The silence in the room became deafening, each second stretching out like the tolling of a warning bell in my chest. My gut twisted, not from surprise, but from the slow, dawning realization that the truth had always been circling, just beyond reach.

I had read the court log. I had seen the vague docket entry, the sealed charges, and the speculation in the press. And like everyone else, I'd filled in the blanks. I thought it was fraud, some internal breach, maybe trading violations. Something clean. Something that fit the narrative.

But now, knowing what I knew, my stomach turned.

I pictured Claudia answering the door. I pictured it, her shock, the moment everything fell apart. The look on her face when the NYPD showed up, not with answers, but accusations. I imagined her shielding their daughter, trying to understand words that didn't belong in her world: possession, hitmen, evidence.

I had told myself he must've done something. I needed to believe that. Because the alternative, that he hadn't, that he was innocent but destroyed anyway, was too unbearable to face.

I hadn't asked questions. I hadn't wanted to. Accepting the worst about him was easier than confronting the possibility that the rot ran deeper, into the walls I worked within—that I played a part in it.

That night, I reviewed the logs from that period. I hesitated before logging in, half afraid of what I might find, half afraid I'd find nothing at all. I was looking for something, anything that would help me understand how this happened.

I was alone in the office, just the glow of my monitor and the hum of the office air conditioning system overhead. It was like standing at the scene of a crime, trying to reassemble the moment of impact. Every flicker of light on the screen felt loaded. My pulse drummed in my ears. I kept thinking: somewhere in here, hidden within these logs, is the truth they tried to bury.

I combed through packet data—snapshots of the information flowing across our network—along with login trails that tracked every digital step, and event logs that time-stamped system activity. These were the forensic breadcrumbs. I remembered Doug's earlier sandbox result, where we'd isolated the suspicious file in a controlled environment. We had only scratched the surface.

"Doug," I called over the phone, even though it was late. Doug had worked with me for years, a quiet but sharp infrastructure guy, known for building a leading-edge server room back in 2005 at a previous bank. He was among my first hires when I landed this job. Not a formal member of the tech leadership team, but someone I trusted. He preferred data to politics, never took sides, and rarely spoke in meetings, but when it came to systems diagnostics, there was no one better.

My voice sounded steadier than I felt. "I need you to come in."

There was a pause. "I don't know, David ... this sounds big." His voice carried tension.

"It is," I said. "But I need your eyes on this."

Another beat of silence. "You're not asking me to open a door we can't close, are you?"

"No," I said. "We're going to open the one they locked."

"All right," he said. "I'll be there in 20."

Doug was one of the few people I still trusted. And maybe the only one who could make sense of the madness. Years ago, he warned me that our system was too open, too easily exploited from the inside. I hadn't listened.

CHAPTER 30
THE HOOK

True to his word, Doug arrived 20 minutes later, jeans, hoodie, and a laptop bag slung over one shoulder. His drawn face and tight jaw were clear. We didn't speak as we walked to the server room, just the tap of our shoes on the tile and the low mechanical hum of machines filling the silence.

We re-ran our security scan, this time looking closely at everything that had opened or run on Alasdair's computer over a single day. One strange program stood out. It looked harmless, but it allowed someone to access the computer from outside his office secretly. No alerts. No notifications. Just silent, invisible access, as if someone had left a back door open, and no one noticed.

Doug showed me the file's hidden details. Someone had tampered with it, making it look as if it had been created earlier than it actually was, to blend in and avoid suspicion. In layman's terms, it's like falsifying a timestamp on a document to make it appear innocent by changing the "created on" date to something that fits the narrative. Doug glanced at me, his expression tight.

"This not only looks planted, it looks professionally engineered. Someone wanted this to pass surface-level scrutiny and fail under deeper inspection, which means they wanted it to be found."

His voice carried a tension that I hadn't heard before, as if he knew we were standing too close to something that could burn him. Then Doug pointed out something even more troubling. Every file has a kind of digital fingerprint. This one didn't match what it should have, like catching someone faking a signature on an important document. This mismatch confirmed that someone had tampered with the file and that it was not what it claimed to be.

The NYPD had already found the criminal content, but what we were looking at now—the cloaked login paths, falsified timestamps, and admin exploits—told a deeper story. We weren't disputing what had been found; we were uncovering how it was planted.

That matched something the NYPD had already suspected.

And someone in New York had smoothed the path internally. The logs showed seamless access—*too* seamless. Permissions had been granted without escalation. Doug flagged the user tag, ECROSS, as having reviewed the audit triggers the night before the Swansea team arrived. I stared at the screen. *Erica.*

My mind jumped back to the second interview with the police. One detective had a file open, but barely looked at it. They weren't asking about me; they were asking about network controls and how access worked. The detectives questioned the methods of content filtering. Whether someone like Alasdair could have ever visited those kinds of sites from a work machine. They also had questions about Erica. It now made sense.

I told them the truth. He couldn't have. Our firewalls and DNS filters would have blocked the attempt before a page even loaded. That was the moment I saw a shift. One detective leaned back and closed his file.

"That's consistent with what we found," he said.

We planned to report what we had found both to the New York police and to the head office security department, who were by now leading an internal investigation.

It added weight, not a contradiction. Evidence such as this might help the New York police build a broader narrative of what had truly happened. Worse, the program had full administrative power; it could do anything without asking for permission, like handing someone a master key to the building and erasing the security footage afterward.

Each of these markers, Doug explained, was a red flag in isolation, but together, they painted a picture of deliberate sabotage.

"You don't write code like this unless you want it to vanish," he muttered.

I nodded, though I barely heard him. My mind was reeling.

"I think this was a kill shot," I said, my voice barely above a whisper. "Not a cleanup."

There was a finality to the data, a surgical precision in how the evidence had been planted. This wasn't about covering tracks; it was about erasing a man.

But it didn't change everything. The shock had already come; Warren's revelation had left me hollowed out. What Doug found didn't deepen my horror. It gave it structure. Proof. It gave the story a frame I could no longer deny. The architecture of the crime had become visible, methodical, engineered to destroy. If anything, it changed what I believed was possible inside a corporation. This wasn't a conspiracy theory. This included code, access logs, and tampered metadata. And it was real.

A few days later, they suspended Rhun. No fanfare. Just a memo from HR saying he was "under internal review." It didn't say why, but we all knew. The NYPD hadn't cleared Alasdair yet, but the tide had turned. Someone upstairs had read the signals and pulled the emergency brake.

From that point on, no one spoke Rhun's name in meetings.

One night as I lay awake at 3 a.m., my thoughts kept returning to Alasdair's face, to Warren's words, to the quiet horror of what I now knew. I felt unclean, as if I had been complicit in something I hadn't even seen happening. The walls of our bedroom felt tighter than usual, as if they were pressing in with each breath. At one point, I gagged into the sink, no vomit, just the dry heave of someone overwhelmed by guilt and rage. I stood at the kitchen window for hours, watching the streetlights flicker off as morning approached, replaying every decision I'd made, every conversation I'd had, trying to pinpoint the moment I unknowingly crossed a line. But there was no single moment. Just a slow erosion of ethics, masked as process, hidden behind protocol.

The next morning, I arrived at the office before dawn. I sat at my desk, staring at the screen, my hands idle on the keyboard. I wasn't sure what I was supposed to do anymore. The rules I'd trusted, the systems, the oversight, the chain of command, had all betrayed me. Betrayed Alasdair. The ground under me felt unstable, as if I were walking across glass that could give way at any second.

That day, Reggie walked by my door, coffee in hand, nodding as if it were just another Tuesday. I looked at him and felt nothing but contempt. My stomach turned. It was like watching someone casually sip espresso in the ruins of a bombed-out building. How could he carry on like this, pretending we were still a functioning institution, pretending we hadn't just witnessed the orchestrated ruin of a man? I felt physically ill at his nonchalance. A tightness crept into my throat, and I had to steady my breathing. He represented every-thing I hated about what we'd become: detached, indifferent, complicit.

And in that moment, I knew this wasn't over. Not for me. And maybe, just maybe, not for Alasdair either.

But what did "not over" even mean?

I was not a cop or a prosecutor. I was a CTO in an office, clinging to the wreckage of a crumbling firm. And yet, I couldn't shake the thought that if I didn't act, no one would. That justice, whatever that word still meant, would rot beneath the weight of silence.

But action had consequences. Not just for Rhun. For me. I opened a shell window, then closed it again. My fingers hovered over the keys, unsure whether I was trying to write code or confess a sin.

I walked away. Came back. Opened a blank text file. Closed it. Stared at the floor. At the framed photo of Sue and me in Portugal, light, laughter, life before this.

What would she say if she knew? Would she still see me as the man she married, or as something else, something darker, forged by betrayal?

That night, I made a decision I can't fully defend.

I remembered something Warren had said, almost in passing, that the Swansea team had been "authorized by Rhun." That line had stuck with me, gnawed at me. Doug had proven how the evidence had been planted. Warren had shown me why. But it was Rhun who made it possible.

And Rhun didn't act alone. I thought of Erica, how she'd pushed for access to the same Swansea audit reports weeks earlier, insisting they were "routine." How she'd deflected when I asked why they needed such deep permissions. At the time, I chalked it up to urgency. Now I wasn't so sure.

Maybe Rhun had seen Alasdair as a rival. A threat to his promotion. Or maybe he was just the kind of man who followed orders, no matter how dirty. And Erica, what did she gain? Protection? Power? Or was she playing a longer game, one I still hadn't seen the full shape of?

And Rhun, despite his suspension, still had his company laptop.

I never understood why the IT security team didn't confiscate it; maybe the headlines distracted them. In normal circumstances, IT would have revoked his access weeks ago.

I sat in the dark with my laptop on my knees. No lights. Just the faint glow of the screen and the ache of something I couldn't name. The monitor reflected in the glass of a photo frame I had turned face down.

I tunneled into his machine using a backdoor program I'd written years ago. No alerts. No traces. It opened like an old safe you still remember the combination to.

I created a new folder buried three directories deep under a system mirror called *user_mgmt/sys/conf*. Inside, I planted a file labeled *RHO-Sync_Archive01*. It wasn't criminal, just damning. Doctored audit reports. Metadata trails implied Rhun had exfiltrated sensitive client data. Inappropriate compliance overrides. Time-stamped notes tied to known whistleblower dates.

All plausible. All fabricated.

Then I erased my fingerprints. Deleted shell logs, bounced through a disposable relay, and reset the system clock cycles to confuse any audit trail. Not even Doug would have been able to reconstruct the session.

When I shut the lid on my laptop, I felt hollow; it felt like anything but relief. It wasn't a triumph. It was something cold. I told myself it was justice. That I was balancing the scales.

But in truth, I had crossed a line. And I knew it.

The worst part wasn't the lie I'd just created. It was how easy it had been. How automatic. I justified my actions like bullet points in a pitch deck: Rhun was guilty of worse; the system was broken, and Alasdair deserved vindication.

But beneath all that, in a quieter place I didn't want to face, was something else. I had wanted to hurt him. Not just to stop him. Hurt him.

That's what chilled me.

In trying to expose the corruption, I'd embraced its logic. I'd become part of the architecture I swore I was dismantling. Not by accident. By design. Mine.

I didn't know what would happen next, whether the file would surface, whether Rhun would go down. But I knew something was different in me. Not broken. Just ... altered. Whatever came, I wouldn't be the man who looked away again.

CHAPTER 31

THE DAY THE SKY FELL
CLAUDIA STEWART

The knock came just after 7:00 a.m. I was in the hallway, bouncing Ellie on my hip, trying to coax Tom into his socks. Alasdair had been up early, sitting on the edge of the bed with his laptop open, still wearing pajama bottoms and a T-shirt, muttering about needing to follow up with someone in London. He hadn't worked at the bank in months, but the charade hadn't ended. Every morning still looked like a workday.

When the doorbell rang, he looked at me. Not confused. Not curious. Just still.

"Can you get it?" he said quietly.

I shifted Ellie to my other side, took a breath as I made my way to the door, and opened it. Three men and two women stood there. Plain clothes. Grave eyes. Badges in hand.

"Mrs. Stewart? We're with the Serious Fraud Office. We're here for your husband."

I didn't understand the words. Not at first. I thought maybe they had the wrong house. Or were here about something minor? A question, a misunderstanding.

Alasdair appeared behind me. I stepped aside, feeling Ellie tighten her grip on my arm.

"What is this?" he asked, moving in front of me. His voice was hoarse. "There must be some mistake."

The officers didn't answer. They read him his rights as he stood in the foyer. And then they handcuffed him.

I gasped. Tom, watching from the staircase, began to cry.

"In front of the children?" I shouted, my voice breaking. "What are you doing?"

"Standard protocol, ma'am," one of them said, not unkindly.

Alasdair looked stunned. Pale. As if his mind couldn't keep up. "Claudia ... call Max."

And then he was gone. Walked out of our house in hand-cuffs, with Ellie still in my arms, Tom wailing behind me, agents already rifling through our home. My entire world was upended in that doorway.

I called our lawyer, Max Berger, and left a shaky voicemail. Then I called my mother. I don't remember what we talked about, only that she kept asking if I was safe, and I kept saying *yes* when I meant *no*.

The rest of the morning passed in fragments. I fed the kids, changed Ellie, and then dropped Tom at preschool. When I came home, they were still there, still searching. I felt so violated. I cleaned the same countertop again ... and again, trying to stay out of their way but keeping busy so I didn't lose my mind. I kept checking the news, but there was nothing.

Just after noon, Max called back.

His voice was calm, measured, but the words cut through me like glass.

"Claudia, there's no easy way to say this. Cambria filed a report with the authorities several weeks ago. They claimed to have found illegal material on Alasdair's old work laptop. The police have since confirmed it through forensic review."

"Illegal material? What kind of material?"

A pause.

" Evidence that Alasdair was planning a murder-for-hire attempt."

I went cold.

Everything in the room dimmed. I sat down without realizing it. Ellie had cried somewhere nearby, but her voice sounded far away.

"They're saying that they found powerful evidence on his work PC that he was in the throes of hiring a hitman to kill someone at the bank," Max said, his voice filled with regret. "His profile was used to access the dark web and contract someone. Everything was stored locally. Timestamps match periods when he had exclusive use of the machine. It's serious, Claudia. I'm so sorry."

I couldn't breathe. I wanted to scream, to throw the phone across the room. To tell Max he was lying. That this wasn't possible. That this wasn't Alasdair.

But the worst part wasn't what he said.

It was the tiny voice inside me that whispered, *What if it's true?*

He had been distant for a while. Detached. Secretive. There were nights he had stayed late in the office, mornings when he closed his laptop the second I walked in. Excuses about "board tensions," or "legal posturing," or "transition meetings" that made little sense.

I had chalked it up to shame. Losing the job. Trying to preserve some shred of dignity.

But now, with Max's words echoing in my head, I replayed those moments differently.

And I hated myself for it.

Hated myself for doubting him.

Hated myself more for needing to.

By late afternoon, the agents had left. Someone else rang the doorbell. It was Rachel, one of my closest friends, who didn't need to ask if she should come. She brought dinner for the kids, let me fall apart in stages, and filled the silence with the presence only a friend who knows everything can provide.

We ended up in the laundry room: me, folding towels again without thought, and her, sitting close beside me. She didn't speak immediately. She waited for me to begin.

"He told me it was all behind us," I whispered. "That the worst had already happened."

Rachel looked at me, eyes red but steady. "I don't know what to say. Only that you're not alone. Not for a second."

"He told me to call Max, like it was just a formality. Like it was all some minor legal blip."

"Claudia ..."

"I opened the door with Ellie on my hip. And they took him away. Cuffed him like some ... monster." I wiped my eyes, realizing I'd been crying without knowing. "Do you think he did it? Do you think he is capable of hiring a hitman?"

Rachel didn't answer. Not because she didn't care, but because we both knew there wasn't an answer that wouldn't break me further. And that, somehow, made it worse.

That night, the kids slept in our bed. One on each side. Their bodies warm, their breathing steady.

His side of the bed was empty.

The air in the room was still.

I didn't cry again. Not then. I was beyond that. Numb, drifting.

But I knew the tears would come when the kids asked where their father was. When the reporters called. When the neighbors whispered.

They would come.

And when they did, they wouldn't stop at grief.

They would hollow me out with shame, confusion, and the unbearable guilt of not knowing whether the man I married was a victim, or something far, far worse.

They released him on bail two days later.

He came home quietly, like a ghost returning to a place that no longer wanted him. We talked little that first evening. I made pasta. He didn't eat. The kids stared at him from across the table, unsure whether they were supposed to be happy or afraid.

We started sleeping in separate rooms. Not out of anger, but because I couldn't lie next to someone I no longer understood. He said he didn't blame me. He said he knew how it looked. But every night, before he closed his door, he told me again, "They set me up, Claudia."

And part of me wanted to believe him.

But trust, once fractured, doesn't heal with repetition.

The kids changed. Tom became quiet, withdrawn. He wouldn't talk about school. Ellie cried more often, clinging to me until she fell asleep. They sensed the rupture even if they didn't have words for it.

There were days I looked at Alasdair and wanted to scream. Others, I looked at him and wanted to hold him until it all went away. But I never did—either. I just ... endured. I kept the house running. Kept the children fed. Kept answering questions with half-truths. But inside, I was falling apart. Because no matter what Max said about timelines or forensic reports, and no matter how many times Alasdair looked me in the eye and swore his innocence, I couldn't stop asking myself the one question that destroyed me: Should I have known?

CHAPTER 32
THE CRACK IN THE DAM

The news broke slowly, like a crack in a dam. First, a blog post. Then a quote from a "confidential source." Finally, the headline: "Evidence Against Former Bank Executive Under Scrutiny." The local New York press had seized the story. By week's end, it dominated the front page of *The New York Times* business section. The language was cautious. "Investigators now believe that the digital material found on the executive's work computer was likely introduced after he left the firm." But the way I read it, the implication was unmistakable. Alasdair was the victim of a frame-up. The world was only beginning to reckon with what it had done to him.

The financial community reacted with confusion and defensiveness. Analysts who had once lauded Alasdair's strategic acumen now scrambled to rewrite history, positioning themselves as cautious observers rather than former allies. Colleagues issued carefully worded statements. No one apologized. No one admitted they'd believed the worst. Social media lit up with outrage, some directed at Cambria, others at the silence of its insiders. A few indulged in shallow commentary, as if the scandal were just another trending topic. It was shocking. To me, it was black and white. They framed Alasdair. Nothing more than that.

The scandal became a litmus test for corporate ethics, drawing comparisons to past financial debacles where aggressive tactics led to unauthorized activities, resulting in substantial fines and tarnished reputations.

For a long time, life for Alasdair and his family had been a quiet hell. After his initial arrest, Claudia, once a respected figure in their community, found herself suddenly isolated. Neighbors avoided eye contact. Invitations to social events stopped. Their children faced whispers at school. People linked his name to scandal, even though no one knew exactly what he was accused of. The isolation was suffocating.

But now, as the truth surfaced, the silence around them began to shift. Slowly. Uncomfortably. Like people realizing they'd turned their backs on the wrong man. No one made amends, but the tone changed, from whispers to awkward nods, from avoidance to uneasy recognition.

Authorities launched a criminal investigation into Cambria's internal practices. The company suspended several employees in Swansea. Whispers of a broader conspiracy circulated, systemic, deliberate, and potentially criminal. The FBI opened a parallel inquiry, citing possible violations of US wire fraud statutes, obstruction, and conspiracy to defraud. Journalists began calling my office. One even showed up in our lobby, waving printouts and pressing for comment. I declined all interviews. I wasn't ready to speak. Not yet.

My intention for the files I planted on Rhun's machine was to remain hidden, serving only to cast just enough of a shadow. But once the investigations ramped up, someone in compliance must have flagged the anomalies. A sandbox triggered. An internal probe followed. Within days, the fabricated metadata had slipped into the official timeline like a splinter. I watched from the sidelines, silent. Not proud. Not relieved. Just resigned. It wasn't restraint. It was avoidance.

The headlines changed. They didn't name Rhun directly, but the language was telling.

"Access Logs Reveal Misuse of Privileged Credentials."

"Unusual Authentication Patterns Raise Red Flags."

"Sensitive Audit Materials Found in Unauthorized Folders."

That was *my* work. And it was working.

I told myself it didn't matter, because what he'd done was worse. Rhun hadn't just framed Alasdair. He had erased him. Maybe Rhun had feared Alasdair more than he let on. Rhun saw Alasdair as a threat, too competent, too respected, too connected. He couldn't get rid of him through normal political maneuvering. Alasdair had too much support on the board, too many quiet allies. So Rhun did what power-hungry men do when cornered: he made Alasdair disappear. I'd simply given the world a new lens. A reason to look again. But over the following nights, something gnawed at me. I had crossed a line, and I knew it.

At first, I constantly told myself it was justice. That I had balanced the scales. That doing the right thing sometimes meant doing the wrong thing first. But guilt doesn't barter; it accrues. It clings. And even in silence, it demands attention.

I began waking at odd hours, heart pounding, unsure of what had jolted me from sleep. I scanned headlines compulsively, watching the ripples my actions created. Some nights, I convinced myself I had done the only thing I could. Other nights, I saw myself as no better than the people I despised, just another man willing to twist the rules when it suited him. And sometimes, in the quietest moments, I admitted something worse: I hadn't just wanted justice. I'd wanted revenge. That part still lived within me, raw and unresolved. And I hated it.

Sue wasn't just worried; she was emotionally present in a way that startled me. Her pointed, insistent questions revealed an intimacy only someone who knows you thoroughly could possess. After one long pause, she reached for my hand, then stopped. Her silence didn't accuse me. It just made the space between us feel heavier than the truth.

The truth? I didn't know anymore. I knew I had acted. And once you cross a threshold like that, you don't get to walk back. You carry it.

At night, I would lie awake beside my wife, staring at the ceiling fan, its slow rotation mocking the stillness inside me. Sue asked once if I had known more than I'd let on. I told her the truth, or at least the version of it I could live with. She didn't press. Later that night, I sat alone in the living room long after Sue had gone to bed, staring at the darkened television screen. I thought about calling Alasdair. I thought about driving to his house. Instead, I poured myself another beer and did nothing. Cowardice isn't loud. It's quiet and comfortable, and it waits for you to get used to it.

Then, one Monday morning, an email appeared in my personal inbox. Subject: *Lunch?* From: *a-stewart64@gmail.com*

No greeting. No explanation. Just a date, a time, and a place. *Oyster Bar. Grand Central. Thursday. 12:30.*

I stared at it for a long time before replying.

I had not heard a single thing from Alasdair for over two years, and now this. It shocked me.

The oyster bar had always been one of Alasdair's spots. He loved the vaulted ceilings, the subway-tile charm, and the clatter of oyster knives behind the bar.

It was noisy, busy, and always packed by noon, but it felt familiar, comforting. I used to go there every Friday with my executive peers. It was our little tradition. Loud conversations, good seafood, a sense of belonging in the chaos. We were kings of our small domain back then. Alasdair thrived on that energy. We all did. We used to come here after major closings. Never fancy. Just honest.

I jumped on the subway uptown to Grand Central Station. Upon my arrival, I found him seated in a back booth, coatless, with a glass of sweating iced tea before him. The restaurant was busy, with waiters delivering plates of fresh, mouthwatering seafood.

The scent of brine and fresh lemon hung in the air. I felt my chest tighten. When I saw him, I had to look twice. I barely recognized him. He'd aged a decade in just two years. His hair was gray, not peppered. His posture, once upright and animated, had softened. But his eyes, those sharp, shrewd, calculating eyes, were still there.

He stood. We shook hands, then sat in silence for a moment. The bench vinyl was cool against my back.

"Thanks for coming," he said finally.

"I wasn't sure I'd hear from you again," I replied.

He nodded. "I wasn't sure I wanted to be heard."

We ordered food: two clam chowders, a plate of oysters, and black coffee. Neither of us touched the menu. The waiter returned with the chowder, setting it down without a word. Alasdair didn't touch it.

Then he began.

"The day they came to arrest me," he said, his voice steady but carrying a trace of lingering pain, "We were just starting the day. I was still in my pajamas. I heard a knock, and Claudia answered. Then I heard her panicked voice." He paused, his eyes distant, replaying the memory. "There were five of them. One held a printout. Another had handcuffs ready. They said they had a warrant. Claudia was in shock, and the kids ... they were terrified. They had no idea what was going on." He took a deep breath. "I stepped in front of Claudia and asked what this was about. They didn't answer. Just read me my rights, and handcuffed me."

He looked down into his coffee. "They took my personal laptop. Searched our house. Found nothing, obviously. But it didn't matter. The damage was done. My wife doubted me. She was the person who knew me best. If I could not convince her I was innocent, I knew I was in real trouble."

He exhaled and took a drink of his coffee. "We had been dealing with this for a long time until the authorities completed their investigation," he said. "Then came the headlines. I was hoping to keep it out of the press. But those vague stories of a corporate crime and the hiring of a hitman, all somehow linked to my name. I became blackened by the headlines. My older kids in Scotland were confused and ashamed. My younger two sensed the tension and became increasingly withdrawn. And Claudia ... even though we were well into this, she started looking at me as if I'd brought something rotten into the house. Everything had started to unravel again."

He paused again, longer this time, his voice dropping. "Back when I was first arrested, that first night in holding, I thought maybe that was it. That I'd vanish into the system. That my kids would grow up thinking their father was a criminal—or *worse*. I cried. I hadn't cried in years. But in that moment, sitting on a mildewy plastic cot under buzzing lights, I broke. It was like being dropped off the edge of the world. Cold, hard surfaces. Fluorescent lighting that never dimmed. Some guy muttering about aliens in the next cell. But the worst part wasn't the place. It was the waiting. Not knowing if I'd ever get back to normal."

He stirred his coffee absentmindedly. "They let me out the next morning, no charges yet—just suspicion and reputation damage. But Claudia ... she didn't look at me the same. For weeks, she avoided eye contact. I'd walk into the room, and she'd walk out. And my twins ... my daughter stopped calling me, and my son asked if I was going to jail."

He let out a shallow breath. "I slept in the guest room for three months. Claudia wouldn't say why she wanted that space. She didn't need to. I remember one night, maybe a week after it all began, I found her in the kitchen around 3 a.m., staring out the window. She didn't see me. She just stood there, holding a cold cup of tea. The silence in the room felt heavy, like even the air was too ashamed to move. She whispered, 'I don't know who I'm supposed to defend anymore.' And then she broke down. Slid to the floor, sobbing into her hands. I watched from the hallway, frozen. I wanted to reach for her, to say something, anything, but I couldn't. My feet wouldn't move. I didn't know if I still had the right. Then, we slowly began to rebuild our lives. I was at home most of the time. It actually helped. We had plenty of time to discuss. I thought we were making excellent progress. But more stories in the press ... it felt as if it all came crashing down again."

"How did you get through it?" I asked barely above a whisper.

"Max Berger," he said. "Attorney. Former federal prosecutor. Old friend of a friend. He took the case pro bono once he saw the evidence, or rather, the lack of it. Said it stank from the start. He was relentless. Filed FOIA requests. Dug through call logs. Brought in his own forensic analyst. That guy found the mirrored browser history file. That's what cracked the whole thing open."

Max Berger was a celebrity attorney, often seen on television offering legal commentary. He had led the defense in several high-profile cases and had a reputation for being both ruthless and theatrical in the courtroom. He was a short, round man with a sharp eye for theatrics, always dressed in expensive, made-to-measure suits and often seen with a large cigar perched between his fingers, as if he were permanently mid-verdict.

"He's known to be a real bulldog," I said.

"He is. But once, after a particularly brutal meeting where the DA's office threatened to take the case to court finally, he stayed behind. Sat with me in silence for ten minutes. Then he said quietly, 'This isn't justice. It's reputation warfare. And we're not losing it.' That was the moment I knew he wasn't just a lawyer. He was in the fight with me. He believed me completely, without hesitation, when no one else did. Max never blinked."

"You're lucky," I said.

"I know. I owe him everything."

He paused. "You remember Project Fortress Manhattan?" he asked. "That's what changed it. I explained to Max, and later to the NYPD, that it would have been technically impossible for me to access that kind of material on the dark web from a company machine. The filters, the firewalls, the DNS blocks, it was airtight. Once they heard that, things changed. That's what led to your second interview. That's when they started believing me."

He smiled for the first time, worn, distant, as if the muscle memory had to fight its way back to the surface. For a flicker of a second, I saw that man again. The Alasdair I used to know. The one who could command a room with a joke and a glance.

"That man saved my life."

A long silence stretched between us, punctuated only by the distant clatter of plates and hushed conversations from other tables.

"Claudia almost left me," Alasdair added quietly, his voice thickening. "Not because she didn't believe me, but after the story broke in the newspapers, she couldn't take the whispers. The looks. The way people crossed the street to avoid us. One night during dinner, she looked at me and said, 'I don't recognize you anymore. You're like a ghost walking through our house.' And at that point, she was right. I'd stopped speaking. Stopped fighting. I was disappearing."

He stifled a sigh. "Our family was facing financial difficulties. I had to reach out to my parents for support. It was humbling, borderline humiliating. I felt like I had failed them all, in every way."

"But she stayed," I offered gently.

"She stayed," he echoed softly, his voice firming up with gratitude.

As we finished our lunch, he half-heartedly inquired about some of the staff in the branch, but I could tell he was done with the bank. The profit-generating powerhouse, the back-and-forth between Swansea and New York, and the small yet powerful team he had built to keep an entire multi-billion-dollar business afloat. He had mentally left it all behind him.

I watched Alasdair leave the restaurant, shoulders squared but eyes still wary. I knew the reckoning wasn't over. Not for him.

That night, Sue was waiting when I got home. She was curled up in the corner of the couch, a book open but unread in her lap, the TV glowing quietly in the background.

"Well?" she asked, not looking up right away.

I shrugged out of my coat, unsure how to begin. "It was ... hard," I said finally. "He's been through hell. But he's standing."

She looked tired, more than tired. There were faint shadows under her eyes, the kind that come from emotional exhaustion, not just lack of sleep. I realized I hadn't been the only one carrying the weight of this. She closed the book and gave me a long, unreadable look. "Did he blame you?"

"No," I said too quickly. "He didn't really blame anyone. He just ... told the story."

We sat in silence for a while. The soft hum of the refrigerator filled the background with white noise. I could feel her watching me, sensing my discomfort.

"What did you say?" she asked gently.

"Not much. I listened."

Another pause.

"Do you think he forgives you?"

"I don't know. Maybe. Maybe he's just tired of hating people."

She leaned forward, elbows on knees, then looked up at me again.

"But David ..." she asked, voice quiet but direct. "Did he actually say he was innocent?"

I opened my mouth, then closed it. The question landed with more weight than I expected. I replayed the entire conversation in my mind, every pause, every look, and realized I didn't have an answer.

"No," I said finally. "He didn't."

I went to bed, but sleep didn't come. I lay there staring at the ceiling; her question echoing in the dark.

Did he actually say he was innocent?

The more I thought about it, the more it unnerved me. Not just because he hadn't said it, but because I hadn't noticed. Somewhere inside, had I already accepted that it didn't matter? That guilt and innocence were just performances in a courtroom, and what counted now was survival, damage control, reputation.

That question haunted me more than anything he'd said. Maybe the truth wasn't what mattered anymore. Maybe it was what you could live with. And I wasn't sure I could. Maybe that was the actual cost. Not the lie. Not the evidence. But the slow rewriting of your own moral code, until nothing felt wrong anymore, just necessary.

CHAPTER 33
THE COST OF TRUTH

The days following our meeting at the oyster bar were a blur of introspection and unease. Alasdair's revelations lingered in my mind, each detail a weight pressing down on my conscience. But the question that haunted me most was what Sue had asked. "Did he actually say he was innocent?"

For all the truths he shared, there was one he never stated. He never actually said he hadn't done it. And that silence now wore on me, not because I thought he was guilty, but because I wasn't sure anymore what I needed to believe to justify what I'd done. If there was even a shadow of doubt, if Alasdair wasn't completely innocent, then the things I'd planted on Rhun's machine became something else entirely. Not justice. Not revenge. Just fabrication. And that thought terrified me.

I found myself revisiting memories of my early time at Cambria. The late nights strategizing over mergers, the celebratory toasts after successful deals, the camaraderie that once felt unbreakable. Yet, beneath those memories lay a foundation of silence and complicity. How many times had I turned a blind eye to the subtle signs of systemic rot?

And how many of those signs had names? Erica came to mind, not as a suspect at first, but as a constant. Always in the room. Always precise. She'd helped facilitate the Swansea team's access, citing operational urgency. I remembered questioning it once, lightly. She'd smiled, assured me it was procedural. I believed her. Too easily, in hindsight.

It was Doug who found the smoking gun. The email chain between Erica and Rhun. It had been hidden in a private archive on one of Rhun's retired profile drives, technically out of our reach. But Doug had been digging, and what he found didn't just raise questions. It screamed.

Subject: *Q3 Compliance Filter Changes.*

Threaded beneath it was a quiet exchange:

Erica had flagged an "opportunity to route sensitive user triggers through non-alerting channels."

"Do it quietly. Remove the audit tags," Rhun replied.

Erica's last note was simply, "Done. Files mirrored. Flags scrubbed."

That was it.

Doug looked at me and said, "You still think she was just efficient?"

I didn't answer. I walked to the window and stared down at the plaza, trying to remember the last time something had truly blindsided me. Disgust, yes. Anger, often. But not surprise. Not lately. The truth was, I had always suspected it. I just hadn't been ready to admit it, not to Doug, and certainly not to myself.

The next morning, I texted her: "No more coffee meetings."

She replied with a single question mark.

I didn't respond. From that point on, we barely spoke to each other. I suspected she knew that I knew.

About a month later, Sue and I decided to have a drive up to Vermont. We needed out, just for a weekend. She didn't ask questions. Just packed light, brought the excellent coffee, and picked a playlist that alternated between The Who, Squeeze, and Depeche Mode—three of my favorite groups. We stayed at an Airbnb. It was a restored farmhouse that overlooked a frozen field. The silence was thick, the kind you could rest inside. The second morning, we walked along a trail near Lake Willoughby. Snow flurries danced around us. At one point, I looked down and saw a child's mitten left on a bench. Red. Frayed. Out of place. I couldn't stop staring at it. It felt like a remnant of someone who had trusted the world to be safe.

Sue touched my arm. "You okay?"

I nodded, but I wasn't.

I had reached out to Alasdair the week before and asked him if he fancied meeting up for coffee. We were going to be in his area, and he had his country house in a nearby town.

Alasdair met us in a tiny coffee shop later that same, quiet morning. No jacket, just a sweater and scarf. He looked even older than when we had met at the oyster bar, but not broken. Grounded. He waved before we saw him. Still the optimist, somehow.

He hugged Sue. "You haven't aged," he said.

She laughed. "That's a lie, but I'll take it."

We all sat and ordered coffee from a young waitress.

Alasdair asked about New York. I kept it surface-level. Mentioned Doug. I told Alasdair that Rhun had been suspended and had vanished from all correspondence.

"Still no reckoning then."

"There's movement," I said. "The DOJ is closing in, but they haven't held anyone accountable. Not really."

He nodded.

We finished our coffee and walked down the tiny high street. Sue browsed in a nearby bookstore. We waited outside. He leaned over to me. "You know the hardest part?"

I shook my head.

"It wasn't the media. Or the police. It was seeing that Claudia believed the worst was possible. Not that I did it. But that someone could make it look like I had. And she wouldn't know."

He paused.

"She told me, 'I don't know who to defend anymore.' And that broke me."

I wanted to ask him then, to press, just once, to hear him say it outright. But the words caught in my throat. Instead, I said, "Do you ever think about setting the record straight?"

He took some time before answering. "There's no straight. Just the version that hurts less."

I nodded, but that didn't help. The version I needed was still missing.

We spoke again of the night that Claudia had collapsed in the kitchen. That image had stayed with us both, but it was something that clearly troubled him deeply.

He invited us back to his house, which was just a short drive away. After arriving, he handed us both a mug of tea and said, "I'm not coming back."

"I figured."

"No, I mean to Wall Street," he corrected. "This life, it's slower. It's better. You should try it sometime."

He gestured toward the garden visible through the frosted window. "I've got 20 tomato plants ready to go. Claudia says, 'I'm overcompensating.'"

"She's not wrong," I said with a laugh.

Before we left, he gave Sue a jar of homemade chutney. She promised to return the jar along with some freshly baked banana bread.

In the car, she turned to me. "He's okay."

"Getting there," I said.

She paused. "But you're not. Not yet."

For the rest of the weekend, we went walking in the snow and read by the fire. We said little, but the break seemed to help me recharge my batteries.

Back in New York, the city hadn't changed, but I had. Meetings felt shallower. Buzzwords louder. I sat through a two-hour presentation on "post-regulatory synergies" and left with a headache and an existential itch.

That evening, I sat on the floor of our lounge in Chatham, laptop open, staring at the last of the logs. Not for work. For truth. And it was all there, buried but undeniable. Erica hadn't just helped. She had orchestrated it.

Later that evening, I stood by the window and watched the snow fall. The porch light cast long shadows across the yard, and somewhere in the distance a plow rumbled past. I thought about Alasdair, what he'd endured, and what he'd rebuilt. And I thought about myself, about everything I'd compromised just to feel as if I were doing something right. This wasn't about absolution. It was about recognition. Of who I was. Of what I'd done. And the cost of finally telling the truth, even if no one was listening.

CHAPTER 34
THE LANDMINE

I t began in Cardiff, where the bank's internal audit team was based. Not with an exposé. Not with a courtroom outburst. But with a memo, a forgotten line buried in the wreckage of bureaucratic noise, waiting for someone to see it for what it was.

One of the junior compliance officers, a quiet, diligent woman named Amanda, was scanning internal memos during a routine audit. Amanda was the kind of person most people overlooked. Thirty-four, divorced, and still renting a flat above a bakery in Grangetown, she lived a life of small, precise routines. She brought her own tea bags to work, used color-coded tabs for everything, and preferred Excel to conversation. But beneath the quiet exterior was a steel-threaded sense of right and wrong.

She didn't speak often in meetings, but when she did, people listened. Her work was tedious, unrewarding, and buried in a digital maze of quarterly reconciliations, policy annexes, and boilerplate disclosures. Her eyes were glazed, her tea cold, and the cursor blinking at line item 447 when she found it, a memo titled "Special Intervention Protocol—NY Branch, 2010."

The language was obscure, but the content was incendiary. It mentioned "coordinated asset isolation" and "targeted forensic review." Most damningly, it noted "post-exit data modification procedures." There were references to third-party operatives and accelerated data path approvals, flagged with urgent red stamps dated weeks after Alasdair's departure. It read like a checklist for erasure, one that had been executed with precision.

To Amanda, it was more than troubling jargon; it was a procedural autopsy of a digital crime scene.

She flagged it, packaged the files, and sent them up the chain. For a moment, she hesitated, aware, perhaps, that what she'd uncovered was no ordinary audit fluke. Her finger hovered over the send button longer than usual. Then she clicked, exhaled, and turned back to her screen. The blinking cursor waited.

Rhun had already been suspended by then. The New York investigation was underway. But what Amanda found would tip it toward something far more risky for him.

Someone in Swansea had incorrectly logged and mislabeled the file, burying it in an encrypted archive long enough for everyone to forget it existed. It was a digital landmine hiding beneath thousands of policy annexes—until someone finally stepped on it.

Upon receipt, Robert Williams, the bank's group head of audit, realized that the investigation had uncovered potentially criminal activity. He immediately reported it to the UK's Financial Conduct Authority, which opened a preliminary inquiry.

Although Cambria's headquarters were in Swansea, the UK government centralized financial regulation. There was no separate Welsh enforcement system. In cases like this, oversight fell to the national authorities, namely, the FCA and the Serious Fraud Office in London. A few emails here, a few phone logs there. But the deeper they dug, the darker it got.

When the inquiry reached a certain threshold of exposure, the file was handed to British prosecutors. And from there, things moved like lightning.

The file wasn't just theoretical. It contained damning forensic artifacts: a complete inventory of client transfer instructions, encryption keys, and offshore routing templates, all tied to entities under investigation by both the FCA and the DOJ in the United States.

Investigators suspected that Rhun had instructed someone to reactivate the code, bringing old systems back online for internal use. He silently approved them through risk channels. But I knew the truth. Rhun did not revive that code. It had been planted. By me. A private key certificate that matched an active bank credential.

Most damaging, investigators found a metadata tag linking the archive to a machine that had been unused since Alasdair's disappearance. Once again, digital material that I had also planted. That same analysis traced the introduction of falsified material, including the contracts and emails planted on Alasdair's computer, to a chain of authorizations originating with Rhun. It suggested orchestration, not coincidence. That detail was crucial. That detail showed a likely creation—or at least staging—of the files during the exact time of his removal. To regulators, that suggested intent.

Within weeks, the New York police, who had been working closely with the British authorities, involved the FBI. This wasn't just a Welsh scandal; it was a transatlantic breach with direct legal consequences in the United States. The memo unearthed by Amanda described activities that also implicated US-based staff and legal processes. Specifically, the memo revealed that someone had funneled manipulated digital evidence into a joint compliance file later used to support an affidavit for Alasdair's arrest. This meant someone planted the material on the PC after the bank fired Alasdair. That affidavit was filed with the New York court.

The crime—fabricating digital evidence—had crossed international lines and directly shaped the outcome of a US legal proceeding. The affidavit that led to Alasdair's arrest was corrupted, thereby violating core federal statutes: tampering with evidence, obstruction of justice, and abuse of process. The DOJ and FBI claimed jurisdiction not only because Cambria operated in the US, but also because actions taken overseas had compromised the integrity of their courts.

To the Feds, this wasn't abstract. It was personal.

An emergency meeting was called in New York by the DOJ task force overseeing the joint investigation. The agenda was clear: review the findings from the audit in Wales, coordinate the federal response, and assess the legal implications of the compromised affidavit that led to Alasdair's arrest.

The DOJ conference room smelled of printer toner and old coffee. Untouched sandwiches wilted in paper boxes beside legal pads stacked at every seat. Tension clung to the walls like static. Silently, I sat in the back. They asked me to attend as the head of technology for the New York branch, someone who could explain the situation in layman's terms. I wasn't law enforcement, but I was close enough to the wreckage to be useful.

Although invited, Rhun and his legal team failed to attend. He remained suspended, following the NYPD's initial investigation into the planted materials on Alasdair's computer. Reports placed him in Singapore, possibly London, but his location remained uncertain. I doubted he had any intention of returning to New York anytime soon, not with federal investigators circling and his name surfacing in cross-border subpoenas.

During the two-day meeting, they asked me only a few questions, primarily about Fortress Manhattan, the technology security platform. They then informed me that my presence was no longer required.

Three days later, they issued an arrest warrant for Rhun.

The charges were technical but devastating: conspiracy to commit digital fraud, destruction of audit evidence, and malicious exploitation of credential management systems.

The indictment read like a manifesto.

"This was not a breach," it said. "This was a grotesque betrayal of fiduciary duty, engineered by those entrusted with the protection of financial systems."

But beneath the control, I began to see something else. Rhun had seen Alasdair as a threat—not a colleague, but a rival. Alasdair had been CEO-elect, a heartbeat away from taking the top job. When the board pivoted and named Rhun instead, it wasn't just a new hire. It was a declaration, and Rhun needed Alasdair out of the picture. Not because Alasdair was weak, but because he wasn't. He was everything Rhun feared: competent, principled, and respected. And this time, they weren't bluffing.

Cambria's stock dropped 17 percent overnight.

The media ran a split-screen: Rhun at a Davos panel, discussing innovation and resilience. Beside it, they ran the text of the indictment, highlighted in red.

Colleagues who once parroted his phrases now deleted old Slack threads. Legal sent a preservation notice to all systems. And Group IT began a full internal trace.

Then came the ripple effect.

The court served Erica with a subpoena. Although they hadn't charged her yet, her name appeared in five separate email chains related to deleted compliance workflows. Doug's forensic analysis had been critical. Between his recovered logs and the DOJ's asset trace, the picture had shifted. Erica wasn't the architect, but she was a willing accomplice. Her signature appeared on risk exceptions. Her credentials were used to validate admin changes. She knew. She *had* to.

I thought about that deleted email chain. The language. Containment strategy. Disciplinary optics. I am sure that of all the people involved, it was Erica who hurt Alasdair the most. Not because she struck the blow, but because she'd once defended him. The woman who had supported his proposals, who had seemed loyal, ultimately enabled his destruction. Not through noise, but through silence.

The fallout wasn't instant. But it had begun.

Almost immediately after issuing the arrest warrant, the DOJ began laying the groundwork for an extradition request. They compiled a detailed dossier outlining Rhun's role in the digital fabrication and its impact on the US legal process. The formal request submitted to the British Ministry of Justice included signed affidavits, evidence logs, and forensic analyses linking the falsified documents to activities permitted under Rhun's command before his suspension.

Privately, US officials reached out through diplomatic and legal channels, arguing that failing to extradite would undermine international cooperation in financial crime enforcement. The request triggered quiet but tense deliberations within the British legal and political establishments. Rhun's team quickly responded by framing the US move as overreach, an attempt to assert American jurisdiction over a sovereign European process.

But the message from the Feds was clear: extradite him or prosecute him yourselves.

Behind the scenes, however, Rhun's well-connected family began working the political levers of London. Old favors were called in, strings pulled, and subtle pressure applied to senior officials within the Ministry of Justice. Though never publicly acknowledged, many insiders realized no scenario would allow the US authorities to receive Rhun. His lineage, wealth, and institutional ties formed an invisible wall around him, one that no diplomatic dossier could breach.

Subpoenas flew like confetti. Authorities seized the laptops. Email servers were mirrored. Internal communications and emails—dissected. And through it all, one name kept rising to the surface like a bloated corpse: Dr. Cadwgan Rhun.

A name that had once carried weight. Gravitas. He was the type of executive who journalists described as "formidable," whose mere presence could silence a room. At Cambria, his word was law. He wore only black suits, spoke in clipped phrases, and insisted on sitting with his back to the wall in every meeting room. The man who drank his espresso without sugar looked down his nose at people who did. A sculptor of careers—and a destroyer of them.

There had been stories over the years, whispered warnings about Rhun's ruthlessness. After a missed revenue target forced him out, Rhun summoned a former executive to his office and bluntly ordered him to pack his things. "Tell your wife the insurance extension will last three months. After that, you're on your own." Another recounted a town hall where Rhun mocked a junior staffer who asked about work-life balance, smirking: "If you want work-life balance, become a poet."

When I saw the language quoted in *The Times*— *user_mgmt/sys/conf*, my stomach turned. That had been my path. My file. The ghost I left behind. What started as a desperate, half-righteous act of retaliation had metastasized into something much larger. Something dangerous.

The evidence building against Rhun wasn't just the email trail tying him to Alasdair's takedown; it also included the payload I had planted. What I meant as a warning had instead pulled back a curtain. It revealed Rhun's fingerprints not only on the frame-up, but on a lattice of illicit financial activity that went far deeper than anyone had realized. I hadn't expected it to go this far. But there was no denying that the data I planted was what triggered the attention of the British financial authorities. It was possible that even without my intervention, the walls were already closing in on Rhun. The planted evidence may have amplified the alarm, but it hadn't started the fire.

I remained conflicted. Riddled with guilt, yes, but also with something darker. A grim satisfaction. Knowing that what I had done, however murky, however wrong, had contributed, in part, to the downfall of a man who had destroyed so many others. I hadn't lit just the match. I'd stood in the glow.

Later, I learned Amanda hadn't been the only one digging. Someone in the Swansea office had flagged a separate set of access logs during an unrelated audit. No one said it out loud, but I caught it in a sidebar comment from one of the DOJ analysts: "Redundant signals. Same conclusion." I didn't ask what that meant. I didn't want to know.

But another thought had gnawed at me, something I hadn't fully faced. What if I'd gotten it wrong? Not about Alasdair, at least not yet. His silence still haunted me. But about Rhun. What if, buried under all his cruelty and ambition, he really hadn't known about the file? What if, in trying to force justice, I'd built a lie so well-crafted it was feeling real? I told myself he deserved it, for everything he'd done, for everything he allowed. But even as I said that, I couldn't ignore the possibility that I was now doing the same thing I accused him of. Framing someone. And the worst part? If I were wrong ... I'd never know. I'd made the evidence too perfect.

And if anyone ever traced it back to me? I wouldn't just be disgraced; I'd be indicted. Obstruction of justice, digital tampering, conspiracy. But that wasn't what scared me. What scared me was that I'd crossed a line I used to police. And now, I couldn't even see where it had been.

And I wasn't sure I'd ever step fully out of its light.

But I wasn't the only one. Erica's name appeared twice in the DOJ's internal documentation, once in a summary of access privileges granted to the Swansea team, and again in a flagged email chain approving expedited folder creation just days before the planted files appeared. Her involvement still wasn't headline news. But it would be. In interviews, Erica claimed she knew nothing of any wrongdoing and insisted she had personally done nothing wrong. Her fingerprints were on the system. Not directly in the payload, but on the packaging that made its delivery possible.

She hadn't built the weapon, but she'd handed it over, knowing what it might do.

Erica blew the whistle on internal fraud years ago at a different firm, believing she would be protected. Instead, HR leaked her identity. Her team turned on her. They pushed her out. Blackballed. She almost left banking altogether. Cambria gave her a second chance.

But she'd learned something: The truth doesn't protect you. Power does.

She had backed the wrong man. Maybe she believed Rhun would protect her. Maybe she thought playing accomplice would be her path to power. I didn't think Erica was evil. But ambition has a way of clouding ethics. And now, she stood on a fault line of her own making.

That detail mattered. Addressed to the FBI. To the DOJ. To Alasdair.

There would be consequences. The Feds weren't done.

And neither, I suspected, was I.

CHAPTER 35
THE FALL

At first, Rhun denied everything. He released a terse statement via the bank's press office, referring to the investigation as a "deeply regrettable misunderstanding." He assured the board that this would be settled quickly. But the tone darkened as more documents became public. The denials became legalistic. Then conditional. Then silent.

Whistleblowers began coming forward, two in Swansea, one in Hong Kong. Their voices trembled at first, then steadied with resolve. They spoke of a culture defined by fear, secrecy, and performance at all costs. Rhun demanded not only performance but also absolute loyalty and total compliance with his directives, no matter how questionable. His authority wasn't just respected; it was absolute and enforced. One whistleblower, a former HR specialist, admitted to creating falsified termination files for multiple executives. Alasdair was just one of many.

It became clear, even to those who once defended Rhun, that Alasdair hadn't just been collateral damage. He had been a target. The plan hadn't been to obscure wrongdoing. It had been to remove a man. To turn a loyal and successful executive into a criminal and rewrite history before anyone could object.

The scandal detonated like a controlled demolition.

News outlets across Britain and Europe ran nightly segments. Sky News featured somber graphics and stern-faced analysts. The British press dubbed it "Rhun-Gate." *The London Times* ran a Sunday feature titled "The CEO Who Faked a Crime," complete with sidebars on digital forensics and corporate governance failure.

In the US, the media frenzy was just as intense. CNN carried a rolling segment titled "Wall Street's Welsh Shadow." Bloomberg TV dissected the transatlantic implications. MSNBC featured Primetime commentary linking Rhun's case to broader ethical failures in global finance. Social media ignited, and *#RhunGate* trended for days. Even late-night hosts took aim, comparing Rhun to Bond villains and calling his arrest warrant "Wall Street's version of Interpol." One Welsh comedian on a popular variety show sneered, "Rhun thought he was invincible. Now he can't even cross the street without a SWAT team."

Then came the raid. Despite his suspension, Rhun had remained in his sleek flat near the bank's head offices in Swansea, either out of defiance or the delusion that he still controlled the narrative. Early one morning, a convoy of unmarked sedans pulled up to Rhun's place. The cameras were already there, tipped off, probably. He emerged in a navy robe and slippers, flanked by plainclothes officers. His face was a mask of fury and disbelief. He didn't resist. He didn't speak. But his eyes burned.

The footage aired on the BBC within the hour.

The charges were staggering: conspiracy to commit evidence tampering, abuse of corporate authority, obstruction of justice, malicious prosecution.

Authorities not only arrested him but also, unusual for a white-collar crime, held him in detention without immediate bail—an unmistakable signal of just how serious the charges had become.

After two weeks, they finally granted him bail.

What followed was nearly a year of legal maneuvering, public speculation, and procedural delays. When the trial finally began, it felt less like a legal proceeding and more like a national reckoning.

The trial took place in the High Courts of London, just outside the old city boundary.

During the trial, the lawyers read emails aloud. Not summaries, but the full text. Word for word. One, sent days before Alasdair's firing, read: "He will not step down. I want a permanent solution." Another: "Ensure that digital traces are irrefutable. This must look organic."

What they didn't know, what I've never said aloud, was that some of those "digital traces" came from me. Quietly. Carefully. Not out of revenge, but necessity. Rhun had orchestrated Alasdair's takedown; of that, I was sure. But the forensic proof that brought it to light? That had been mine.

I told myself it was about justice. That the system would never expose him without a catalyst. But perhaps I also did it out of fear. Fear that without action, I'd remain complicit. That Alasdair's ruin would stain us all. Maybe I needed to believe that the ends justified the means, because the alternative was paralysis. And even now, as the courtroom listened in stunned silence, I wondered if I'd done the right thing. Or just crossed a line I could never *uncross*.

The court summoned me to testify early in the trial, primarily concerning system architecture, audit trails, and digital evidence authentication. I was careful. Precise. Factual. But inside, I was terrified.

Every question felt as if it might veer toward something I couldn't truthfully answer. I kept waiting for the moment they'd ask about the file paths, the logs, the anomalies I knew wouldn't stand up to scrutiny. I prayed they wouldn't dig that deep.

When the US forensic expert took the stand, I nearly stopped breathing. If anyone could see through what I'd done, it would be them. But the testimony was confident, unequivocal. They hadn't found the flaws. They hadn't seen a ghost.

I hadn't perjured myself. I answered every question they asked. But I hadn't told the full story either. They didn't ask me for it, and I was grateful. Every minute on that stand felt as if a trapdoor might open beneath me. I'd walked a tightrope between disclosure and self-preservation, heart hammering, sweat prickling behind my collar. And once I'd taken the stand, I stayed. Day after day. Not for obligation. For reckoning. I needed to see how far the rot had gone. I needed to watch it unravel.

Then Rhun took the stand. His voice was flat but firm. "I don't know what those files are," he said. "I didn't create them. I've never seen them before."

The prosecutor pressed. Showed him a folder structure. A file name. A path. Rhun looked genuinely confused. "That's not my file."

I believed him. At least about that.

Then came the experts.

A DOJ forensic technologist testified: "Our investigation revealed no evidence that a third party planted the file," he said. "The metadata, user credentials, and access history all point to a single source: Dr. Rhun."

Cambria's own head of infrastructure corroborated it. "There's no evidence of tampering. Everything we've seen supports the file originating from Rhun's machine. There's no trail beyond that."

I sat frozen.

The trap had worked too well. The evidence pointed to

Rhun like a spotlight, and none of the experts questioned it. I had built the frame so perfectly that even now, under the harshest scrutiny, it held. And I didn't know if that made me clever, or monstrous.

The courtroom was dead silent during the readings. You could hear every creak of a wooden bench, every flick of a legal pad. One former colleague testified that someone had ordered him to install monitoring software on Alasdair's computer, supposedly as part of a routine performance review.

"I told myself it was just policy," he said, voice cracking at the admission. "But I knew it wasn't about tracking work habits. We weren't reviewing performance; we were fabricating a justification. I realized we were not uncovering the truth. We were creating a narrative."

A low cough echoed from the gallery as the judge paused. No reporters stirred. It was as if the room itself held its breath, unwilling to interrupt the sight of a man being unmade. His lawyer shifted nervously beside him, sliding papers into a folder with the resigned cadence of someone who'd already lost.

The defense insisted Rhun was merely delegating, unaware of his subordinates' actions. But the emails said otherwise. The directives had come from his own account, in language too pointed to misinterpret. The intent was too clear, too personal.

They also showed something else.

They admitted into evidence the NYPD forensic report that stated conclusively that emails, images, and documents found on Alasdair's machine were planted. Someone had tampered with the timestamps. The signature hashes showed they had not originated from his user profile. There were no access logs showing his opening or moving any of the material. The tech who had arrested him testified under oath: "In retrospect, it was a mistake. We didn't know at the time. But it wasn't him."

That mattered.

Alasdair was innocent.

Even as the trial continued in London, US authorities pushed for extradition, submitting a formal request to the British Ministry of Justice, along with a multi-page DOJ dossier. It outlined Rhun's alleged role in the manipulation of digital evidence. But the British courts refused, citing constitutional protections against the extradition of citizens. Rhun's legal team seized the moment, framing the American charges as political theater, a noisy deflection from the US's own regulatory lapses.

British headlines split down the middle. *The Times* called the US demands "provocative," while *The Telegraph* argued they didn't go far enough. American outlets were harsher still, painting the UK as a haven for elite fugitives.

Ultimately, the British authorities agreed to prosecute Rhun domestically, which appeased no one. The US warrant remained active, and Rhun's name stayed on the international watchlist. He would never travel freely again. Every border crossing became a calculated risk. Even neutral jurisdictions posed a threat. He canceled a planned trip to Zurich. Interpol drafted a red notice, never executing it, but it always loomed.

The jury didn't take long. After six weeks of proceedings, they returned a unanimous verdict: *guilty on all counts.*

The sentence was historic. Seventeen years in prison, with no parole before 12. Not just a sentence, but a seismic rupture. A thunderclap in the world of white-collar crime that echoed through executive suites from Swansea to Wall Street. For once, the punishment matched the deception, and the courtroom didn't just deliver justice; it sent a warning.

I left the courtroom and didn't rush back to New York. I didn't want to return to the place where silence had passed for neutrality. I'm not sure whether I'll work in this industry again. Maybe I'm done. Or maybe I've changed, someone who now understands how easily systems can be manipulated, how a man can disappear unnoticed, and how loudly one must whisper the truth for it to be heard.

As I stepped outside, I caught Erica watching me from across the road. She didn't wave. She didn't smile. Just a single, unreadable glance, long enough to wonder if she knew. Or suspected. And then she was gone.

CHAPTER 36
THE ERASURE

Rhun lost everything. His C-suite position. His job and his pension. Cambria literally chiseled his name off the boardroom wall at its Swansea headquarters. Even his family, reportedly, had gone silent.

A newspaper published an alleged email from Rhun's daughter to a university dean asking for the dissociation of her name from her father. Rumor has it, his son changed his surname altogether. Whether true or not, the symbolism was devastating.

The court froze his assets pending civil suits from Alasdair, Owen, and at least three other similarly targeted executives. One of them, Thomas Wellington, who was head of trading in Swansea, had spent months in psychiatric care after his firing. Another had moved to the Welsh mountains and disappeared from public life entirely.

It was over.

But for Rhun, the fall was far from clean. During the last week of the trial, his composure began to unravel. The tailored suits were gone; instead, he rotated between two rumpled blazers, each bearing the faint shine of fabric worn too many times. His once-imperious posture had collapsed into a defensive hunch. On the third day of sentencing arguments, he rose shakily to address the court. His voice, once so commanding, faltered. "There are nuances ..." he began, but the words stuck. A tremor passed through him as he reached for a glass of water with both hands. The judge, perhaps recognizing the desperation masked as dignity, cut him off. Rhun sat down slowly, staring straight ahead, the color draining from his face.

Earlier in the trial, he had lashed out at a clerk for mishandling a binder, snarling, "Do you know who I am?" The courtroom froze. Even the reporter stopped typing. The judge issued a warning. From that point, Rhun spoke only when spoken to.

His family didn't attend the sentencing. Not his wife. Not his adult children. Their absence wasn't just noted; it was palpable. The prosecution glanced once toward the empty gallery seats reserved for family; the judge, too, hesitated for a beat before proceeding.

Reporters stationed outside Rhun's estate described a once-pristine home now blanketed in silence, with dead leaves curling on the steps and the mailbox overstuffed. A neighbor said they hadn't seen anyone enter or leave the house in over a week. The official family statement read only: "No comment."

Inside the courtroom, the weight of that absence was louder than any outburst.

Quickly, the bank also began the process of removing him. The chiseled wall in Swansea became a symbol, a surgical removal, as if cutting out rot from the heartwood. Workers repainted the hallway where his portrait once hung in neutral gray, discarding its original brass nameplate. A custodian who had worked there for 20 years told a reporter, "They made us scrub the wall twice. Said it still stank."

A curt memo circulated internally, ordering the destruction or sealed archiving of all materials bearing his name, effective immediately. A commemorative plaque from the bank's centennial gala vanished. The legal department granted a special exception to delete Rhun's video archives of internal messages. It was as if the man had never existed.

The removal team worked overnight. By morning, the only trace left was a slightly discolored patch of marble where his name had once gleamed. Staff whispered that it still caught the light the wrong way, like a scar.

But the shadow he left behind remained.

And yet, not everyone was gone. Reggie somehow survived the purge. His name never surfaced in the trial, not directly. While whispers lingered about his proximity to Rhun, nothing stuck. He kept a low profile, attended every board call, and followed directives to the letter. His email was untouched. His name was absent from the subpoena. In a world collapsing, he was in Switzerland, neutral, silent, effective. Reggie had never spoken about Rhun. Not once. And maybe that's why he survived. Silence was his currency.

Dmitry also kept his head down and his role intact, even as the building hollowed out. Silence didn't just replace ambition; it calcified it. The continued presence of both Reggie and Dmitry felt less like resilience and more like the residue of the collapse.

But the damage was permanent.

I watched the verdict on a muted television in our almost-empty downtown office. The screen showed a wide shot of the courtroom. Rhun sat rigidly at the defense table, jaw clenched, arms folded like a man trying to hold himself together by force. His skin had lost its patrician glow, now sallow, waxy, worn. He didn't flinch when he heard the verdict. Not even a blink. But I saw the twitch in his left cheek. The only telltale sign was that the man who once orchestrated empires was beginning to crack. It was a small betrayal, but just enough to show the world he knew. That he felt it. That the mighty don't fall all at once, but in stuttering fragments, twitch by twitch.

Erica was beside me. She remained silent. She refrained from clapping. A sigh escaped her lips. "Finally," she said.

We both kept our eyes on the screen. A reporter tried to shove a mic toward Owen as he left the courthouse. He didn't speak, just walked with his hands in his coat pockets and his head down. He looked older, thinner. A man who'd carried too much for too long. Even in that brief moment, he radiated exhaustion. Not just physical, but moral. The weight of knowing he'd once stood inches from the truth but couldn't stop it.

I remembered when Owen used to stand straight-backed in every town hall, always with a question, always pressing for clarity. Somewhere along the way, Rhun had bent him too.

Erica didn't move for a long time. When she finally stood, she didn't look at me. Just reached for her coat and said, "We should've stopped it sooner." Then she walked out.

But before she reached the door, she paused, not long, but just enough for me to wonder if she was waiting for me to speak. I didn't know if she meant the bank—or us, so I held my tongue. She turned to leave and never looked back.

In the footage of Owen, he never looked up. Even after they pulled the mic away, he kept staring at the sidewalk as if it owed him something.

Alasdair wasn't there. I didn't expect him to be. He'd vanished again after the media storm. Someone said he'd moved north, maybe living in his Vermont vacation home. Others said Canada. I figured he didn't need to witness the end. He'd lived it already, through headlines and depositions and the lonely ache of betrayal. He'd gotten his answer already.

I'd crossed a line, and I knew it. Maybe it wasn't justice in its purest form. Maybe it was vengeance wrapped in ones and zeros.

But the system had failed Alasdair once.

I would not let it fail again.

In the years since his arrest, I had carried a quiet guilt, a sense that I could have done something sooner. I never lied, never obstructed, but I hadn't exactly lit a torch either. I'd moved incrementally, always calculating the risk. In the end, though, I hadn't just helped crack the seal; I'd forced it open. I bypassed our compliance logs, buried the breadcrumbs deep in a sub-folder marked by a harmless audit code. No one saw it. No one was supposed to. But I ensured someone could find the trail if they knew where to look.

I remember the day I opened that first memo, the one Erica forwarded without comment. Someone had sanitized it; it was clinical, yet unmistakably coded. I could've closed it, pretended it wasn't my concern. But then I thought of Alasdair's face the day he cleared out his office, the shock in his eyes. That was when I knew I couldn't let it stand.

I spoke to Sue about it often, late at night, when neither of us could sleep. She told me I had done what I could, that I had helped in the end. But I wasn't sure. Maybe I just needed to believe it.

Deep down, I knew I'd played a role in Rhun's downfall, not by accident, but by intention. And that knowledge didn't feel like justice. It felt like guilt. I had spent so long wrestling with my conscience, torn between loyalty to the institution that employed me and the quiet conviction that something terribly wrong had happened.

I had acted quietly, from behind the firewall. Alasdair might eventually have been recognized as a victim with my help, but I ensured it. Maybe I hadn't been a hero, but I hadn't been a coward either. And somehow, in the strange calculus of justice, that had to count for something.

I remembered sitting across from Alasdair at that sushi place, just months before it all began. I didn't know it then, but I was face-to-face with a man who would later be buried in silence. I shuddered at the thought.

I remember sitting on the deck in the garden one cold evening in Chatham, wrapped in a blanket while Sue dozed beside me. The sky was clear. My breath rose in quiet spirals. And all I could think about was the first time I shook Rhun's hand years ago. How firm it was. How cold. Like something engineered, not human. A grip designed to dominate. In that moment, I realized justice wasn't just about verdicts; it was about confronting the ghosts we'd allowed to take root.

And justice never fixes everything. Neither time nor reputation is mended by it. It cannot restore sleep and old friendships. It doesn't erase years of fear, confusion, and complicity. It doesn't dissolve the scars etched by watching your back, measuring your words, or wondering when the axe might fall. But it puts a pin in the chaos. It says: *this far, no further*. And when it finally arrives, it changes the temperature of a room. It allows people to breathe again.

That day, we breathed. But we didn't smile, not because it wasn't over, but because we knew how much we had lost along the way. The lies, the fear, the self-preservation. No one came through it unscathed. Alasdair had been vindicated, yes, but at the cost of exile. Owen carried the cold reminder of guilt down his spine. I still woke at 3 a.m. many nights, staring at the ceiling. And Rhun? Rhun was gone, but a part of me was too. The scar he left was in every line of code I touched, every sentence I second-guessed, every silence I let settle.

Justice had come. But it hadn't spared us. It simply marked the end of one story, and the weight of what we'd let happen.

CHAPTER 37

THE SPACE BETWEEN

SUE WALLACE

He came home late. Not unusually so, lateness had become part of him, but something in the way the door shut made me look up. Not his exhalation of exhaustion or the shuffle of his guilt, but the clean, precise thud of the closing door.

David always tried to smile when he saw me. That night, he didn't bother.

"Long day?" I asked, keeping my voice even.

"Yeah."

That was it. I don't want any elaboration. No kiss. No attempt at normal.

He took off his coat and folded it carefully over the back of the chair. He sat down at the edge of the couch as if he wasn't planning to stay long. I could feel the air between us, brittle with something unsaid.

He stared at the wall—not the television, not me.

I watched him in silence. The man I married was still in there, but he was buried beneath layers of armor I hadn't seen him build. It was like watching someone drown in slow motion, each gasp covered by another task, another secret.

"Did something happen?" I asked.

He shook his head. "Nothing new. Just ... things moving."

He was lying. Not in the obvious way, there were no tells, no shifting eyes or stammered deflections. It was the calm that gave him away. He was no longer unsettled. He was resolved. And that scared me more than the anxiety ever had.

"You look different," I said.

He turned to me. "Different how?"

"Like you finally did something."

His face twitched, just once. Then he looked away.

We sat like that for a long time. He didn't say a word, and I didn't press. I could have. Maybe I should have. But part of me was afraid to know. Not because I didn't want the truth; I did. I always had. But I could feel the weight of it, whatever it was, and I wasn't sure either of us could carry it if he said it aloud.

Later that night, I heard him in his office, typing, closing drawers, and shuffling papers. He was meticulous again, just as he used to be when solving something big. But this time, it didn't sound like creation. It sounded like closure.

As I lay there in bed, I drifted back to when we first arrived in the US. We had two suitcases and one shared dream. David was so full of light back then. Restless, yes, but always laughing, always moving forward. We didn't have much, but we had momentum. We had built a life from scratch. Both of us worked too many jobs, skipped too many holidays, and counted every dollar until we didn't have to.

And through it all, he never lost his spark. Even when he was tired, even when we worried about the kids or the mortgage or the next round of layoffs, he always had a joke, a story, or some ridiculous theory about how we'd one day retire by the sea and write a book about it all.

Now?

Now he barely looked at me. He spent more time with encrypted spreadsheets than he did with our own children. And yet, those children, our children, had made it. Graduated.

Excelled. They were steady, kind, and curious. We had done something right. But I wondered if David even allowed himself to feel it anymore.

I knew the stress had changed him. I just hadn't realized how completely. Whatever he was doing, whatever line he had crossed, he thought it was necessary. He thought it was about survival.

He crawled into bed at 2 a.m. and didn't touch me.

I lay awake beside him, eyes on the ceiling, and thought: *Whatever he's done, it's already too late.*

Not for him. *For us.*

And that was the first night I wondered if I'd lost him entirely.

CHAPTER 38
THE WIND DOWN

The board in Swansea quickly named a new CEO. It was an internal promotion and was hastily arranged. Douglas Smyth. He was formerly the CEO of Norton Securities in London.

He promptly decided that the bank no longer had the appetite to operate in the United States. It was a combination of the recent losses we had suffered and the risk profile of our traditional businesses.

Even before informing the staff, the bank issued a press release announcing the branch's imminent closure.

Unfortunately, with our distressed assets, selling off the portfolio was not an option. The losses would have been more than the group could support. So, it was a case of winding down the business quickly, but minimizing the losses.

We were told we'd receive significant retention bonuses if we stayed until the end.

For once in my life, I didn't need the money, but I said yes. So did the others. We weren't staying for the bank. We were staying for each other. Four people tied together not by loyalty to the institution, but by the wreckage we'd quietly survived. We'd been through something no outsider could understand.

That counted for something. It made us stay when we probably shouldn't have. It made us carry the body to its grave.

But there had once been seven of us.

Erica didn't retire. She didn't take a redundancy package; she was not offered one. She was under investigation. But she was still in the office every day.

There was no satisfaction in it. Just a hollow ache. She'd sat beside me in meetings, offered advice in whispers, smiled at my jokes, and had coffee with me almost every working day. And then she'd buried the knife. And maybe I had let her stay too long. Maybe I didn't want to see it.

A few months into the wind-down, Warren came to my office with a sealed envelope. "You need to see this," he said, his voice low.

Inside was a memo from the Department of Justice, shared via formal disclosure through Swansea. It confirmed what I'd already suspected. Erica had been complicit, not passively, not ignorantly, but *actively*. Her credentials had authorized several of the flagged access attempts. She'd approved at least one of the deletion commands. And her name appeared in internal messages discussing compliance risk mitigation strategies that matched the timing of Rhun's most aggressive interventions.

I sat there staring at the printout, my stomach churning. Warren said little, just stood by the window, arms crossed. When I finally looked up, he nodded slightly.

"They're charging her," he said. "Conspiracy. Obstruction. A few counts, reduced. She's pleading out."

She was finally fired by the bank. No ceremony. No statement. No severance. Just an HR email and a quiet escort off the floor. On her last day, she cleared her desk in under 15 minutes. No goodbyes. No fake smiles. Just the sharp click of her heels against the marble and a silence that said more than words ever could.

I caught her in the lobby.

She saw me this time. Paused. Assessed. Her eyes, still razor-sharp, betrayed nothing.

"You always loved a quiet exit," I said.

She tilted her head. "I didn't think you'd come."

"I didn't come for you."

We stood facing each other, two ruins in tailored clothes. Her black coat hung looser than usual. She looked thinner, older. But her voice still had that clipped efficiency, the one that used to carry entire meetings.

"You said you were loyal," I said quietly. "You told me we were building something that mattered."

"I told you what you needed to hear."

"You lied to me."

Erica blinked. Once. Slowly. "We all lied to each other."

I stepped closer, low enough that no one else could hear. "You tried to ruin Alasdair. You tried to ruin me."

She didn't flinch. "You made it easy."

"Why?"

Her jaw tightened, but she didn't look away. "Because I was tired of cleaning up other people's messes. Because they always picked men like you to protect. And because no one ever picked me."

"So, you sold us all out."

"I survived. That's more than most of you can say."

I let the silence sit.

"Was it worth it?"

She hesitated. Just long enough.

"Ask me again in five years," she said, then turned to leave.

I didn't stop her. I didn't want to.

Some betrayals come with speeches. Hers came with nothing. And that, somehow, felt worse.

The evidence wasn't overwhelming, but it was enough. She pleaded guilty to a lesser charge and received a five-year suspended sentence. No jail time, but her career was over. I never heard from her again. But rumors persisted, Erica advising a shadow firm in Zurich, Erica seen in Dubai, Erica quietly consulting under a different name. No proof, of course. Just whispers. And if anyone could disappear and reemerge without a trace, it was her.

But thinking about Erica brought me back to Sanjay.

He had been part of my team; sharp, temperamental, loud, prone to a lunchtime drink, but even though I had only worked with him for a relatively short time, he was unwavering in his loyalty.

But after his layoff, he unraveled quickly. He sued for wrongful dismissal, alleging that Erica had directed him to create a sensitive access profile and then scapegoated him when it was discovered. The bank denied it, of course. But those who knew Erica knew what she was capable of when threatened. And in those last years, she was always threatened.

Sanjay couldn't land another job. The rumors followed him quietly, persistently, infecting every interview, poisoning every opportunity. He began drinking more, missing appointments, couch-surfing until there were no more couches. Eventually, he ended up at a motel in Jersey City.

Six months before his case was due in court, his sister found him there. Whiskey. Pills. A note that simply said: "Tell the truth."

When I heard the news, I sat in my office with the door closed for nearly an hour. Just staring. I don't know what I expected, maybe that he'd move on, rebuild, disappear into another life like so many others. I hadn't spoken to him since the day he left the firm, and now I never could.

I told myself it wasn't my fault, that I hadn't given the order. That Erica had set him up, not me.

But the excuses didn't hold. Not when I'd gone along with it. Not when I'd chosen silence over risk. His death wasn't just tragic. It was damning.

For weeks after, I saw his face in flashes, in glass reflections, in strangers on the street. I'd lie awake wondering what he meant by the note. Who was the note for? Whether it was an accusation or a plea. Maybe both.

The weight of it never left. Not really. I still remember the way he used to laugh, loud, jagged, defiant, as if he were daring the world to outpace him. Even now, there are days I wake with a heaviness I can't name until I remember: Sanjay. Brilliant. Difficult. Loyal. *Gone.*

The bank settled quietly with his mother. No admission. No regret. Just a quiet check and a closed file. Erica never said a word.

He vanished from every official record that followed. But I never forgot. None of us did. Erica managed to keep her title until the end. Sanjay didn't survive.

That left four of us—survivors, at least in name.

The wind-down management team comprised me, Reggie, Warren, and Carolyn. Dmitry was already gone by then. No warning. One day, he was in the office; the next, his badge was disabled, and his desk was cleared. An audit team from Swansea had flagged inconsistencies in the system architecture reports, ones only Dmitry could have explained. But they did not request an explanation. Just a quiet removal. I tried calling. No answer. He disappeared like so many before him.

The next year passed in a strange rhythm, equal parts tedium and tension. We weren't building anything. We were taking it apart and selling whatever we could. Quietly, we buried it. Slowly, deliberately, with checklists and procedures and boxes that needed to be ticked. Sometimes it felt as if we were erasing ourselves in slow motion.

One afternoon, I walked onto the trading floor just after lunch. Half the desks were empty. Monitors were on, but no one was behind them. Phones blinked silently. A pair of junior analysts stood by the espresso machine, whispering.

"I heard London pulled the plug on three teams last week," one said.

The other shrugged. "We're next. Just a matter of time."

Neither looked surprised. Neither looked angry. Just ... done.

I turned back toward my office, the silence trailing behind me like smoke.

We laid off staff as we sold the financial assets. Every week, our headcount got smaller. Eventually, we got to the point where most of our systems and applications were retired and archived. The last remaining application was our accounting system.

I oversaw the shutdown of our data center. We decommissioned every server. Cataloged every tape. Archived every file according to retention rules. It was compliance by design, but it felt like surveillance disguised as order.

Maybe we weren't survivors. Maybe we were witnesses, keepers of a silence no one else wanted to inherit.

I knew the signs. I'd once mirrored that same surveillance, not because I was told to, but because I had to. Planting the seed that would crack Rhun open wasn't just technical. It was personal. And the weight of that choice hadn't left me.

They watched every step. Compliance from Swansea issued instructions for even the smallest tasks, some bordering on the absurd. Legal had to approve nearly every form, down to badge deactivations and desk inventories. At times, it felt less like a wind-down and more like a quiet internal investigation where they treated us as suspects and had already collected and labeled the evidence.

One of the last physical tasks was removing the Cambria Financial Group signage from the lobby. I watched as they unscrewed the metal letters from the marble wall, one by one. A banker from Swansea once told me a specialty metalworker forged those letters in Newport.

They had designed the letters to last 100 years. They lasted 13.

Thirteen years of ambition, misdirection, and consequence. Not even long enough for a generation, but enough to change a life. Enough to burn a hole in one.

Reggie's silence also carried a weight. Not just habit, but defense. He'd watched too many good people fall and learned that staying quiet was the safest path through a storm. Once, I walked in on him sitting alone in the server room, lights off, screen dimmed. He didn't hear me coming in. Just sat there, staring at a log file as if it held something sacred.

Warren had started sending long, late-night emails, mostly procedural, but padded with fragments of thought and unfinished sentences, as if he were trying to say more.

Carolyn snapped once when the courier was late for a file pickup—then apologized. She never used to apologize. And then she was gone. No goodbye, no farewell email. Her desk cleared overnight. Some said she returned to Europe. Others insisted she had never left the city. I never saw her again. No online footprint. No updates. Just gone. Like so many in our world, erased, willingly or otherwise.

We didn't talk much, the four of us. But there was mutual respect. We got the job done. Warren, ever the lawyer, kept us out of trouble. Reggie had been through hell, too, in his own way. You could see it in his eyes sometimes, the quiet, second-guessing, the weight of what he'd carried. Carolyn ran logistics like a battlefield quartermaster, always one step ahead of the paperwork. Sometimes we'd meet in the old boardroom—now empty save for folding chairs and a dusty whiteboard—and just sit. Talk about nothing. Complain about the coffee. Make dark jokes. More than once, Reggie left early without a word. Warren would refill the sugar jar and say nothing.

Some nights, I found myself walking the empty floors alone, just to hear my own footsteps. The silence echoed off the walls like something sacred and final. Once, I sat at my desk for hours staring at an unsigned certificate of destruction, a routine form. But for some reason, I couldn't bring myself to sign it. It felt like the last nail. Not just for the servers or the systems, but for all of it. For Alasdair. For Rhun. For the part of me that once believed we were building something important.

There was another document too. The summary log of flagged access attempts showed Alasdair's credentials being used two weeks after his departure. Maybe to clean up loose ends. Maybe to muddy them. Either way, it meant he'd never really left, not in the data, and not in the consequences. An anonymous source in IT had quietly forwarded it to me. No one had asked me to include it in the closure package. No one had told me to destroy it either.

There were whispers that Rhun had ordered digital traces scrubbed long before the first subpoena landed. That Alasdair's downfall wasn't a defensive move, but a warning to others. Examining those access logs, I wondered if someone, possibly Erica, had been told to complete Rhun's work. Or protect what he left behind.

I did not log it. I didn't shred it. I just kept it. In a plain manila envelope, slipped into the bottom of my briefcase, under some family photos. Maybe out of guilt. Maybe as insurance.

I already knew what a breadcrumb could do. A single digital trail could destroy a man or unmake a lie. I'd seen both. Left both. And I wasn't sure anymore which side of the firewall that put me on.

Maybe because I wanted to believe I still had some control. Or maybe, more honestly, because someone needed to remember. Maybe that someone had to be me.

Once, near the end, I opened it again. Just looked at the logs. I thought about sending it to a journalist. Or burning it. I did neither. I slid it back into the envelope and closed the drawer. Maybe I was just waiting for someone else to carry the weight. Or maybe I knew no one would.

But the truth has its own shelf life. And by then, perhaps no one cared.

I knew I was finished when I started counting lightbulbs. Literally. One day, I caught myself auditing how many lightbulbs remained in the supply closet and calculating whether we had enough to last until the final walkthrough with the property management firm. It wasn't a task. It was an escape. A way to feel useful when everything else felt emptied of meaning. When I closed the supply closet door, I lingered there longer than I needed to, staring at the shelves as if they might explain something back to me. That was the moment I knew. I was done.

CHAPTER 39
THE LAST DINNER

We didn't get a send-off. Just a calendar alert and a locked account. But before we scattered, we had one last dinner. There were things we'd witnessed, and things we'd allowed, each of us carrying a version of the same unspoken story.

None of us had emerged untouched.

We chose a tiny Italian place on Fulton Street. The chairs were too close together, and the lighting was too warm. It felt like a memory before it had even ended. We toasted with red wine and said all the things we hadn't said before. There were tears. There was laughter. But mostly, there was relief and weariness.

"I thought we were building something special," Reggie said, his voice barely above a whisper.

"We were," I replied. "For a while. Until it became something else."

Carolyn smiled sadly. "We kept the lights on. That's not nothing. But it's not everything either."

Warren just lifted his glass. "To survival. And to knowing when to walk away."

The wine was too warm; the pasta was overcooked. But

none of that mattered. We were saying goodbye the only way we knew how, with stories and silences.

I never told them what I'd done.

Not even Sue, not entirely. Some truths belonged buried deeper than any server. But I kept the memory like a live wire under my skin, both a warning and a tether. There were moments I thought I was doing the right thing—planting data, pushing leaks—but sometimes I wonder if I was just trying to ease my conscience. I fought from the shadows and told myself it was enough. But maybe cowardice wears the same coat as strategy, just with better tailoring.

Nobody said what we were all thinking: that we'd survived, but we hadn't come out clean. Not really. Our paperwork showed no damage, but inside, what we'd seen and allowed to happen had scuffed, scraped, and stained us.

When the check came, we lingered. Nobody moved. And for a moment, I almost spoke. Almost said it. But I didn't. I let it pass. Some truths stay buried not because they are dangerous, but because no one is ready to hear them.

After that dinner, we didn't see each other again, not in person, not really. But fragments reached me. Updates passed along in emails, in whispers, in the professional rumor mill that never quite dies.

We all drifted in different directions, like pieces shaken loose from a larger structure.

Doug Saito had left quietly months before the wind-down began. He never said much, and he didn't hang on to get his redundancy package. I knew he'd seen too much of the systems, the setup, and the cracks no one else wanted to acknowledge. Last I heard, he was in Seattle, working on clean energy infrastructure. He never looked back. I never expected him to.

Carolyn stayed through the very end, then completely vanished. No goodbye, no farewell message. I heard whispers;

some said she had returned to Kent. Others said Geneva. Stylish to the end, even her departure was enigmatic. No one really knew. I stopped asking. I never saw her again.

I always wondered whether she had seen it coming. During those last few weeks, her eyes followed Erica like a hawk. Not accusing. Just ... recording. There were nights she stayed hours after everyone else had gone, typing without pause. She never told me what she had been writing.

Reggie remained until the final walkthrough, then disappeared almost as quickly. There were rumors of a heart attack, of a quiet retreat upstate, of a silent, private retirement. I was never able to confirm any of them.

Warren kept to his careful routines. Legal work. Late-night emails. But even he looked rattled toward the end, pausing in conversation, errant thoughts half-spoken. It was as though the effort of keeping his secrets polished was wearing him down.

We each found our own exits. Not triumphant. But honest. It ended not with justice—not even with truth—but instead, with silence, and the lingering burn of decisions that had saved someone but damned another. It ended with bureaucracy, with clearance logs and shutdown memos, with people pretending that nothing had ever happened. Just another branch closed. Another file marked complete.

We buried it quietly and walked away as if the bleeding had stopped.

But I remember. And I will carry that memory longer than the bank carried its shame, because the truth doesn't fade just because someone filed it away.

On my last day, I went out for a quiet drink on my own. My mood was calm, reflective. After, I took a different route and returned to the office instead of going straight home. I stood in the lobby of the Freedom Tower, staring at where the signage used to be. Relief was what I thought I'd feel. I didn't. I felt hollow. There was a phantom pressure in my chest, like a conversation I'd forgotten to have. When the night guard nodded at me, I couldn't even nod back. I stepped into the dark, not sure if I was walking away from something—or toward it.

Manhattan, unbothered, kept moving. But inside me, the code still hummed. The silence wasn't peace. It was a memory.

THE AFTERMATH

Some mornings, I wake before dawn and sit in the silence, wondering how it all came apart. I live in Georgia now. A large regional bank headquartered here scoped me out for the chief technology officer role. I managed to time my exit from Cambria perfectly, wrapped things up, took a few weeks off, and moved south with Sue. It was a clean break. Not the coast. Not the mountains. Just a quiet suburb north of Atlanta, where the air smells like pine and people wave when they walk their dogs.

I still work in banking, but this time, in retail. This challenge is more about people and systems than politics. That's a relief. The job is stable and straightforward, which suits me. But I'd be lying if I said I don't miss New York sometimes. The bright lights. The pace. It's always in motion. Here, things happen more slowly. People still trust institutions. That trust feels fragile now, like something inherited but rarely examined.

Sometimes when I'm driving home from the office, I think about that tall glass building near the downtown water's edge, about the floors we once occupied. About the buzz, the energy, the sense that we were building something extraordinary, until we weren't.

There was a night I stayed late, long after the cleaners had left. The office was empty except for the hum of the machines. I sat at my terminal, watching a line of code blink like a cursor on a confession. I remember hovering over the "execute" command, my hand trembling. No witnesses. No second thoughts. Just the sound of my breath in the dark.

Sue had always sensed there was more I wasn't saying. She waited. I wasn't ready.

Then one night, about a year after we moved, I told Sue everything. We sat on the back porch. I couldn't look at her. Just stared out across the lawn as the cicadas hummed. I told her about the server logs. The envelope. The planted structure on Rhun's machine. I told her about Warren. About Sanjay. About what I'd done.

When I finished, she said nothing for a long time. Then she reached over, took my hand, and said, "You did what you had to do. To survive it. To make it mean something."

I didn't reply. I couldn't. Her words didn't absolve me, but they held me upright. That was enough. We sat there for a long time afterward, neither of us touching nor speaking. Just breathing in the dark.

I lost touch with almost everyone. Carolyn vanished. Reggie had a heart scare and dropped off the grid. Warren resurfaced in legal journals, cool and polished as ever, but never returned my emails.

And Dmitry? I searched for him once. Found nothing. Not even a trace. It was as if he had never existed.

Of all of them, only Doug responded. He'd moved out west and taken a role at a tech firm in Seattle. Still drinking cold brew. Still swearing by standing desks. We exchanged pleasantries, but it wasn't the same. Too much time had passed between us.

Although I never saw Erica again, she still crosses my mind from time to time. She lost everything: reputation, position, legacy. Inside the industry, she became a cautionary tale. A reminder that plausible deniability doesn't absolve you of the truth. Sometimes I wonder if she ever regretted it. Or if she convinced herself, like we all did at some point, that it was just business. It doesn't matter now whether someone coerced her or she was complicit. The damage was done. Sanjay was gone. And some things are impossible to undo.

I think about Owen, quiet, brilliant Owen, who took the same bullet but somehow stood up again. I regret not having talked to him again. There's a hollowness in that silence that time doesn't fill. We will never know what was on the thumb drive Alasdair gave him. But I suspect that it would have vindicated them both, without my help.

And Warren, he returned to private practice. His name still surfaces from time to time, quoted in journals, tied to new clients. We've never spoken since. There were no consequences for him, at least none that I saw. He always played things carefully, never leaving fingerprints. But I'll never forget the day he told me the truth. It was a crack in the facade, small but unforgettable.

I've talked to Alasdair a few times. The fund he and Owen tried to build after their departure faltered for a while, choked by lawsuits, blacklists, and the fallout of scandal. Eventually, something took root. Quiet. Steady. After Owen's death, Alasdair took on a new partner. I never learned their name. We haven't spoken in years. We all walked away changed. A few found meaning. Some found quiet. Some never recovered.

I've looked back a thousand times and still believe I acted correctly. I don't feel guilt, only a quiet frustration that I wasn't able to do more. There were moments I wished I'd had more power, more access, more leverage.

And then I remember: I had access. I used it. Quietly, deliberately. I planted the string that unraveled Rhun's tapestry. It wasn't revenge. Not exactly. It was a necessity. But it left a mark on him—and on me.

I made my choices honestly, with the information I had.

Except when honesty gave way to action. When I stopped watching and started interfering.

No one sanctioned it. It wasn't part of any strategy. Just one moment of absolute clarity, followed by a keystroke I can't take back.

I've never told anyone. Other than Sue. Not even Doug. And I won't. Some truths aren't for confession. They're ballast, meant to be carried, not released.

So, I walk. I lead. I remember the quiet hum of a truth I buried just far enough down to keep breathing. I did what I had to do. I'm not proud of all of it. But I'm not ashamed either.

I've never written a memoir. Never given an interview. Never sat down to "tell my side." Maybe I never will. There's too much I'd have to leave out. Too many corners I'd have to darken. What I did, what I enabled, doesn't fit neatly into a redemption arc.

And sometimes, when I wake before sunrise and step outside with my coffee, I look at the sky and think: we *almost* built something great. We had vision, talent, and just enough belief to think we could bend the rules without breaking ourselves. But ambition without integrity is a fault line, and eventually, everything cracks. That lesson stays with me, etched deeper than any memo or resignation letter. It's what I carry forward.

And then I go back inside, where I find comfort, warming my hands on the steaming cup of coffee. The sky brightens. The day begins. And, as always, I'll head to work, lead my team, and attend meetings. Life moves forward. But part of me is still there. Within that glass structure. In the data trails and secretive meetings. In the choice that changed everything. The warning stands: institutions forget, but people remember. And because forgetting would mean none of it mattered.

Last week, I received a call from a reporter in London. Said he was writing a retrospective on Cambria's collapse and had come across an anomaly in one of the forensic audit reports.

"There's a reference," he said, "to a user-created log entry on Rhun's machine. But no trace of the user in the system. Almost as if it were ... added later."

I kept my voice steady.

"Interesting," I said.

We agreed to speak again next week.

After the call, I sat in the dark for hours, thinking. Not about being caught; if they found something, so be it. What unsettled me was something else: the reporter had mentioned new leads. A cross-reference from an old compliance archive in London. He said that others were already on it. That the data pointed to offshore transfers, encrypted credentials, and emails that Rhun couldn't explain.

Actual evidence. Not fabricated. Not planted.

And that's when it hit me; Rhun would've gone down, anyway.

I didn't need to do what I did.

I told myself I'd acted in the name of justice. That I was balancing the scales. But what if I'd just tipped them a bit sooner than they inevitably would have tipped? What if I planted the truth before it had time to surface on its own?

That's the part I carry now. Not just what I did, but the knowledge that it may have been unnecessary. In trying to fix something, I may have corrupted it further.

I haven't decided whether I'll take the follow-up call.

Maybe I will.

Maybe I won't.

Some truths I've learned don't live in confession.

They live in the silence that follows.

ABOUT THE AUTHOR

D.P. Dart is an author of financial thrillers who spent over thirty years in senior leadership roles across global banks and fintech companies.

His work in technology and operations exposed him to the inner workings of Wall Street, the high pressure of corporate boardrooms, and the gray areas where ambition and morality collide.

Retired in 2021, David now lives in Florida with his wife, where he writes part-time. *Planted* is his first novel.